Urbex Predator

Take nothing, but pictures. Leave nothing, but bodies.

This edition published in 2024 by Amazon KDP

ISBN: 9798867566128

(Independently published)

URBEX PREDATOR

Dear Reader,

I'm thrilled to have you embark on this journey into the depths of horror, suspense and survival. I hope you'll find this book to be a thrilling and captivating experience, filled with heart-pounding moments and unexpected twists.

If you enjoy the book and have a few moments to spare, consider leaving a review on Amazon. For independent authors like me, reviews are invaluable. Your honest feedback can make all the difference in reaching more readers and shaping the future of my work.

If you'd like to stay updated on the latest news, exclusive content, and upcoming releases, I invite you to join my e-mail list at jensboele.com. Be the first to know about new stories, special promotions, behind-the-scenes insights and much more.
And as a special treat, download a character cheat sheet from my website! Many readers have found it helpful in keeping track of the diverse cast of characters. Find it at www.jensboele.com

Thank you for choosing "Urbex Predator." Now, turn the page and let the adventure begin!

Chillingly Yours,

Jens Boele

Urbex (short for Urban Exploration or Urban Exploring) is the private exploration of facilities of urban space and so-called Abandoned Places. This often involves exploring old industrial ruins, as well as sewers, catacombs, rooftops, or other spaces of unused facilities. The photographic documentation and artistic processing of such urban explorations founded the still-young genre of ruin photography and is gaining increasing popularity in social media.

Apex Predator (from Latin apex peak or apex) is the not strictly defined term in biology for a carnivore that is at the top of the food pyramid in an ecosystem. It is thus a predator that has no predators of its own.

PROLOGUE

Silence was all that was left. Neither the shouting of the officers nor the marching thunder of the soldiers had remained from the Cold War. Finally, it was time itself that had defeated all enemies.

Unwavering, indifferent, and relentless, it gnawed at the foundations of what the Allied forces had left behind. Heat had cracked the asphalt, rain washed out the concrete, wind and storm had smashed doors and windows. Tar paper had melted in the sun and frozen in winter. Tiles had cracked in the freezing cold. Weather had crept into the woodwork and driven the paint out of the wood. Moss and ferns clung to exterior walls, clogging gutters, and water pipes. The forces of nature had achieved what those of the enemy had failed to do.

In the cold moonlight, Scott and Billy wandered between the former apartment blocks near the barracks. Six-story residential silos had probably housed the soldiers' families at that time. Today they were surrounded by trees that had not been planted yet when the houses were abandoned. In the moonlight, the open front doors of the house looked like the entrance to a more sinister and terrifying world than the darkness of the woods. The night wind carried the heavy smell of forest soil and damp cellars to their noses. Now the nocturnal animals came to life and mingled their calls with leaves rustling.

"Wait!" Billy put his hand on Scott's shoulder. "There's something up ahead."

They stopped on a grassy path that once had been a road.

"What's supposed to be there?" Scott folded his arms in front of his chest.

"Look ..."

A black shadow emerged from the forest. Billy froze, Scott held his breath. It appears the animal was slowly approaching them. Gosh, let it be just a dog that has lost its way.

"It's a wolf," Scott whispered.

Billy felt Scott's arm pushing him back.

"Damn, what do we do now?" Scott breathed frantically.

The animal approached slowly; head bowed.

"That's a wolf," Scott kept whispering, "that's a wolf ..." Breathing frantically, his voice grew louder with each word.

"That! Is! A! Wolf!" he shouted energetically, stamping his foot with each word, and waving his arms.

When Billy came out from behind his back, the animal had disappeared. His shoulders slumped. Scott exhaled in relief.

"Was that really a wolf?" asked Billy in a low voice.

"I don't know," Scott went on. "Anyway, it's gone."

"Can't you even turn on the flashlight?"

"No, man. Not until we get inside. I don't feel like getting caught by security anytime soon."

Taking a deep breath, Billy let go of his tension. "And how is this even going to work? We've been walking through the forest for about half an hour now."

"Yeah, so what?"

"How are we supposed to move those cables back to the car? Do you think I will run the route back and forth umpteen times?"

Scott abruptly stopped and glanced at Billy. "You aren't even listening to me, are you? We will get all the cables out of the ceilings that night and stash them here. Then we'll see what we got, and tomorrow night we'll break down the gate and drive up here with the transporter. All right?"

Billy chewed on his lower lip. "Yes, but why don't we go with the van already?"

"Because the broken gate would attract the security service in the morning, which would then catch us, stupid."

Waiting for an answer, he glanced at Billy, "It's not that hard to understand, though, is it?" Billy nodded mutely.

"But do you think there's still a lot to earn here anyway? This place is kind of old, you know. I'm sure others have been here before and pulled the copper outta the walls."

"Take a good look around. Do you see any graffiti? Do you see any trails? Has anyone been partying here?" Billy let his eyes wander. No, no one has been here for a long time. "Don't ask me why, but this place is hot."

Scott raised his eyebrows. "Now let's get going." Forgivingly, he patted Billy on the shoulder. "Otherwise, the Big Bad Wolf will get you right away."

Sighing, Billy kept walking.

"This is probably just too far away from civilization. We're just out here in the middle of nowhere. Nobody gets lost here ..."

A bloodcurdling scream echoed throughout the night.

Frozen, Billy stopped, Scott took a step back.

"What was that?" Billy's voice trembled.

Scott stared into the night. "I'm sure it was just an animal."

Billy shivered. "Was no animal, dude."

Scott turned to him. "What else would that have been? The wolf probably took a deer. You know what kind of noises animals make when they're scared to die?"

Billy shook his head quietly as he remained in a state of shock.

"See it like this—the wolf will feast now and leave us alone." Scott smiled. "Is even better for us."

After a brief silence, he added, "Think of the money!"

The wind had eased, the dark forest path lay in silence. Behind them, the moon illuminated the clearing where the houses stood. In front of them, there was darkness.

Billy whispered, "Wait," and then walked on hesitantly. His legs were heavy as lead, his breathing shallow. "Wait for me."

"Hurry," Scott whispered softly.

As the path narrowed, the trees came closer, denying them the last light of the moon.

They could barely see anything when they noticed a motion in the shadows.

A large shade moved slowly between the trees.

It walked upright on two legs.

This was not an animal.

Billy felt an icy chill as his arms felt numb. He felt an invisible band tighten around his chest, draining his breath as Scott disappeared into the darkness.

"Scott?" He gasped for air.

"Run! Run Billy!"

Billy's stomach clenched. He heard Scott try to shout something, but his voice turned into an uncontrolled gurgle. Like he was going to throw up. Then a rattle.

Billy wanted to run away, but he just stood there, unmoving and trembling, paralyzed with fright. He grabbed his cheek. His eyes stared into the forest, widening.

"Scott?"

A branch cracked.

Darkness surrounded him.

Silence.

FOLLOW THE TRAIL

The meadow was flooded with warm summer light. There was the scent of straw in the air. At the end of the clearing, nettles lined the adjacent spruce forest. Amidst the chirping of birds, one could occasionally hear speeding cars from the distant state highway. Nela and Tess followed a path through tall grass that hadn't been mowed in years. The meadow must have once belonged to someone, which was remarkable because somebody must have parked the cars that were slowly rusting away here.

"Look!" Smiling, Nela gently touched her friend's shoulder.

"Hello, hello, hello! What have we got here?" Excited, Tess jumped past Nela and ran toward the rusted pickup truck. "Pretty rad, that mopa!"

Nela laughed as she took the backpack off her shoulders and set up her equipment. Good to see that her friend was thrilled.

"Check out all the other cars."

She looked across the meadow and saw a green panel van at the edge of the forest. Branches had already grown through it. A station wagon and a Camry were parked next to each other. The station wagon was rotting away, while the Camry was in good condition. The pickup truck would be the first subject, the panel van the second. Both cars looked just perfect.

Untouched by human hands yet destroyed by time.

"Like they were just waiting for me ..."

Nela carefully extended the legs of the tripod, attached the SLR camera and finally put on the lens. On the camera's display, the old car looked small and inconspicuous. The engine block's rust tones blended into the spruce forest background and were framed by the meadow's green and the trees' needles. The body's former white paint was the only thing that stood out. Yet, the rust underneath was blistering and breaking through the coating.

Rain, moss, and sunlight had rendered it dirty and brittle, giving it a hint of green. Nela focused on the seats, of which little more than wooden planks, foam, and the remnants of plastic trim had remained. The tire-tread, however, was surprisingly deep. So, whenever the car had last been driven, it hadn't been long ago.

Nela took a look at the sky and was satisfied. Passing clouds provided a dynamic motif. This would be a perfect start for her shoot. Just get a little closer and move the perspective further down to have a more inter-esting view.

"Do you want me to sit in it, or do you prefer me to lie on it?"

Tess had propped herself up, elbows on the engine block. Her long blonde hair fell down on one side while she stuck her butt out on the other. Her short jeans revealed more skin than they hid, and the knee socks in her hiking boots seemed more flirtatious than practical. Blinking at her,

Tess pursed her lips.

Nela took a deep breath and gazed up at the sky.

"Come on, move your tasty ass to the other side" she prompted Tess, who changed her position and, with tilted head, positioned behind the car. "Like this, or would you rather do it just so?" Tess put her head in the other direction.

"Neither. You're going to squat until I can't see you anymore!" exclaimed Nela with a grin.

Tess scrunched her nose and folded her arms. "A little bare skin wouldn't hurt your bachelor thesis …"

"… but also, wouldn't improve it," Nela replied. "The theme is 'natural decay.' And it's not like you've reached that point yet."

Tess sighed at Nela's joke. "For once, can you do me a favor? How else am I ever going to succeed with my Instagram?"

"Yes, we can schedule a photo session for sure. However, I think that displaying one's body for the mere generation of likes is a first step into prostitution. But that's for you to decide."

Now Tess had to laugh. Nela's cynical comments were having an effect. Slowly, with swaying hips, she approached her friend. "Mrs. Dubois, maybe we should prostitute ourselves together. This brown exotic beauty and the blonde angel are available for the paying customer for frivolous photos."

Grinning, Nela shook her head, "Yeah, right. Now extend your wings and fly out of the picture, blonde angel. You are ruining the subject."

"Excuse me? Am I not playing by the rules?" With feigned indignation, she recited the Urbex code "Take nothing but pictures, leave nothing but footprints."

"You do, but you are also leaving a trail on my picture." Taking a step behind Tess, Nela straightened the blades of grass to restore the illusion of pristine.

Tess watched her friend struggling to brush through the grass like she was wielding a Japanese Zen rake. It was a fine line between cynicism and humor, and she was never quite sure which side Nela was on. Her gaze remained glued to Nela, becoming fixed and hazy.

Tess knew she was attractive before she had worked as a nude model at Nela's college, where they had met. She was captivated by Nela's determined nature from the start, but at moments like these, Tess wished Nela took her more seriously. She was confident that she would do better than the social media celebrities she followed. At least well enough for her not to have to wait tables anymore. And have a little more glamour in her life. And could afford to live in the sun, too.

Tess stretched out her arms and squinted her eyes. Her gaze focused, as she watched Nela make adjustments to her camera, press the shutter button, turn the camera again, make new adjustments, and press the shutter once more. Her loving way of working was somehow fascinating. Tess approached and glanced over her friend's shoulder.

She admitted, "This looks great," when she saw the old pickup truck in the picture, like it was a part of nature. And yet, it was obvious that it was not of natural origin. While everything around it grew and thrived, the car decayed and died. The image had a unique magic that was hard to escape.

"Do you like it?" Nela asked without turning around.

"Yes, I do. A lot."

"Me too, it's perfect the way it is. We couldn't have found a better day."

Tess laughed. "So, now it's my turn!" With quick, short steps, she hurried to the car and posed. "Go ahead and shoot, cowgirl!" she called out to Nela.

"You are a pain! Get out of my …"

But Tess ran away before Nela could finish her sentence. "Hey there!" Tess yelled.

Two young photographers set up their equipment on the green box truck at the edge of the clearing. Astonished they paused.

"Would you guys like to take my picture?" With hands on her hips, Tess sauntered toward the speechless boys. She pivoted her upper body from left to right and gave them a bright smile. "You know, my friend back there is more into rusty sleds than hot curves." Tess paused, batting her eyes. "But I'm sure you'd appreciate such hot bodywork, wouldn't you?"

"Um…" was all the two photographers could say.

"Okay, okay," Tess echoed, "I can show more skin if you'd like." She pulled her shirt up and tied a knot under her breasts. "That's better, right?"

Just as speechless as her male counterparts, Nela watched Tess' performance. She wondered if it had been a good idea to take the photos for her final exam alongside a lovely but crazy wannabe model.

"Sorry, but we're about to …" the young man stuttered, "we would rather …"

"You don't have to be afraid," Tess tried to relax the situation.

"Nah, it's just that today we want to do more …" he struggled for words,

"Well, we would like to do more nature photography."

As if not accepting his justification, Tess gave him a smiling, playful look.

"We just have a real plan for today" his partner interjected, "and an awful lot to do."

Tess blinked in disbelief. "You're aware that some chances only occur once in your life, right?"

"Hmm, yes, that's right …" he pondered, perplexed.

"But if we're going to throw our plan overboard, it's got to be for a superb reason," his friend added.

"Well, thus it has to be an exceptional motif."

"Yes, something special."

"So, we could just say, 'Good thing we shot the subject and not the old cars'."

"Uhu." Confirming nod.

"If it was, like, a rare butterfly in the meadow or something …"

"You guys are real assholes, you know that?" Nela interjected angrily. "Come on, Tess, they're not worth it."

At the same time, the women held up their middle fingers to the shy boys. "You better keep pushing your cameras' buttons, you sissies!"

While Nela packed her gear, they both had to hold back their laughter. Some of their Urbex colleagues were more uptight than altar boys.

"Come on, let's get out of here," she urged Tess, pointing toward the end of the clearing. At the end, there was a small path that led into the unknown, where the forest opened. "Always follow the trail!"

"We still have a long way to go."

"However, that's the shortest way!" Out of the corner of his eye, Zander Regan watched the rest of the group with his arms crossed.

"Are you telling me that I have to crawl through a bush and then climb over a wall for a photo shoot? Really?" Yelka handed Vivian her sneakers. She was carrying her flip-flops in her right hand, like she was carrying a purse. Vivian's outfit for the trip to the abandoned barracks was far from practical, especially her choice of hot pants and a spaghetti-strap top.

"I must admit, Yelka," added her manager Damon, "I'm quite irritated about this location too. Isn't there an official entrance to the site?" He lifted his sunglasses and glanced at Yelka and Zander, eyebrows raised.

Zander ignored Damon's gaze, pretending to check his watch. Vivian and Damon were already starting to get on his nerves. This could have been a fun trip, but he was used to their behavior. It was likely that one of them would become dramatic at the slightest opportunity. The other sure bet was that Yelka would try to appease her sister, his pretty Yelka.

Oh, if only she knew how much he desired her ...

"Zander really tried everything, Viv. This is the fastest way to the barracks—and your photos." She smiled. "You're going to look more than gorgeous, darling sis. The barracks make an impressive backdrop, right, Zander?"

There she was again, Yelka with her velvety voice and twinkling eyes that made his legs feel weak. Zander didn't understand why Vivian, not Yelka, was the Instagram model. It was like a joke.

I am a model on Instagram.
Yes, and I'm a mercenary in Call of Duty.

"Isn't that right, Zander?" repeated Yelka.

"Huh? Oh yes," Zander stuttered as if he had been caught in a lie. "The barracks were abandoned after German reunification and have lain fallow ever since," he explained. "The area is in the middle of a 6,000-acre woodland and consists of barracks, a civilian settlement, and a military hospital. All areas are separated from each other, but are supposed to be connected by underground bunkers ..."

"For fuck's sake, can you please wake me up when he's done with his monologue?" Annoyed, Vivian glanced at Damon.

"Viv, please."

"6,000 acres is pretty darn big," Damon hooked in. "I hope we don't have to trek for miles through the woods. Tonight we have to post our stories, and by tomorrow morning the pictures. And our designers still must retouch them before."

"This is the fastest way. We'll be there in half an hour," Zander meekly assured.

"I'm supposed to spend another half hour ..."

"Get down! Down!" shouted Zander and Yelka at the same time.

As they walked along a dirt path next to a weathered stone wall, a car approached.

Yelka pulled her sister behind a bramble hedge. Zander had already dropped to the ground, and Damon followed suit. A blue, old station wagon approached, kicking up dust. Zander spotted a single driver through the bushes. The man was older, perhaps in his late 50s, with a brown dog in the back. The driver seemed vigilant, guarding the compound. They remained motionless until the car disappeared from sight.

"What was that all about?" Vivian vented her anger.

"If they catch us here, the photo shoot is already over," Zander explained.

"That's the reason it's both risky and quick."

"The other option is to walk a long distance from the old junkyard through the woods."

While Damon was straightening his men's purse, Vivian was still fiddling with her outfit, upset. Her top had ridden up so that Zander could catch a glimpse of her belly. The muscles stood out a little, but not enough to look athletic. It was then that his gaze reached the top button of her jeans. If only she were not so arrogant …

"So, what's next?" Damon was impatient.

"There should be a dune over there in front of the wall …" Zander pondered aloud.

"Yes, I can see it already. Come on, come on, darling sis!"

Excitedly, they ran through the bushes and reached a section of the wall in front of which wind and weather had piled up a small mound of earth. It was hard to see from the path. Only a few people had chosen to go to the barracks from here.

"Come on, you go first," Damon prompted Zander.

He put on his black safety gloves and approached the wall with slow steps. Even though the pile of earth reduced the height of the wall, Zander was forced to stretch his arms further in order to reach the top. The concrete was brittle and had gotten tanned by the elements. Cracks in the wall revealed rusty metal struts.

"Do you want me to help you?" Yelka stood behind Zander, watching him. "Uh-uh."

He braced one foot on the wall and pulled himself up. When he shifted his weight forward and got his first glimpse of the other side, he pulled his left leg up and sat upright.

Below him was a withered meadow that some distance away merged into a dark spruce forest. Between the treetops, he spotted the roofs of the residential complex, which lay in the middle of the woods. His heart began to beat faster. What lay there was the first part of the old barracks. He bent back to Yelka.

"I can see them."

"Is that true?" Her eyes lit up as they finally arrived at the place she had longed to visit for ages—it had been her idea to come here.

"Come on up!" With joyful excitement, Zander reached out to her.

Yelka quickly climbed up the wall to get to him. He pointed over the top of the forest to the dark roofs of the housing blocks. "See?"

"Oh my God, there it is!" exclaimed Yelka enthusiastically. Her joy was so great that she hugged and squeezed Zander.

He felt ashamed and smiled shyly. "Okay, I'm going down." As he leaned to the side to lift his right leg over the wall, his head unintentionally settled into Yelka's lap. When his cheek touched her thigh, he almost lost his balance. At the last moment, his hands clung to the wall and Zander was able to hold on. Yelka grabbed his forearm. "Hey, watch it," she shouted, both startled and amused.

Zander took a deep breath and dropped. The soft ground cushioned his fall as Zander landed in the deep grass.

"Everything okay down there?" Zander gave Yelka a thumbs-up sign, nodding. "Okay, come on up then, Viv!"

"This will be fun." Damon propped his back against the wall below, squatted down, and offered her a boost. Vivian gave Yelka her flip-flops and let Damon lift her onto the ledge.

"Poor, poor guy," Vivian whispered. "When are you going to let him have it?" Yelka rolled her eyes. "Stop it!" She then grinned and gave her sister a nudge.

"Don't you think he is cute when he blushes every time you touch him?"

"Shh!" Yelka definitely didn't want Zander to overhear their conversation. "If you don't behave, I'll set you up with him."

"Nah, he's been in love with you since kindergarten, even spending a night with me wouldn't change this."

Amused, Yelka smiled and swung over the wall. "Yeah, you'd like that, wouldn't you?" she grinned as she dropped herself down.

Only now did her sister realize how deep it was. She hesitated.

"Come on, it's not that high, you can do it!"

But Yelka's words could not convince Vivian. She took a deep breath.

"Damon, come up, you have to help me."

After a few moments, her social media manager appeared at her side. He was visibly upset that his new red sneakers had gotten dirty in the process. "Come on starlet, get down, I'm holding you" he instructed his model, but she didn't listen to him.

Routinely, Vivian pulled out her cell phone and put on a simper smile. "Selfie time," she chirped and pulled the trigger. "Last story before the leap into darkness!"

"Hey, no coordinates!" shouted Yelka. "We're not posting any location."

"Oh my God, you and your weird Urbex rules ..."

Zander had walked a few footsteps through the grass, ignoring the rest of the group. He would rather be here alone with Yelka. It wasn't clear to Zander anyway why she was going all out with a photo shoot for her self-absorbed sister instead of taking photos herself. They could have stayed here overnight easily.

She would surely like that better than to be put under time pressure by Damon. Yelka had loved Urbexing ever since she had been on that California vacation. Her chip card was full of photos of abandoned towns and resorts. Since then, she had infected Zander with the Urbex virus. He loved going on adventure trips with her, feeling the magic of these special places. With Yelka, though, he would have gone just about anywhere.

"Hey!" shouted Damon, upset. Meanwhile, he and Vivian had climbed down from the wall and were looking at him in bewilderment. "How are we supposed to get back up there?"

In fact, it was almost impossible to climb over the wall from this side without any tools.

Damon's face turned a shade of red, and his jaw clenched as he balled his fists. Vivian's eyes widened, as she vigorously shook her head, her hair bouncing with each motion. Yelka's chest rose as she inhaled a slow, deliberate breath, and her lips pressed together in a thin line, the tension in her body evident.

It's not my problem.
I didn't want to be with you guys anyway.

Zander smiled, "We'll find a way."

"Did you see the Camry? It hasn't been here for long."

"So does the van. Looks like it had just been parked."

"Well, who knows? Maybe we're not alone in the barracks."

"Okay, fine by me. Fingers crossed we don't meet any more morons like those in the junkyard."

Tess laughed. "I would still prefer a couple of uptight guys than a bunch of rioters."

"Hey, that children's hospital we visited last year burned down a week ago."

"Really?"

"Yeah, it was pretty battered, though."

"I'm glad we had a chance to snap some pics back then."

"Can't understand why people do that? What do they get out of it?"

Nela and Tess had already hiked through the dense pine forest for an hour. The rain of the last few days had left swollen ground and deep puddles. It was humid, mosquitoes circled their faces.

"Damn!" Tess slapped her forearm where she had just felt a sting.

Nela kept her arms moving, scaring away the insects.

"How much further is it?"

"I don't know, don't have any Wi-Fi here," Nela replied. "But if I'm guessing the distance correctly, we should be there soon."

"It's about time, I don't like walking through the forest anymore. Mosquito bites mess up my skin. And itch."

"I have got spray with me. Tomorrow morning we'll use it, the way back will be less stressful, though."

"I wonder if it's such a good idea to spend the night in the barracks ..."

"Right, we can go back too."

"I'll sleep in my own bed then ..."

"... and don't get any sexy photos of yourself!"

"Pft! Come on!" Nela laughed.

Talking quietly, they walked through the dense forest when a clearing opened up in front of them. The path widened and from under the grasses, faded asphalt appeared. A few decades ago, there seemed to have been a road here. To the left and right, there were other roads and paths to be found.

"Look, this is an intersection," Nela exclaimed in surprise. "Cars used to drive here!"

"Look at that!"

The first apartment block rose behind the trees. Six stories of gray, windowless concrete surrounded by conifers were the last witnesses of the Cold War. The entrance to numerous apartments was once visible on a wide path, but now ferns, shrubs and branches have spread. The remains of a seesaw were visible in the undergrowth, next to it a climbing frame.

"Unbelievable, isn't it?"

"Feels like I'm in the jungle of Cambodia."

"Can't even imagine; we are in the middle of Germany here."

With long strides, Nela stalked through the thicket, always careful not to lose her balance.

"Look," she called out to Tess, "a light!"

At first glance, the moss-green concrete pillar of the streetlight was invisible in the green of the forest. Only when Nela leaned against it did she feel the hard edges and the cold rock.

"It hasn't lit up in years, though."

"Awesome!"

"Hey, do you think they'll light up tonight?"

"I don't think so."

As they walked along, Tess and Nela approached the entrance to the house. The windows of the lower floors were boarded up, but the front door was missing. Under a moss-covered shelter, they found the dark entrance to the interior.

Warm sunlight, chirping birds and lush green plants took away the dark, scary side of the building. Inside, raw walls, crumbling stairs and wet concrete gave a hint. The closer they got, the heavier and colder the air smelled. That sinister magic of abandoned buildings was what Nela and Tess were looking for.

"Should we go in, or do you want to take a lap around the block first?" Tess asked.

Nela was hard to stop. "Are you afraid?"

"No, it's okay." The summer air was humid and hot. In the cool shade of the abandoned house, it would be pleasant.

Cautiously, Nela took her first steps into the darkness of the block. It felt as if she was entering another world. Suddenly, the warmth of the summer day had disappeared, and the chirping of the birds had stopped. The damp cold made Nela shiver. Her grinding footsteps cast a soft echo through the stairwell. Quite naturally, she lowered her voice to a hushed murmur. She whispered to Tess, "Watch out, the stairs don't have any railing anymore."

The first rooms they entered were empty. Plaster trickled from the ceiling; paper rolled off the walls. In the glow of their flashlights, they could make out old newspapers whose pages were as faded as their contents.

"Hey, those are from the era of the collapse of Eastern Germany," whispered Nela

"Yeah, that certainly looks like the Berlin Wall. How long have they been here?"

"Pretty much thirty years." Nela had to stifle a laugh.

"Yeah, right …"

For a moment, the friends were silent and let the place take effect on them. The atmosphere was surreal, as if they had entered a parallel universe where the passage of time had changed direction a quarter of a century ago. And yet not much of it was tangible.

"Let's get further up. I sense the upper floors might have more to offer."
"Maybe it's warmer there, too."
"The difference is crazy, isn't it?"

The stairwell was dark even in the glow of the flashlights. Few windows were boarded up or overgrown by nearby trees. Condensation dripped silently from the ceiling, creating a dull echo on impact. Tess shined her lamp down the stairs, but it couldn't see through the dark.

"Just keep looking up," Nela encouraged her.
"Uh huh …" Tess had pressed herself against the wall and slowed her pace.
"Grab my hand."

Tess did not hesitate and took her friend's hand. The cold and the altitude became more bearable.

"We're there," Nela now said in a clearly more confident volume.

She had been right, the apartment they now entered was almost untouched, with only the ravages of time gnawing away at it. The shelves had collapsed, and walls had turned green from exposure to the elements.

Beneath the clothes rack were shoes the likes of which Nela and Tess had never seen before. They seemed so old that they had gone out of style even 30 years ago. Trash lay on the floor, fused to the musty carpet. It smelled of mold and wet paste.

"Before we spend the night here, though, we need to air it out" Tess joked.

"Good idea, open a window."

"Come on. The wood is so swollen that the handle can no longer be turned."

"You'd better leave it then. Maybe we can somehow get up to the roof and spend the night there. Fresh air would be great."

"Hey Nela," Tess now whispered again. "There are people down there."

In fact, Tess recognized three or four people among the trees.

"Did those uptight boys follow us?" Nela grinned.

"Well, there seem to be several of them."

"Urbexers, too, I'm confident."

"Probably wannabe YouTubers, as ill-equipped as they are."

From above, they could see that most of them were wearing shorts and T-shirts. They seemed to have little concern for their safety.

"But I think they're photographers too" Tess reflected, "They have tripods with them".

"Unfortunately, they are quite noisy."

"They probably think they're alone out here."

"And they do not carry any backpacks or bags with them. Where do they keep their photo equipment?"

They watched the group, which appeared to be having a lively discussion. Nela and Tess heard laughter.

"Come on, let's go downstairs and scare …"

She choked on the word as one of the group banged his tripod against a tree.

"Those aren't tripods. They're steel pipes," Tess whispered in a trembling voice.

"They're coming."

"Come on, let's get out of here."

Jesse slammed his steel pipe against a young tree's trunk. His stare was rigid, and the force of his blows increased. Jesse was bound in the act of destruction, would not rest until the goddamn tree was shattered. The bark had already begun to splinter when he heard the sound of shattering glass. He spotted Mike, breaking one of that lousy ruin's windowpanes. A tiny splinter hit him on the cheek. Abruptly, he lowered his pipe and yelled at Mike.

"Are you fucking retarded?" He stroked his cheek, looking for traces of blood. When he found none, he again shouted at Mike. "Can't you be careful? I got splinters!"

"Cry me a river, man!" Leaning his head to the side, Mike grinned at his buddy. "What a sissy you are."

"Fuck you, asshole." — "Fuck you!"

Mousey watched as the two older boys attacked and pushed each other. He liked these moments when violence was in the air. As long as he wasn't the victim, he felt that tingling sensation in his stomach. A mixture of sensationalism and voyeurism was what triggered him. But Mousey was distracted. His gaze wandered over to Tami. The older girl had dyed her hair dark and wore a top cut off below her breasts. Mousey didn't want to miss the moment when she stretched, when maybe he could catch a glimpse of her tits.

Dave and Ryder had also noticed that Tami was getting dressed up. The two top dogs were constantly swarming around the girl. Mousey was pretty sure Ryder and Tami were dating, but they weren't officially together. If only Mousey were three years older, he'd chance his luck as well.

Tami had sat down on the old swing next to the rotten seesaw and carefully began to swing back and forth. Every so often she moved her pelvis forward, and occasionally, she stretched out her chest to gain momentum.

"Would either of you like to give me a nudge?" she asked with an innocent undertone, yet aware of her cockiness.

Standing wide-legged, Ryder kept a tight grip on his dog, Gazoo, while Dave pushed Tami lightly from behind. "If you want it harder, you better get on your knees."

Tami rocked forward. Her and Ryder's eyes met, smiling, and anticipating. As she slid back, Ryder's and Dave's eyes crossed. They flashed full of challenge.

"Most importantly, you shouldn't have a wimp standing behind you then."

"Is this something a sissy would do?" With a grin, Dave grabbed Tami's butt before giving her another shove.

"Uh!" Tami exclaimed with wide eyes. Dave's importunity seemed to please the girl.

"Mousey!" Ryder didn't take his eyes off her. "Mousey, come here!"

The youngest homeboy turned back to reality. For a moment, he had forgotten everything around him. When Dave touched Tami's butt, she threw her head back and let out a cocky squeal of delight. Her top slipped up, and for a second Mousey could see her nipples.

"Yeah?" he asked, still in a trance.

"Yo, take Gazoo and go for a walk."

Without looking at him, Ryder handed Gazoo's leash to Mousey. Disappointed but dutiful, Mousey grabbed the leather strap and pulled on it. The brown mongrel with the short fur and the flat muzzle barked at him but obeyed. Gazoo was big, and if he had escaped, Mousey would have needed all his might to hold him.

Ryder, however, was not interested in that. The little fellow had to parry and do his bidding. Otherwise, he'd gotten his ass spanked. Just so.

Seeing Dave so close to Tami made him angry. She was his girl, and Dave shouldn't think he could do as he pleased.

"Tough guy, huh!" he called over to Dave. "Haven't had a shot in a while, have ya?"

"We'll see who's scoring today" he boasted back.

Tami knew that she would go with one of the boys today. The only question was whether Ryder or Dave would prevail in the end.

"You absolutely won't, that's for sure!"

Now with both hands free, Ryder smiled at Tami and took a step toward her. As she spread her legs, their loins touched, and Ryder put his hands around Tami's hips. She gazed at him in amazement. Ryder did not let go of her. As she threatened to slide backwards, she wrapped her legs around him, then let go of the swing and snuggled up to Ryder, who was holding her. As the swing swung back empty, Dave kicked it aside in frustration. Silently, he walked past the couple, joining Jesse and Mike. Ryder threw a kiss after him. "Should the two of us get out of here?" Tami giggled.

Silently, he watched Jesse and Mike standing in the entrance of a house, banging their steel pipes against the walls. Their wicked laughter indicated they were having some kind of perfidious fun. Behind them stood Mousey, holding Ryder's barking dog with both hands.

Dave pushed Jesse forward. He turned around and looked at him, grinning maliciously.

"What are you doing?" Dave snubbed Jesse.

"There's a cat down in the basement."

"Filthy animal!" shouted Mike.

"We'll scare the hell out of it, and then we'll go down." Jesse raised his eyebrows and gestured with the steel club in his hand.

Dave nodded with his jaw clenched. They'd waste the darn cat. "Hold that mutt, I'll get that critter!"

Hastily, Dave rushed down the stairs into the dark cellar, Jesse and Mike following close behind. The steps led down to the lowest floor. There was a half-open door in front of them. This must be where the animal was hiding.

"Kitty, kitty, kitty," Dave whispered as he carefully opened the door. "Come to Daddy." In the dim twilight of the basement, he could glimpse the cat in a corner. "I've got you now!" He feinted a step toward her, but jumped into the right corner, the only escape option. Jesse backed him up while Mike secured the left flank. There she was,

Dave grabbed the cat's neck and yanked the snarling animal upward. Its eyes lit green. "Now we're going to twist your little neck," Dave fantasized. He was ready to take out all his rage on the defenseless cat.

But when he tried to grab it, the animal slammed its claws into the flesh of his forearm. He cried out in pain and shock, throwing the cat away into the cellar. "Close the door!" But it was too late. The cat had disappeared.

"Fucking hell!" Dave was frantic, running up the stairs, where he caught Mousey watching Ryder and Tami. Gazoo sat in the grass and panted.

Smack! A juicy slap hit Mousey. "Are you jerking off right now, little fucker? Where'd that feline go? Can't you even pay attention?"

Upset, the three came back from the cellar. Mousey didn't know what happened to him. Even Ryder and Tami had interrupted their smooching.

"What's going on?" roared Ryder, while Dave, Mike, and Jesse had lined up around Mousey. Mike shoved the boy and Dave went for another slap, but Ryder grabbed his arm.

"Cut the shit. I'm calling the shots here, got it?"

Dave yanked his arm out of Ryder's grip. "Oh, yeah, but it looks to me more like you're making a love birdy of yourself."

For a moment, hostile silence hung over the scene. Ryder was about to retort, but Dave was faster. "Look at our womanizer," he urged the rest of the gang. "We have to hang out here every day while he's having fun with his ..." Dave hesitated, "... birdy."

"Watch your mouth!"

"Or else?" They stared at each other challengingly, but this time it was not a contest, but anger that was in the air. Ryder clenched his fists and tensed his torso.

"Come here!" But Dave took a step back and lowered his tone. "Come on, even your dog doesn't care about you anymore."

Indeed, Gazoo was lying in the grass and did not rush to help his master.

"I don't need him for you either, you little shitbag."

Mousey was no longer interested in Ryder and Dave. His cheek was still burning from the slap the older boy had given him. He squinted over at Tami, but she had pulled back. She kept her arms crossed in front of her chest and scowled over at Ryder. She had to realize that she was the cause of the argument. Mousey sensed it, this time they'd snap, Dave had gone too far. Ryder would beat the shit out of him, no doubts. Yet then Mousey saw something that should relax the situation. For the moment.

"Hey," he whispered just loud enough to interrupt the two adversaries. "There are people over there."

"We better find a way out quickly. The editorial's deadline is getting close, we can't afford any further delay."

Damon's words lay upon the group like a heavy burden. He was good at making his personal problems everybody's business. When he felt spoiled, he meant business. And Damon wasn't done yet.

"Moreover, we have no Wi-Fi here. Zero, nada, not a bit."

He let the words sink in, then added, "Even if I wanted to, I couldn't post anything out here." He put his phone away and joined Zander.

"Here's how it's going down: While the girls are taking photos, you're looking for an exit that will get us out of here A–S–A–P. Get it?"

"We'll take the pictures, don't worry about it" Yelka hooked in from behind. "And tonight, from our hotel, we'll be able to watch your follower numbers skyrocket in no time."

"I assume so," Damon replied curtly. "The sore point in the planning is the way back. But Zander will take care of that. And I know for sure he'll find a really fast way out for us." Appreciatively, he patted his shoulders.

"Damon, when do you think we will break the 30,000 mark? I really want that to happen by this weekend."

"Yes, starlet, we can definitely do that. Your pretty sister will do a fantastic job and Zander will get us back to the hotel in no time."

Zander wasn't concerned about Damon's problems at all. If it were up to him, Vivian should just do blunt erotic shots on the beach or in a studio. Or better, shoot soft porn. That was what it was all about, after all. Maybe he would watch that too. Vivian naked in the sand. Hmm ... Anyway, none of this had anything to do with the fascination of abandoned places. And this barracks had so much of it to offer.

"If we continue along this path through the forest, we will soon reach the residential block. From there, another path leads to the recreational facilities. There is a pool, a sports field and a theater, but it could also be used as a cinema. In parallel ..."

"Sis, shouldn't we take a picture of me in this outdoor pool?" Lasciviously, Vivian played with the strap of her top.

"Absolutely" laughed Yelka.

Why wasn't she actually on his side? After all, he had planned the whole trip just for Yelka. Zander wanted everything to be perfect today. Yet, that wouldn't work with Vivian and Damon. Honestly speaking, they shouldn't have joined in the first place. When the forest suddenly opened up to reveal a settlement, Zander's heart began to pound faster.

Weathered multi-story apartment blocks rose into the sky, overgrown with birch and fir trees. Moss clung to the entrance areas; ivy sought its way upwards. The scenery looked like a modern Sleeping Beauty castle, sprung from the premonition of a sinister dystopia.

For a moment, the group stopped and let themselves be captivated by the magic of the place. Speechless, their eyes wandered up the multi-story buildings, lingering on the dark building openings and absorbing the surreal atmosphere.

"This is incredible," Yelka was the first to return to her words. She put an arm around Zander and hugged him. "Just incredible."

Zander felt overwhelmed. His excitement was looking for a channel. "Considering that the residents lived here for 40 years, and nature has taken over for 30 years, then … well …" He didn't know how to finish the sentence. Zander was overwhelmed, both by the place and by Yelka's closeness.

"Darling sister, you can start thinking about whether you want to be photographed on the steps or the old climbing frame" Yelka indicated as she dug her camera out of the small backpack.

"The steps are great!" exclaimed Vivian, settling down on the moss-covered steps.

"Perfect," Damon joined in again as well. "That looks excellent, starlet! Lie back, let your hair fall to the right."

Zander walked thoughtlessly over the moss that covered the former street. Here, families must have once walked home, children played on the sidewalk, and vehicles drove north to the barracks. With a kick, he plucked the green from the ground and looked at the dark asphalt. This was how the place had been left nearly three decades ago.

He squatted down and let his fingers slide over the old pavement. A shiver came over him. At that moment, he felt the same fascination for these places as Yelka. Stealthily, he glanced over at his secret love as she took photos of her hot sister.

Vivian had leaned back dramatically, her chest up, her hair hanging down behind her. Her belly was exposed, her breasts pressed against the top. She stretched her long legs, like she was riding a bicycle.

Zander's gaze drifted off to Yelka, who held her camera with both hands. She was shifting positions from time to time. Although she was wearing cargo pants, boots and gloves, she didn't look one bit less sexy than her younger sibling.

He averted his eyes and let them roam over the facade of the apartment block again, only to look back over at the sisters.

"So, now …" Damon was about to intervene in the shooting when heavy dog barking made their blood run cold.

Yelka stopped her shots, Vivian lost body tension and Damon turned his head.

The big, short-haired yapper hung on the leash of a young guy in his early 20s. His tattooed arms were pumped up, stretching a red shirt. His chest jutted out as he stood wide-legged, holding the dog. A sharply cut face framed his full lips. He wore a gold necklace, his hair was shaved short. Behind him, four boys and a girl had set up. Two of them held metal pipes in their hands, brandishing them menacingly.

"Good day to you all!" The words didn't sound like a greeting, but more like a threat. "This is private property. No trespassing!" As if to underline his words, the dog growled insistently. The group slowly approached. Those two men carrying the batons grinned menacingly. "The whole compound is surrounded by a concrete wall."

Yelka was the first to speak up, "Hey, we're just taking pictures, we're not destroying or stealing anything."

"So what?" told Ryder Yelka. "Fuck it, you guys are still illegal. There are signs on the outside walls and gates that state that this place is off limits."

"Yeah, but you're still coming here," the dark-haired boy with the scratched forearm shouted.

"Even though it's forbidden."

The group had surrounded the four, leaving no way out. Gazoo barked at Vivian, tugging at Ryder's leash.

"What you are doing here is forbidden, you know that."

"Okay, we made a mistake," Yelka tried to concede. "How about we pack up and get out of here?" Seeking help, she looked over at Zander, but he was transfixed.

"Yeah, you just thought so." A grim smile played around Ryder's face. "I want to see everyone's IDs!"

"IDs out!" repeated Jesse, roaring.

Yelka looked at Zander first, then at Damon. "Please, let us just go our merry way and everything will be cool," she offered the boys.

Damon had regained his composure and was surveying the situation. Yelka and Zander getting married would be more likely than these guys being security guards. There was danger in the air. They were in the middle of nowhere and were being threatened by a gang of rednecks, carrying a loose dog.

Dave lifted the steel pipe and touched Yelka's chin. "Ain't nothing cool here," Ryder told them. "Either you show us your IDs or else."

As if to make an example, Dave hit the ground with his club.

Yelka flinched. Gazoo jumped up at her, held back only by Ryder's leash. "Chop, chop, IDs out!" Ryder roared indignantly.

"I think we need to make a cut here!" With a brisk step, Damon put himself between Yelka and Ryder. "To me, it seems like a misunderstanding."

For a moment, there was silence. Gazoo stopped barking, Dave's steel pipe hovered in the air, and Ryder waited to see what Damon would say.

"My name is Duke. Damon Duke, of Duke Executives." He spread his arms and stood between Ryder and Yelka.

"We rented this location today to hold a photo shoot."

He pointed to Vivian, who was still sitting on the steps. "This is Vivian Donahue, one of our most important models, known as Violet-D."

Damon waited a moment, watching the gang as they stared over at Vivian. He could see the aggression draining from the young men's faces. Desire appeared in their eyes.

"We are taking pictures for the centerfold today. Vivian's work needs a relaxed atmosphere. So, I'd be grateful if we could do the shoot without any further disruptions. Later, I'm sure she'll have time for a short meet and greet with autographs. If you have any further questions, please contact Councilor Wilbanks. Please carry on, we don't have any time to lose. Hush, hush!"

A stunned silence hung over the scene. The gang hadn't quite taken their eyes off Vivian when it dawned on them that they had just been set up. Yelka and Vivian were already preparing to resume the photo shoot when Ryder suddenly straightened up again. "Are you kidding me? I want to see your fucking IDs—no photos until I say so!"

"Good," Damon turned abruptly and held out his ID to Ryder, "that's me, Damon Duke." He gave him a moment to compare ID photo and face, then pulled out his cell phone. "And now I'd like to know what company you're with."

Damon held the phone to his ear and waited for Ryder's answer. But he remained silent.

"Mr. Wilbanks, this is Damon Duke speaking. I apologize for the interruption. Contrary to our agreements, we were evicted from the place by security." His and Ryder's eyes met. "They didn't hire any security at all? Then I assume this is a misunderstanding."

Dave looked at Ryder, waiting for any reaction. But he just stared at Damon indecisively.

"No, I don't think we need police here. Thank you very much, and again, I'm sorry to bother you."

Damon dropped the phone into his purse, then pulled out a slew of business cards. "Here you go."

First, he handed Ryder his card, then to the rest of the gang. "We're still looking for security employees. If any of you want to make money, you're more than welcome to contact me."

Dazzled, the gang looked at each other. "Have a nice day! Now, starlets, we'll move on to the next location."

Ryder looked grimly after the Urbexers as they walked on. Soon they would find out what kind of a nice day they were going to have.

NIGHTFALL

They held their breath, tiptoeing down the dark stairwell. Tess held on tightly to Nela's backpack. Just don't look down into the darkness. Quiet as they were, each step seemed to echo through the abandoned, dark house. Nela thought they could even be heard outside, just too well. She reached into her pocket and picked up the pepper spray she usually carried for animal defense.

Once they were on the first floor, she peeked out of the window. At first, the game of hide and seek seemed absurd as they felt the warm sun again, saw the tall grass and heard the birds chirping.

However, the gang they had seen from above still lingered at the end of the apartment block. There were five boys, one girl, and a mean-looking dog. The leader of the gang was a big guy in a red T-shirt who wore silver chains around his neck. His sidekick, who he was talking to, was wearing a black shirt and big tunnel earrings. The girl standing between them was slim, had her brown hair tied back in a braid, and stared with a cold glare. The boys were loud, laughing maliciously, the mood seemed testy. However, Nela and Tess could not understand what they said.

"If we walk out of here, they'll see us right away."

"The dog runs free. If it senses us, we're done."

"What are we going to do? Should we hide until they leave?"

"Absolutely not," Nela decided. "We're going to look for a window at the back of the first-floor apartments and climb out of there."

Quietly, with careful steps, they retreated and disappeared into the apartment at the end of the hall. When they had closed the door behind them, Nela switched on her flashlight. Tess did the same. The apartment was empty, the boarded-up windows letting in only a little daylight. The dampness produced an oppressive, musty smell. Silently, they crept from room to room, but all the windows seemed to be barred with thick wooden boards.

Tess sighed and had already given up the search, when Nela opened the door to the bathroom. A bright light shone towards them. However, the window was unlocked, but the pane had been smashed and sharp pieces of glass stood out of the frame. Tess reached for the latch to open the window, but Nela stopped her.

"You don't know what will happen if you open it," she whispered, "if it opens at all." Indeed, the frame was old, and the wood swollen. "If it falls toward you, it will make a terrible noise."

"Right."

"Let's climb through it carefully." Nela pulled a few pieces of glass from the frame and silently tossed them into the tall grass. With a cautious step, she climbed onto the toilet and crawled backwards out of the window, careful not to touch any of the sharp edges.

"Come on, I'll hold you," she urged Tess.

She hesitated, but after a quick breath, Tess climbed outside as well.

"We will be far enough away if we keep going to the next apartment block."

The two friends quietly sneaked through the tall grass. They heard voices from one of the other apartment blocks. It didn't sound like a gang, but they avoided the group just in case. Who knew if it was friend or foe? And whether they were not attracting the attention of those hoodlums.

Upon reaching the last apartment block, they took a deep breath. They were safe. For now.

"Hey," Nela nudged Tess. "Look, there's a supermarket."

"Really!" In amazement, Tess looked down the weathered steps that led to a small store.

"Come on, let's go inside!" When Nela attempted to push the handle against the door, it gave way.

Cobwebs tore as Nela and Tess entered the abandoned place. They held their breath. Surely, no one had ever entered this shop before them. The floor was covered with a layer of dust and dirt. Lint swirled in the air. The gray cash register in the entrance area displayed the amount of 49.75 Deutsch Marks. On the shelves in the room and on the walls, old soda bottles were covered with dust. At the end of the large room was an old meat counter with milky glass and rusted metal parts.

"This is unbelievable," Nela said, deeply impressed. Unable to take her eyes off the room, she reached into her bag and set up her photo equipment.

"You don't want to leave any footprints here."

"Can you help me out here for a minute?" Nela was actually worried that Tess's cluelessness would ruin her motives. "Could you please hold my backpack? I would rather not leave it in the dust."

While Nela adjusted her camera, Tess gazed around. She would look great as a sexy cashier or as a hot saleswoman at the meat counter. She giggled. But Nela wouldn't take pictures with her here anyway. The girl was a perfectionist and a gifted photographer, but unfortunately far too stubborn. She got that from her mom. Her father came from the Caribbean and was far too laid-back to have passed this stubbornness on to her.

Still, she often wondered why Nela didn't respond to her as well. It certainly wouldn't diminish the aesthetics of her photos if she took a few shots of her in between. After all, she wouldn't have to share them with her prof. Lost in thought, Tess strolled through the entryway and squinted outside through the tarnished windows. She would rather be in the sun, smiling cheekily at the camera, almost on the plane to Dubai...

"Hey, pretty girl, turn around!" Nela's calling woke Tess from her daydreams. Irritated, she turned to her friend and looked straight into her camera.

"Smile, you are on camera!" Nela laughed, the shutter buzzing.

Tess lowered her backpack, fixed her hair, and posed. She put on her brightest laugh. Finally! Tess put her torso back, stretched her breasts forward, tilted her head, turned sideways, tossed her hair back, stood on one leg, flapped her arms. She turned on full blast, showing off every pose she had ever learned. In front of her, Nela and the camera disappeared, the room becoming her stage. Even the click of the shutter soon faded away. Tess grinned, pouted, kissed and laughed. This was what she always wanted to do. Determined, she started moving and headed for the meat counter. Now she would...

"Stop, stop, stop!" Nela snapped her out of her concept, "I haven't taken a picture over there yet."

Tess stopped in consternation. Was her shoot already over? "So what?"

"The counter is still untouched," Nela explained. "I want to take pictures of that, but I need to reset the equipment first."

Tess looked at the counter and understood. Why couldn't she have done that before? "Yeah, okay, you're right," she replied quietly.

"Uh huh …," Nela murmured as a matter of course and screwed her tripod.

"This sucks." Tess folded her arms.

Confused, Nela looked at her.

"I think it's dumb, I really do," she admitted. "I won't feel it anymore."

"Just be glad I'm taking pictures of you at all," Nela replied flippantly.

"I just think …"

Their conversation came to an abrupt pause, shattered by a sudden, loud thud against the window.

Startled, they tried to look outside, but the windows were cloudy and fogged up. They felt like they had seen a shadow run in front of the store.

"What was that?" Nela whispered. Her hand searched for the pepper spray. Tess was trembling, scared. "I have no idea."

They paused for a moment and then inched toward the door with hesitant steps. Nela pushed her head through the gap and tried to spy outside but could not spot anything. Up the stairs, the path led back into the block. There was only the slight rustling of the trees, while the grass lay still.

"Do you see anything at all?"

"Nothing."

"Maybe it was just a branch or something."

"Yeah, might be."

Insecurely, they looked at each other and listened for another moment.

"We should probably find a place to sleep."

"That's probably for the best."

"We can come back here tomorrow."

"Okay, that's fine."

Nela gazed at Tess. The impending quarrel was forgotten. Tomorrow, she would dedicate more time to her. Yet, they had to find a safe place to stay for the night now.

For there could be wolves out here.

"Close call," Yelka chuckled to Damon.

"Let's hurry before they realize you weren't on the phone at all."

"Girls, don't worry about your safety. Everything is under control."

"However, though, we need to talk about my new stage name!" They laughed.

Wrapping his arms around the girls' shoulders, Damon walked ahead of Zander into the apartment block. As the three of them cheered, Zander felt a pang of bitterness welling up inside him. Damon was not controlling anything. In fact, he was dependent on him, had no idea where he even was.

That shady sense of safety was nothing more than an overinflated self-esteem and an overinflated self-assessment. Anyway, they would see that they need to rely on him to get home quickly.

He was frustrated that he had not planned for the height of the wall and now had to look for a new way back. It wasn't that he minded staying longer in the old barracks but having to submit to Damon and follow his orders pained Zander. He would not let that happen to him again.

"I'll search for a new way back," he shouted to Yelka. However, she was already busy setting up the camera. "Alrighty!" she replied, smiling at Zander.

"We're going to need about another hour here," Damon interjected again. "Be nice if you found a solution by then. Right?"

Vivian laughed. "Otherwise, we'll call Councilor Wilbanks again!" Damon laughed smugly.

Silently, Zander turned and followed a small path between two houses into the forest. Having had enough, he needed a break from Damon and Vivian.

If only Yelka would not let herself be blinded like that ...

Disgruntled, Zander walked into the forest, the voices behind him fading away. This must have been the original path to the open-air swimming pool, he assumed. It was located northeast of the apartment block and within easy walking distance. From there, it wouldn't be far to the old open-air theater or the actual military complex. However, this path led deeper and deeper into the terrain. The path to the junkyard, which they would have to take, was in the opposite direction. It would have been a shame to ignore all this, though. Perhaps he could simply lead the group home via a detour. Yelka would surely be grateful to him.

The forest was light, the ground flat. They would make good progress. If they hurried, it would be possible. While walking carefully through the undergrowth, Zander heard the shrill call of a bird of prey. Only now did he notice the eerie silence. No bird was singing, only the rustling of leaves could be heard. His eyes fell on what Zander had at first thought was a withered bush. But as he approached, he realized that this was not a dead plant. Long, curved bones jutted upward in front of him. The outer flesh was partially rotten. This must have been a rib cage. Probably from an animal. Maybe a deer.

At first, he was startled, but then curiosity got the better of him. Zander had never seen a carcass before. Fascinated, he took off his gloves and squatted in front of the carrion. He inhaled and was surprised to notice that it didn't smell. It was only the dark scent of the forest that penetrated his nose.

Hesitantly, Zander touched the bones, letting his finger run slowly over the smooth surface until he reached the splintered end. He felt fracture marks. The animal had apparently not died just like that. A predator must have torn it because a hunter would not have simply left his prey here. If it was an animal … Whatever the remains were, it was very likely that a wolf had preyed here. Perhaps, it might have been better to get out of here before nightfall.

He decided to return to the group. Maybe he could discuss his plan with Yelka in a quiet minute. Zander enjoyed the silence of the forest until he came back to the settlement. From a distance, he heard Damon's voice and loud laughter. The sinking feeling in his stomach returned. It was one thing to take Damon and Vivian with him on their tours. Yet, it hit him even harder when Yelka didn't see this as a burden, as he did. Anyway, he would be alone with Yelka again on the next trip. For sure.

As he took the path between the two apartment blocks and turned around the corner, he saw Vivian sitting in a window, posing. She was lolling around, laughing affectedly and enjoying the attention. Below her, Yelka had set up the camera. Damon, who had an arm around her, had the operation of the device explained to him with mock interest. They laughed.

Zander had a lump in his throat. His feet stuck to the floor, and he was unable to move. Seeing Yelka and Damon like this cut off his breath. Paralyzed, he perceived Vivian pausing and nodding over to him. Her lips also moved, but Zander did not hear her words, only a low hum inside his ears. Damon and Yelka turned to him. She waved at him and laughed, but he just couldn't return it.

Zander closed his eyes and shook his head until he regained consciousness.

"Say, did you find a way back?"
Zander nodded. "Yes, it is right there."

He pointed into the forest.

Twilight cast long shadows on the abandoned settlement as the sun set behind the block. An owl's distant call announced the awakening of the nocturnal hunters. Bats awoke from their slumber and set out to find food. Deep in the forest, a lone wolf was out hunting for prey. Unlike the owl and the bats, the wolf had no rivals. Deer and wild boar were his preferred prey. He raised his nose and took up the scent. But after a few moments he retreated. This was not a good night for hunting. He smelled humans.

In the shadow of the old buildings, Ryder, Dave, Jesse, Mike, Tami and Mousey stood in silence. They stared at those "Duke Executives" business cards and heard how the voices of the other group slowly faded away, finally disappearing between the buildings.

Gazoo had laid down on the grass next to Ryder, panting. While the boys considered the snob's offer, Tami was overwhelmed by it. Never had she met the CEO of a modeling agency. Much less in a professional environment. After all, she would have had to have worked in the first place, and that was far from her mind, as it was from everyone else in the group. The fact that they had been offered a job at all was astonishing. Silently, Ryder and Dave both realized they had been set up. The two young men, who had been fighting, looked at each other with suspicion. Finally, Dave was the first to chime in.

"Hey, what do you think they are paying?"
With a lurking look, Ryder eyed his rival. "Why do you care?" he hissed

back. "Wanna work all of a sudden?" His undertone sounded growly and erased any sense of humor in Ryder's question.

"Naw, absolutely not," Dave replied. "I just thought it was probably a good offer from the guy."

"You think?" Ryder was irritated, sensing hostility in Dave's feigned naïveté.

"Well ..." Dave hesitated. "He seems to have convinced you," he finally continued with a smile.

The rest of the group had also realized that Dave was messing around with Ryder. Mike grinned broadly, Tami openly smiled, and Mousey smirked, looking at the floor. Only Jesse kept his cool.

Ryder stared at Dave, breathing in and out slowly. Inside, he was boiling with rage. A few minutes ago, he had been on the verge of giving Dave a beating, but now the tables had turned. They seemed to be laughing at Dave's comments, though in reality they were laughing at him.

"Maybe" Dave continued, "you can take Gazoo with you." His hesitant smile had disappeared and given way to a broad grin. "To the shift."

Mike laughed silently, Tami held a hand over her mouth, and Mousey turned to the side, hiding his smile. Jesse was the only one standing behind Ryder with an icy expression.

Ryder knew he had to put Dave in his place, but he couldn't just beat him. That would have been a sign of weakness.

"Night Watchman Ryder reporting for duty!" Dave raised his hand and saluted.

It was Tami who burst into cackling laughter. She leaned forward and dropped her hand from her mouth.

A triumphant laugh was written all over Dave's face. Mike smirked mockingly. Mousey bit his lip.

Ryder abruptly grabbed Tami's neck and pinned her down. Her smile froze on her lips when he grabbed her hair and yanked her head back.

"What's so funny, bitch? Did anything he said amuse you?"
Reflexively, Tami shook her head, but Ryder's firm grip hurt her scalp.
"Didn't? Then why are you laughing?"
"Sorry, sorry. I didn't mean it, it wasn't funny!" she shouted.

As Mousey turned away, smiles disappeared from Dave's and Mike's faces.

"You didn't mean it? Didn't mean it at all?" Eyes wide, Ryder stood before Tami. His grip lingered on her hair, but he didn't pull it back any further.
"No, no, no ..." she sobbed, with tears in her eyes.
"All right, then." Ryder grinned as he forced a kiss on Tami. He pressed his lips on hers, pushing her head forward. It wasn't long before he felt her tongue in his mouth. Satisfied, he let her go and gave Dave a challenging stare.

"So, you want me to get you back on track, too?" Ryder smiled sarcastically at the two of them. "Don't wanna get your balls in an uproar no more?" Gazoo had stood up and barked at Dave as if in confirmation.
"Piece of shit," Dave hissed. "I'm not your bitch!"

"That's right. For you are a carpenter's dream," laughed Ryder. This time, Jesse joined in. Tami lifted the corners of her mouth, looking at Dave's skinny chest.

"I have long arms, though, you know!" Dave and Mike built themselves up, preparing for a fight.

"Mousey, what about you?" shouted Jesse. "Are you with us or with team bitch slap?" Mousey shrugged his shoulders, but stood next to Ryder, remembering his sore cheek.

"Oh, fuck you!" Dave spat out. "We're getting the fuck out of here."

"Better get lost then, you two faggots!"

While Dave and Ryder were trading final barbs, Tami sat down on a stone and wiped the tears from her face. With a glance at the display of her cell phone, she checked for runny makeup. The most important thing was to look good. Maybe she would find Duke online. Stealthily, she glanced at the business card and typed in the address. But she got no result.

"Hey!" she shouted to the arguing group. "We don't have any Wi-Fi here at all."

The argument died down, all eyes turned to Tami.

"So, they couldn't make any phone calls at all."

The mood in the group darkened. Furrowed brows replaced the once amused expressions, and a palpable sense of betrayal was in the air. Ryder was the first to speak up.

"They screwed us!" He glanced at Dave.

"Yeah, man!" Jesse cut in. "They messed us up."

It was more a rallying call than a statement.

"Those bastards!" Dave vented all his anger at the photographers.

"Come on, let's get them!"

"Yeah, man!" — "Let's go!"

Clutching the handle of the leash, Ryder charged ahead with his dog. Behind him, Jesse, Dave, and Mike closed in, while Tami and Mousey followed at a short distance. Marching resolutely through the tall grass, they continued on their way between the two houses through which the group had recently disappeared.

But there was no one there.

Neither to the left up to the dilapidated houses in the forest, nor to the right on the side of the last apartment block. The group was simply no longer there. Perhaps they had disappeared into the dark forest. The sun had set, its last rays dimming.

"Where the hell did they go?"

"I don't know. They just left, I guess."

"Fuck."

"We weren't fast enough."

"Never mind."

"Yeah, maybe we should haul ass, too."

It wasn't that Mousey liked to make other people's lives hell. He would rather have been at home now. Even Tami didn't appeal to him anymore right now. After what Ryder had done to her, she seemed to have become somehow ... shabby. Mousey no longer desired her at that moment. But he didn't have anyone else, either.

Without those boys, he would have been all alone. And he certainly wouldn't have found a girlfriend. Thus, it was more the fear of being alone that drove him to bring something to Ryder's attention.

"Take a look over there!"
With a dirty, hoarse laugh, Ryder tapped Dave on the shoulder. "Come on, let's get them!"

The sun set early, leaving the firmament above the old blocks red. There was not a single cloud in the sky. It would be a starry night.

Nela was the first to leave the supermarket and was standing in a stooped position at the bottom of the stairs. Cautiously, she stretched her head upwards and observed the surroundings. But nothing was stirring. The rising wind swept through the tall grass and treetops. Whatever had been scratching at the window had disappeared. Perhaps it had only been branches or leaves. Or a bird that had flown against the window.

"Do you see anything?" Tess was still standing in the doorway, waiting for a sign from Nela.

"No," she whispered, "It was probably nothing. Let's find a place to sleep for the night."

"Are you certain this is the right decision?"

Tess was torn between excitement and fear. On the one hand, she found it thrilling, but on the other hand, it worried her to be so far away from civilization. The gathering darkness didn't make it any better.

"Hey, don't worry about it. We're well-equipped and we'll be safe." Nela gave Tess a hug. "We'll set up camp in a minute, prepare some food, and enjoy the summer night."

Tess sighed, "All right, whatever you say."

Nela smiled. There was no way she would miss the sunrise. The early morning light would lend the abandoned settlement an indescribable magic. With these photos, she would pass the final exam with flying colors. Nela had planned everything in advance. She had compared images, tried camera settings, and tested lenses. When the sun rose behind them, the red morning light would color the entire block and contrast it with the green of the forest. It would be just perfect. Later, they could search for the outdoor pool and stage. Tess would definitely want photos there. Nela had planned for that, too.

"Yeah, that's what I say." She grabbed Tess's hand and walked purposefully toward a house on the edge of the settlement.

"Why this house?"

"We can get a better sense of direction here. Imagine we go out in the dark, and we're in the middle of the block. Where would you run to?"

"Hmm ...", Tess pondered. "No idea?"

"That's right. But when you get out of here, walk down to the right and around the settlement. You'll automatically end up on the path that leads back to the junkyard and our car."

"What if I go around to the left?"

"Well, then you'd be walking straight into the woods."

Tess nodded. "But why would we leave the house at night anyway?"

Nela remained silent. The fact that Tess didn't come up with the answer on her own was good, on the one hand, because she didn't seem to be worried; but on the other hand, it was also naive. It would be better not to unsettle her.

"Oh, I don't know, either," she fibbed. "Just turn on the flashlight, it's getting dark."

The house seemed to have been an administrative building. No apartments were leading off from the corridors, only individual rooms. Now, the already dark building was finally pitch black. In the glow of the flashlight, they could make out gray walls, wallpaper falling off. The lower floors smelled of damp and mustiness. With each floor, the air became more pleasant. Apparently, this was since the windows there were not boarded and some of them stood open.

On the top floor, Nela chose a room in the middle of the main hallway. Tess sat down her backpack and gazed around.

"Nice place. Really." Cheekily, she grinned at Nela. "This is really where I'd like to be with you."

"Is that true?"

"Yes, at least this apartment has an intact window and most of the wallpaper is still hanging on the walls."

Nela laughed. Her friend's deadpan humor was one of her most beautiful traits.

"And there's no mold here at all, either. Neither green nor black."

"Well, this seems to be a true dream home."

They unrolled their camping mats, laid out their sleeping bags, and stowed their gear in their backpacks. But Nela wasn't finished yet. Armed with wire and a multifunction tool, she went out into the hallway.

"Come on, you have to help me."

"What's up?"

"We play it safe."

Back in the stairwell, Nela stretched a wire across the steps. It zigzagged across the steps of the lower floors and then went up.

"How many yards will you use, for heaven's sake?" Confused, Tess watched Nela as she laid the tension wire all the way to her room. At the end, she attached a little bell.

"If someone comes into the house now, we'll hear it soon enough and be warned."

Tess nodded. "But you do know there's another stairwell at the other end of the hall, don't you?"

"Yes, I realize that," Nela confirmed. "We're going to barricade that. Give me a hand." She lifted the door of one office off its hinges. Together, they placed it in the opposite stairwell doorway.

"If someone wants to go through here and opens the door, it falls towards them. The noise will waken us up."

"Possibly," laughed Tess, "I just hope I can sleep soundly, though."

"I think so. But in case of an emergency: If the bell rings, we run around to the right. If the door rumbles, we flee in panic to the left stairwell." Nela laughed. "Okay?"

"Stop scaring me." The humor had gone out of Tess's voice.

"Hey, everything will be fine," Nela assured her. "I just like to be prepared for anything."

"Fine by me. Now, can we eat something, please?"

"Love to, I'm starving."

They put the flashlights in the room for lighting and set up their camping stove. It wasn't long before it smelled deliciously like canned ravioli. Silently, they sat on their sleeping bags and enjoyed the warm meal. It had been an exhausting day.

And while Nela was excited to finish her bachelor's thesis, Tess was thinking about the photos Nela had taken of her at the supermarket. Surely, Nela would help her retouch the photos, and then she could post them on her Insta. However, she didn't know how she would end up making a profit from it. Sure, plenty of followers were important, but then what? She would need someone to organize it all for her. If only...

Tess's eyes closed. Finally, it was bedtime.

Tomorrow will be another day.

"Girls, your photos turned out pretty good, no doubt about it."

"I was not expecting anything else from a photographer like that."

"Dear sis, I love you." With a kiss on her sister's cheek, Yelka detached herself and joined Zander.

"Hey, check out the footage." She hooked up with him and showed him her new pictures on the camera's display. "What do you think?"

Her sudden closeness snapped Zander out of his grumpiness. Feeling Yelka so close to him was confusing, but at the same time he felt incredible joy. Overwhelmed, he stammered, "Uh, what?"

Yelka laughed and nudged him in the side. "The photos of Vivian, how do you like them?"

"Yes," he began, looking at the image on the display. Vivian, head resting in her hands, on the weathered climbing frame. The picture was indeed beautiful; Zander liked the play of colors. But what he liked most was the fact that Yelka had taken the photo. "It's gorgeous," he admitted blatantly.

"Look, this one is my favorite." She zapped forward, stopping at a shot of Vivian standing in the block's open doorway, arms stretched, holding on to the door frame.

All the magic of the place came into full view–the crumbling, dirty plaster; the moss and ivy on the walls; the trees close to the facade—and Yelka's little sister right in the middle. She had captured all this just perfectly.

"This is spectacular," he had to admit.

For a moment, Zander felt a twinge of remorse. It was more likely the doubt of the correctness of his little deception maneuver. Yelka surely would be happy as well, if they were back at the hotel in time and Vivian could post her photos. Then again, maybe she'd be thrilled to still see the old swimming pool and open-air stage?

However, it was already dawning. In a short time, it would be pitch black anyway. Nonetheless, they were on their way, and now Zander would be their guide.

"Are we really on the right track?" Like Yelka could read his mind. "The forest is getting denser."

Zander smiled sheepishly. "Yes, but we still must hurry. It's still a little way to the junkyard."

"Are we going the long way back after all? I thought you found another one?"

Embarrassed, Zander looked down at the ground. She almost sensed his lie, just had to dig deeper.

"Nah." He pressed his lips together and shrugged his shoulders in embarrassment.

"Okay, hopefully we can still make it in time."

Zander got lucky. But his happiness did not last long. They had almost reached the outdoor pool when Damon put his hand on his shoulder. In the twilight, he looked fierce.

"We may not have Wi-Fi here, friend," he approached Zander, "but I can see pretty clearly that you're leading us astray."

He held the display in his face and pointed his finger at the map of the apartment block. Vivian stood next to him, her hands on her hips. Yelka broke away from Zander in surprise.

"Here" he pointed to the wall where they had started, "is where we started. Here is the apartment block. And this" he continued swiping and pointed to a spot in the woods, "is where we should be now. Where are you taking us?" With eyes wide open and a deep frown line on his forehead, he waited for Zander's answer.

Zander felt caught. However, it was not Yelka but Damon who had busted him out–which didn't make it any better. She, too, was now looking at him in irritation. Zander was at a loss for words, he searched for an excuse, but apart from a quiet murmur, he couldn't say anything.

"What?" Harshly, Damon moved in on him. "I can't hear you."

"We have to go to the junkyard," he now blurted.

"To what junkyard?" Damon was still holding his cell phone right in Zander's face. "Where's that?"

"Let me show you." With frantic finger movements, Zander swiped left on the map. "Here."

"It's right in the middle of nowhere!" Damon shook his head in frustration.

"Tell me that's not true." Vivian was aghast.

Yelka looked at him in wander. "Zander, this is supposed to be in the east, but we're walking up north."

"Damn right!" Damon cursed. "Why are you doing this? Tell me!"

Paralyzed, Zander was still staring at the display. In the dim light of the forest, the glow of the cell phone turned their faces blue. Zander felt alone. Damon was upset, his frown line looking like a deep furrow. Vivian had closed her eyes and raised her head to the sky, while Yelka looked at him, waiting for an answer.

"This is the old way," he finally explained, "the same way the soldiers used to take. Take a look." With his shoe, he scraped the dirt aside and finally hit asphalt. Damon shined his cell phone to check Zander's statement.

He regained his composure; the explanation had occurred to him at the very last moment. "If we walk cross-country through the forest, we may run into obstacles and not get anywhere."

Damon shook his head. "That's a long detour. I should have checked myself. Seems, you can't even be trusted with route planning!"

"Hey," Yelka interjected. "Calm down, stress isn't doing anyone any good right now."

"I'm very calm," Damon replied tersely. "And I say we turn left and walk straight ahead. Because there's one thing you don't know either—who knows whether any obstacle might be waiting for us along the way?"

Silently, Zander gazed at him. He was doomed.

"Okay," Vivian chimed in. "All in favor of turning left?" she asked around the room, raising her hand. Almost simultaneously, Damon raised his hand as well. If Yelka sided with Zander, they would have a split decision.

However, Vivian's sister was not bent on conflict. She wanted to keep the group together, as peacefully as possible. Therefore, Zander was not surprised, but all the more disappointed, when she, too, raised her hand.

As Damon stared at him, victorious, he glanced down at the ground.

"All right, decision made. Let's go" called Damon.

Ugh, they should go to hell!

Ryder held Gazoo's mouth shut as they stood in front of the house, watching the flickering light on the top floor. The dog was restless, eager to bark. It didn't matter that there was basically no reason to do so—the mere fact that his mouth was shut aroused the urge to resist within the animal. Just like his master, he never learned to control his anger.

"We'll sneak in and once we're inside," Ryder whispered to his gang, "we'll smash the place to pieces. We'll fuck shit up, scare the hell outa them!"

Glancing into his eyes, Dave grinned wickedly.

"All right?" asked Ryder to the group.
"We'll just scare them, though, wouldn't we?" Tami struggled.
"Sure thing," Ryder grinned and kissed her. "We're just scaring them."
He gazed at his gang, raising his eyebrows. "Let's go!"

In the darkness of the stairwell, Dave followed Ryder and his dog. The steel pipe in his hand felt good. He looked over his shoulder and saw Mike close behind, followed by Jesse, Mousey and Tami, who was using her cell phone as a flashlight. Jesse and Mike both looked determined, brandishing their batons. They wanted to strike, finally. It was still silent, in the barren hallway only their footsteps and the dog's pressed panting echoed. Adrenaline blocked all warning signals, suppressed any hesitation. If any of them had any doubts about their raid, it was too late now.

"Go!" roared Ryder, releasing his dog from his grasp.

He shot forward, barking and growling like a rabid beast, tugging at the leash. Ryder laughed, enjoying the rush of escalation. Behind him, windows shattered. Loud clangs drowned out his cronies' screams of rage. Uncontrollably, they hit everything that got in their way. Tami raised her hand in front of her face. Either from rage or fear, Mousey roared without hitting anything.

Once on the top floor, Ryder saw lights burning in the hallway. That's where they would be crouching, the damn backpackers. He slowed his walk, preparing for the moment of encounter. Ryder enjoyed the way Gazoo pulled on the leash. A ravaging beast, under his control alone! Dave smashed a window; Jesse dragged the steel pipe across the floor.

"Three, two, one …" he shouted, "we're coming in!"

Yet when they stormed the room, only the light of a camping stove was burning. Two sleeping bags lay on the floor. Whoever had wanted to spend the night here had already fled.

Instantly, the roar and raucousness of his gang died away. They entered the room with hesitant steps, their eyes wandering over the remaining belongings in disappointment.

"They heard us" Jesse stated razor-sharp.

"We should have just gone for it."

"Who gives a shit, they won't get far anyway." Ryder grabbed a backpack from behind the door. "They forgot their luggage."

"Look inside!"

"Yeah, maybe there's money in it."

With one hand, Ryder dumped out the contents of the backpack on the floor. The boys cheered when they found women's underwear among a set of cutlery, dishes, a sweater, and long pants.

Ryder let the gray panties circle around his finger. He smelled them, closed his eyes, and delightedly inhaled the scent. "They certainly haven't been washed yet" he lustily laughed.

Dave pulled out a few papers from the pile. "Hotel reservations. But not until tomorrow." He grinned. "For today, the girl still needs a place to stay." He proudly showed around a copy of her ID. "Tess Walker, sweet 24 years young."

"Holy crap, we really let something slide here."

"She's too old for you, kid."

"I dig sexy mamas."

Tami looked down at the floor in embarrassment. This was so humiliating. Not only had Ryder put her down in front of the whole gang, now they were even getting off on a strange bitch, of whom they only knew the ID photo. This wasn't what she had expected!

Out of the corner of her eye, she watched the boys. Ryder seemed to be fighting a duel with Dave to see who could bang this tramp the hardest. Jesse and Mike cheered them on, probably would have loved to fuck her, too.

Only Mousey watched the four of them silently. When he looked at her, she smiled at him. That small, uptight kid. The blink of her eyes was enough to upset him. If it hadn't been dark, everyone would have noticed that he immediately blushed.

Her gaze wandered around the room, away from the little bitch's belongings to a small bell discreetly placed next to the door.

"Ryder," she interrupted the gang briskly, "they had an alarm system." She pointed to the wire stretched just above the floor, leading into the stairwell.

"Well, well, well." With amusement, Ryder marveled at the construction. "A smart cunt. You rarely have that." The boys laughed out loud.

"Maybe she was here with her guy, too."

"Nah, she was a lick sister."

"What makes you think that?"

"The second person on the booking is a chick. Nela Dubois."

"What kind of name is that?"

"It doesn't matter. Two chicks are better than one." Ryder examined the room. "They're out there all alone. We should go find them."

He left the room and stood by a shattered window. From here he had a clear view of the forest, which would probably have been much better in daylight. However, now only the dark blue of the sky remained over the black forest.

Ryder breathed in the cool air. "See that down there in the woods?" Several lights wandered among the trees.

"This time we'll be quiet. Until the very last moment."

MANHUNT

Ben Marshall opened the tailgate of the old station wagon, letting out his golden retriever Athos. His best friend was getting on in years. Indecisively, the dog stood at the edge of the trunk. He used to jump out of the car in anticipation of his dog bowl being filled. Now his hunting instinct had waned, and he slept a little longer each day.

"I guess you don't feel like going yourself, huh? I can well understand that."

He grasped his dog with both hands and carefully lifted him out of the car. He had gotten Athos as a puppy after his wife died ten years ago. Cancer had taken her away from him—that relentless bastard. Since then, he lived alone, with only his best friend Athos.

When he opened the garden gate, he could smell the lovely scent of roses blooming in the front yard. His wife had loved them, and Ben tended to them as best he could. While he wasn't exactly green thumbed, the plants were robust. His wife Gabby had done a good job preparing them. He would have to water them on Sunday if it continued not to rain.

Ben unlocked the door and let his dog into the house. It had always been like that. Athos was always the first to enter the house. Even at his age, he has not let this privilege be taken away from him. He watched the animal walk wearily to his basket and curl up on the soft cushion. On Monday, during his lunch break, he would take him to visit Doc Wally. The old quack was not an excellent veterinarian, but he was the only one in town.

For several years, Ben had been working as a security guard in the civil service. He was responsible for the old barracks area outside the city. The Allies had left the area 30 years ago and nothing had happened there ever since. Like so many Cold War properties, this barracks was slowly rotting away. Eventually, the buildings would collapse, and it would only be necessary to clear the debris to sell the site as building ground. But that was too costly right now.

Ben's job, therefore, was simply to make sure that no one strayed onto the site and came to harm.

He went into the kitchen and put on a pot of pasta for Athos's dinner. While the water boiled, Ben opened a beer and took a deep sip. He stretched and yawed. His hair was falling out, his bones ached, but still, he could not retire. He would not be able to live on his pension alone just yet. He would have to hold out for seven more years before he could retire completely.

Ben let the noodles cool and went up the spiral staircase to the second floor. In the living room, he turned on the light and went to the window where his telescope was. It was a ritual he got into when he got the municipal job. Every evening, as he prepared food for his dog, he would drink a beer and take one last peek at the barracks over in the woods.

With his binoculars, he could see that little satellite town where the families had lived back then. Further back, the former radio tower loomed, with the barracks buildings at its feet. The military hospital could only be glimpsed; the old Infirmary hid too deep in the forest. It was not until Ben had checked out the barracks one last time that he was ready to call it a day.

He put down the beer, opened the protective cover, and put his eyes on the telescope. In the dark, he could usually only guess at the outlines of the buildings, but not today—bright lights burned on the top floor of apartment block 2B. Not a yellow light like flames, but a white light like one or more lamps. Ben watched the house for a moment. There had to be some people there because the lights were wandering around. Ben sighed.

He had made sure that all access points to the area were closed. The surrounding wall was still there from occupation times, but it was in good condition and completely intact. The gate was locked with a heavy padlock. To the east, the forest was the only natural entrance to the block. The actual barracks inside the area was once again secured by a high fence.

Usually, no one entered the forbidden city, but occasionally teenagers managed to sneak into the area. They took photos and wandered around. For them, it was all just a great adventure, but they were unaware of the dangers of the place. There was no covering cellular network on that gigantic site. If something happened out there, you were lost. No one could come to help, and civilization was half a day's walk away. Given that, he had equipped his station wagon with a CB radio. That was the only means of communication that worked reliably.

Ben closed his telescope, went down to the kitchen and prepared Athos' bowl. Tired, the golden retriever crept to his food. Ben gave him a pet on the head. "I'm going to go out for another run. Be right back."

When he started the car, it was shortly after 9 pm. At half past nine he would be at the gate, ten minutes later at the settlement. He steered the car out of town the usual way, turned left at the main road, and found the lights of his hometown growing smaller and smaller in the rearview mirror. The night swallowed them up.

Between the corn fields, he turned right onto a road that only farmer Weimer was driving his tractor. Once upon a time, this had been the main road into the military complex. Tanks and trucks had rolled down here day after day. Now the asphalt was broken up and weathered.

At the end of the fields, the headlights shone into the wooded area that Ben would now follow for about ten minutes. By night, the forest looked dark and threatening. Branches protruded onto the lane; shrubs overgrew the roadway. Apart from Ben, no one else used this road. The closer he got to the barracks, the more the asphalt was covered with dirt, leaves, and mud. The many cold winters and hot summers had left potholes and bumps. This was the reason Ben had to spend a fortune repairing his car again and again.

As the forest opened up before him and the massive gate reflected the light of the headlights, Ben parked the car in the middle of the road. To the left and right around the barracks led the old security road, which he drove twice every day.

He opened the car door and peered into the darkness. Ben reached into the back seat and picked up his heavy flashlight. Just for safety. In an emergency, he could also strike it.

Ben left the engine running and walked carefully to the large main gate, whose double doors towered over him by about three feet. After taking down the chain, he pushed the doors open with both hands. Rusty rattling sounded through the night. He was not a fearful person, but there was something eerie about being alone in this place at night. No one could come to his aid, and civilization was far away. The sound of the night was strange. An owl was calling, rustling in the undergrowth. Maybe, it was time to get a gun license. Just in case …

Ben walked back to the car and quietly closed the door. He would leave the gate open behind him. Then he would drive to the end of the road until it was overgrown with trees and bushes. From there, it wouldn't be far to apartment complex 2B. He just hoped he didn't run into any rioters or cable thieves there. If he did, he would have to call the police for help. But maybe it was just the local youngsters. Ryder and the other kids were good-for-nothings and occasionally caused trouble, but at least he knew them.

After all, they were only children.

That cheerful mood had abruptly vanished after Damon's proposal had been accepted by the group. It wasn't that Vivian and he cared about Zander's opinion, but Damon's goal to return to the hotel as soon as possible was ambitious, and he transmitted his own inner pressure to the group through silence. The sun was completely gone, and night had wrapped up the forest.

Yelka and Zander had turned on their flashlights and led the way, closely followed by Vivian and Damon. Sticks and rotten branches broke under their steps; tripping hazards that actually made Damon's route imponderable. With their lights pointed at the ground, the group trotted along.

"Watch out, there are roots sticking out from under the foliage."

Yelka knew that Vivian was frustrated. As a model, she was not prepared for such a trip. Pressing her lips together angrily, she tried not to lose her sandals.

"Dear sis, don't lose your composure. Better think about that cozy hotel room."
"I do nothing else," Vivian grudgingly replied.
"We're going to have a really nice meal and watch TV in bed later."

"That sounds really wicked!" a strange voice called out. "I'll bang you bitches right there."

In the darkness of the forest, a group of about six people confronted them. In the glow of the flashlights, they recognized the same gang that they had so brazenly duped that afternoon. Their sinister grins indicated that they would not succeed a second time. Three of the boys had raised their batons ready to attack, that mean dog kept growling badly. The only girl in the group had her cell phone pointed at Yelka and seemed to be filming.

They stood frozen in fear, unable to utter a word, and their wide-eyed expressions revealing their shock. Their hearts pounded. Damon cautiously took a step back.

"Hey Duke!" shouted Ryder into the darkness behind the group, where he suspected Damon. "You don't mind if we have a little fun with your models, do you?"

This time, Damon did not reply.

"That's what I thought ..." Ryder enjoyed his triumph as he yelled, "Go! Get 'em!"

Yelka panicked and shouted, "Run!"

Behind her, screams of rage and dogs barking echoed through the forest. The gang swung their steel pipes and chased after them. Adrenaline fueled them on and on. None of them knew where to run. In the frantic glow of the flashlight, Yelka saw Vivian running, Damon in front of her. "Run!" she yelled again, screaming in horror. The gang had to be up close. To the left and right, trees and bushes flew by.

Soon the turnoff to the right had to come, which would lead them back to the settlement. Just don't fall! The attackers' screams did not cease. The dog barked louder and louder. She jumped to the right, over a branch, hooked to the left, then ran down an embankment.

Yelka realized that if she kept the flashlight on, they would not outrun the gang. In a high arc, she threw it through the woods, almost hitting the thugs. Now she was alone, running aimlessly into the dark. She didn't know where the others were. As the darkness embraced her, the screams died away. The gang seemed to be running in a different direction. From a distance, she heard the leader roar.

"Duke, why don't you call the cops!" Ryder thirsted for revenge. "Come on, smart guy!" He gave the leash more play and kept pushing Gazoo. "Sic 'em, boy!"

Ryder enjoyed this outburst of crushing fury and blind violence. Jesse, Dave, and Mike cut a furrow of destruction through the forest. Even little Mousey had taken a stick and was punching holes in the air.

"Fuck 'em up!" He cheered on his gang. "Smash everything!"

Gazoo yanked so hard on the leash that even Ryder had a hard time keeping the dog under control.

"Bring me that motherfucker!" he yelled after the boys.
"Duke, we're going to get you!" The boys joined in.

Ryder turned to Tami, who was running behind him, filming the hunt. Tightening his biceps, he stuck his tongue obscenely out at the camera. Tami was turned on by this. She loved it when he went nuts like that. He would do her tonight so bad!

Almost like they could dispel the darkness, Jesse and Mike rushed ahead. Yet, they saw only shadowy figures fleeing from them through the forest. Didn't matter—they wanted to be first! They were going to get Duke! That fucker who had duped them all!

"There he is!" shouted Mike, seething with rage. Even in the darkness, his red sneakers were clearly visible.

"Fuck, yeah! Come on! We'll get him," Jesse cheered him on.
"Yeah, man!" Mike swung his steel club like a riding crop.

Like a rabbit, the guy in front of them raced through the forest. They could watch him struggle to keep his balance. His arms flailed wildly, lurching to the left and to the right. He set and jumped over a tree trunk, sank to his knees, slowed his pace.

"Come on, we've got him!" Jesse gave Mike a pat on the back. "Let's grab him!"

But Mike lost his balance, tripped over the very tree trunk that Damon had jumped over a second ago. His upper body tipped to the left, falling in Jesse's direction. The two collided. Jesse managed to hold on, but Mike fell and wound up in the leaves.

"Moron!" Jesse roared. "What kind of stupid bitch are you?"
"Shut the fuck up, man! You're the one who pushed me!" Mike jumped

up and went after Jesse.

"Pushed whom?" Jesse raised the metal pipe. "Come here!"

"Hey!" Ryder yelled between them. "Calm down!"

"Because of that bastard, we lost Duke."

In fact, Damon had vanished. One short moment had been enough to disappear in the darkness.

"And where did the others go?" Ryder was furious, spitting rage.

"I don't know, we were chasing Duke."

"Come on, let go of Gazoo! We'll can still get him!"

"Yes, let go of the dog!"

Jesse and Mike felt it was their last chance to find the runaway. Yet, Ryder took Gazoo tightly on a leash. The dog barked one last time and joined Ryder's side, grunting.

"No," he replied brusquely. "You fucked up, you morons!"

Tami now joined them and held the camera on the three of them. Their gazes turned to her. "Turn that thing off," Ryder snapped. Tami lowered her gaze and pocketed the phone as Mousey returned to them. With a stick in his hand, he looked like the little boy he was. It was obvious that his prey had gotten away as well.

"I don't get it," Ryder yelled. "Do I have to take care of everything myself?"

"No, you don't."

From the darkness of the forest, Dave's voice rang out. He was leading someone in front of him, head pressed down.

"See what I got!"

Pressed deep into the soil, Yelka was lying on the ground. She was struck by the earthy, sour scent of fallen leaves and dirt. It was dark around her. She felt the weight of her backpack—at least it was still there. Deep in the forest, she heard voices. Loudly at times, quietly at others. Her breathing was slow. Yelka did not dare to make more noise than necessary.

Cautiously, she raised her head and tried to spot something in the darkness. But it was in vain, she could not see further than a few steps. She still felt shell-shocked. Just a few seconds ago she had tried to cheer up her sister, now she was hiding in the dark forest, hounded and chased. Knowing that thugs were lying in wait didn't make things any better, though.

Yelka lay motionless for a while, listening into the forest. The voices were further away. No one seemed to be near her. Cautiously, she straightened up and tried to get her bearings. On the run, she had lost all sense of her location. The settlement would have to be to her right. But that was just a guess.

And even if it were, should she really return there? Wouldn't her pursuers show up there as well? And where were the others? Her friends couldn't be too far away. She would just cautiously sneak through the forest and…

From behind, Yelka felt two arms wrap around her. She was about to scream when someone covered her mouth. The arms tightened, squeezing firmly. No sound came from her mouth.

"Don't scream," someone whispered softly in her ear. Yelka was trembling, trying to recognize something, but she could not. "It's me, Damon."

Yelka relaxed. She nodded her head in relief. Damon loosened his grip and took his hand from her mouth. She turned around and hugged him. Only now tears came to her eyes. She hugged Damon tightly, suppressing a sob.

"Shhh …" Soothingly, he stroked her head.

When she had her feelings back under control, Yelka detached herself from him.

"Are you okay?" she softly asked.

"Yeah, yeah, I'm fine," he replied. "They chased me quite a bit, but I was able to shake them off, thankfully."

"Thank God. Did you see the others?"

"No, I had to cast off those three goons. In the process, I lost sight of you guys. Do you still have your gear with you?"

Yelka fumbled to the back and reached for her backpack. "I think so, everything should still be in there."

Relieved, Damon nodded. "That's good, for we haven't lost anything."

Yelka was astonished. "What do you mean? The equipment is probably the least of the problems!"

"Yeah, yeah. I guess you're right." He put a hand on her forearm. "I meant the photos aren't lost." Damon smiled. "That's why we were here, weren't we?"

With a skeptical eye, Yelka watched him. She raised her voice to say something in reply, but Damon interrupted her.

"We should find the others in the first place and then get out of here as soon as possible." He smiled. "A-S-A-P."

Yelka nodded in agreement. "Yet, how can we make this happen without being discovered?"

Damon pointed backward, in the direction from which he had approached Yelka. "I came from there. Vivian was behind me and in front of you, right?"

"Yeah, right."

"She must have passed somewhere between those two lines," he speculated. "So, let's go in that direction. Quietly. Carefully."

Yelka nodded. Damon's plan was better than nothing.

"That makes sense, doesn't it? We would run into these psychopaths going the other way."

"Yeah, probably."

"Once we find Vivian," he continued, "we will return to the old settlement and then make it through the forest back to the original route."

Yelka listened to him, but then another idea came to her. "We could just go back to the wall. Back to where we started.”

Defensively, Damon raised his hand. “What are we going to do there? It's a dead end.”

“No, wait!” Energetically, Yelka shook her head. “If we move around a bit, we might find a Wi-Fi connection and be able to call for help.”

“You want to call the cops?” Damon gazed at her with wide eyes.

“Sure–we got robbed.”

“Yes,” he agreed with her, “but we're also trespassing. We'll get in trouble.”

“Come on, that's …”

“And they're going to confiscate your camera. Is that what you want?”

Yelka pondered. “Nonsense, why would they do that?”

“Standard procedure,” Damon asserted. “This is more trouble than we want.”

“Damon, I beg you.”

“Shh, quite,” he hissed. “They'll find us if you make such a fuss.” He put his index finger to her lips. “This is all taking far too long. Remember, Duke Executives funded the trip.”

Oh, that's how the land lay. Yelka understood Damon's bidding.

“I still have a schedule to meet. That still hasn't changed.”

For a moment, they were silent. Yelka was unsure what she should do. She knew Damon–when he had set his mind on something, it worked. But could she trust him in a situation like this?

“Yelka,” he said appeasing. “We'll head off, that way. We'll find Vivian, we'll go straight home, and tonight you'll be in your cozy hotel bed.

And tomorrow," he assured her, "we'll go to the police and press charges. Are you in?"

Yelka nodded hesitantly. That sounded convincing, but hadn't he missed something?

"And what about Zander?"
"Oh, come on, he's a pro."
Yelka gave him a questioning gaze.
"Eventually, that freak will show up."

Running wasn't his natural instinct. Zander lacked any reflex to flee. However, he was not without fear. Instead, his body released adrenaline, causing him to immediately go into a state of shock rather than panic. He would tense up on the spot if he was startled. Where others would scream and run away, Zander would stop and stay. His whole body was so tense, every muscle hardened. Just as the cramps were about to set in, he was able to finally move again. It was a trait that had initially led his classmates to a series of pranks and hoaxes, but which ultimately led them to ignore him. They aspired to see the fear of their victims, hear their screams, and run after them. Just like that gang, they thrived on the visible terror they inspired in others.

Over the course of his life, Zander learned to control his body and to release himself from those cramps. So, he had turned off the flashlight and disappeared behind a tree. He wore a black hood over his face and paused there, his hand clasped tightly around his pocketknife. It was a black folding knife that he could use for sawing, to cut a plant, or thorn bushes. Unfolded, it could easily be a defensive weapon. Zander felt the cold in his hand. He tried to loosen his fingers to open it, but he couldn't. His muscles refused to serve him yet.

He heard the screams and the close roars, the dog yapping like the beast it was. Someone was calling for help, the gang's cries of rage were getting louder. The voices were now in proximity, It was supposed to be happening right behind his back. He saw a blond boy waving a stick. Even in the dark, his light blue jogging suit was clearly visible. Behind him, the girl ran and filmed him, punching off into space. Zander knew they were acting silly, however if they found him, he would be in big trouble.

Usually, the youngest were the worst because they wanted to prove themselves. They would come up with any cruelty to get recognition. And in the end, when it was all over, they would sneak up to him and meekly ask for apologies–in such a way that no one would notice. They were no better than him, but at least they had their group. Zander had none.

His muscles trembled with tension. He closed his eyes and prayed. His black clothes were the only camouflage he had. As the voices quieted, he dared a glance at the gang, but they were gone. Their screams had died down. They must have run further into the woods. Zander swallowed. Maybe he could break away and disappear in the other direction. He tried to take a step forward, but his body refused. All the muscles were hard as stone. Tomorrow, his whole body would ache.

"Do I have to take care of everything myself?" Behind the tree behind which Zander was hiding, someone shouted.

Zander's body began to tremble again. They were not gone, had only lurked. The dog barked. Zander felt his limbs begin to tingle. A buzzing reached his ears. The dog was getting closer, he heard it grunting right next to him. In a second, he would be over him.

"No, you don't," another voice called out.

The dog disappeared, was apparently recalled. Behind him, the gang cheered. Something must have happened that made them stop the hunt.

"What have we got here?" — "Ah, something quite fine." — "Let me see." — "Where did you get that?" — "Nice piece." — "Feels good." — "Hands off!"

The voices rolled over each other. Obviously, they had captured someone. Apparently, it was a woman. Hopefully, it was not Yelka. You could take Vivian, but for heaven's sake, not Yelka. His fingers still clutched the knife.

"Let's move, off to poolside!"

It was the voice of the leader. Beneath it, the gang began to hoot. They started to move noisily, trampling down what came in their way. The dog's barking quieted. Zander's trembling subsided, he felt his muscles relax. They were gone! He inhaled deeply, sucking the cold forest air into his lungs. He then pulled his hands out of his pockets and spread his fingers.

It felt good to feel life in his limbs again.

His body relaxed. A warm feeling filled him, moving from the center of his body down into his legs. Zander looked down at himself. A dark spot had formed in his crotch. He had wet his pants.

Alone in the darkness, Nela crouched behind a bush. She had lost all orientation and without hesitation had run into the forest. To her, it seemed to be the only safe hiding place. Eventually, the gang would have found her in the settlement. But what the hell did these guys want? If she was correct, they were the same thugs they had observed from the apartment block that afternoon. Everything had happened just too fast. Only a few minutes ago, she and Tess had been eating canned ravioli when the alarm bell rang. It couldn't be a false alarm, for it had been ringing far too long and often.

Peeking cautiously around the corner, Nela noticed several people downstairs. She was still thinking about whether it could have been other Urbexers. While she was educating Tess about the situation, the roars, screams, and dog barking started. They grabbed what they could and ran off in the other direction, barricading the hallway with the door unhinged. It was not a second too soon; through the slits they could see the flashlights and hear the bawling gang hitting everything in their way.

Tess had run ahead, while Nela still carried her backpack with the camera. As they in a panic had run into the woods, it slipped off her shoulder. At that very moment, heads appeared at the upstairs windows. Nela had jumped for cover, hiding behind a tree. When she looked up again, the gang was already on their way down. Feverishly, she searched for her backpack, but it was not to be seen in the darkness.

When the dog handling shot-caller left the house, Nela grabbed her pepper spray and prepared herself. She would not go down without a fight. The gang was following a small trail, had come right at her. But their aggression had passed, they were behaving quietly, even cautiously. The guys seemed to be up to something.

Whatever it was, Nela would sell her skin as dearly as she could. When they reached her, the dog sniffed something. Nela took a deep breath and held it. She would pepper spray the dog first, then the gang, and then flee deeper into the woods, running as fast as she could.

But the dog was pulled back. From her hiding place, Nela could witness his owner covering his mouth. What were they up to?

On their excursions they met many weird characters. Most of them were lovable screwballs and were more afraid of women like Nela and Tess than they were of them. Once they had met a Dutch candyman who tried to make them think he was a security guy. Another time, they had stumbled into a porn shoot. And they had also met cable thieves and junkies. But they had kept to themselves in their presence, remained peaceful. The most dangerous people you could usually meet in abandoned places were the owners or private sheriffs.

Yet, this gang seemed to be cut from a different cloth. What were they doing out here, right in the middle of nowhere? You didn't come to this place just to hang out and fool around. There were other possibilities. What if they were security guards? The city wouldn't have chosen a good person if it had. Yet maybe just one of them was officially employed and had brought his no-good friends into the barracks? It couldn't be. Even if they did, they wouldn't go on a rampage of violence and attack people who were harmless. No matter how she looked at it, Nela could not come up with a solution.

When the gang disappeared into the forest, she took a deep breath. Where was her backpack? She spun around and let her eyes wander back and forth, but she was unable to find it. For a moment, she searched for a reference, then looked back to the house. All she would have to do was go back the way she came. Somewhere there, her luggage would have to be found. Yet where was Tess at all? Actually, Nela had expected her friend to emerge from her hiding place when the gang disappeared.

Suddenly, she heard screams. The dog was barking. Fierce shouting resounded through the forest. Had they caught Tess?

"Tess?" she called in a lowered voice. "Tess! Are you there?"

But Nela received no answer. She listened to the voices in the forest. Obviously, there was another group of victims of these psychopaths. Too many voices were calling out, and they couldn't have been chasing only Tess. On the other hand, this did not mean that Tess could not have been there.

Damn it, where was she? Why hadn't her friend been able to wait for her? If only Tess hadn't stepped out of line, they'd be in a better position now! In the very next moment, Nela regretted her thoughts. No matter what had happened, she had to find her. That was her very priority.

Determined, she straightened up, tensed her muscles, and pointed her pepper spray forward. Now, she would go straight in the direction from which the noise came. Period!

Zander was a little strange, but her childhood friend was far from being a freak. Yelka was still upset by Damon's words. She always tried hard to keep the group together, and to offer a bridge to everyone. But Damon would always be the one who just thought of himself. If it hadn't been for Vivian, she could well have done without this cocky jerk! Smiling, he still stood in front of her, waiting for her to agree to his plan. Damon and his shitty schedule!

Well, so be it, now was neither the right place nor the right moment to argue. First, they needed to find Vivian and Zander. Damon, meanwhile, could walk home on his own. She had the photos, and she was Vivian's older sister. Period.

"We will ..."

But that was as far as Yelka got. Footsteps crackled from behind, some-one approached them. Damon again put his index finger on her lips and a hand on her shoulder, pressing her down. They crouched behind a bush, trying to make out something through the branches. But the darkness blocked their view. A person approached the two of them, stopped indecisively, and waited. Yelka pressed her hand against her mouth. With eyes widened, she stared into the darkness. Please walk on, let this moment pass.

At that moment, Damon stood up and with brisk steps walked towards the figure.

"Don't be alarmed," he said half aloud, raising his hands innocently. "I think we can settle this peacefully."

Yelka froze. What was Damon doing, for God's sake? Was he freaked out of his mind?

The figure whirled around, apparently having stood with its back to him.

"Hey, I'm the one you're looking for, Damon Duke," he candidly admitted. "But I'm also the guy who'll pay you 200 bucks to get us out of here safely. Right now, right here."

The person looked at him but did not respond.

Damon, backing up his words, reached into his pocket and pulled out his wallet. "Take it, no problem," he said. "We can forget all about this. The only consideration you have to give is to bring us back to the city."

The person chuckled softly. "I'd like to, but I don't know how," a female voice replied.

Yelka jumped up. Vivian! Taking three long steps out of the bushes, passing a stunned Damon, she embraced her sister.

"Vivian, I was so worried" she sobbed.

But Vivian did not return her embrace; on the contrary, she raised her hands in irritation. "Um," she whispered in a trembling voice, "I think there is some misunderstanding here."

Yelka detached herself from her supposed sister and looked at her. Blonde hair, an athletic figure and about the same clothes, but that was where the similarities ended. In daylight, the differences would have been more obvious. The girl in front of her had freckles, a curvy figure, and wore her hair wavy to her shoulders. She was visibly attractive, but in a thoroughly different way than Yelka's sister.

"My name is Tess, not Vivian," she said in a slightly firmer voice.

Yelka's joy collapsed. Where did this girl suddenly appear from, and where was Vivian? Yelka had to gather herself before she answered.

"Hi Tess," she finally said. "I'm Yelka and ..."
"I am Damon. Damon Duke. You are safe with us."

Yelka couldn't believe her sister's manager. Just a moment ago he had asked Tess for help, now he claimed to be able to protect her.

But Damon was back on his game. "Did the gang rob you? Are you traveling alone?"

"There were two of us," Tess replied, "My friend Nela and me. But those bastards ambushed us in that house over there."

"They chased us through the forest just now." Yelka stroked her shoulder.

"What kind of assholes are they?" sobbed Tess, "Why would they do that?"

"They're a bunch of idiots," Damon said, "posing as security. Surely, they'll disappear soon."

Tess sobbed. "All our stuff is gone. And Nela's gone, too."

Yelka gave her a hug and stroked her head. "We'll find them again," she assured her. "My sister and my best friend have disappeared, too." Yelka felt Tess shaken by tears. "Shhh," she whispered, "everything will be okay."

When they heard voices from a distance, Damon put his arms around the two girls and gently pushed them down. "Take cover, someone's coming." They crouched down and fell silent.

The voices were scattered, at times loud, at times soft. Yelka thought she heard men's voices. They seemed to be moving through the forest.

For a while, they huddled together in silence.

Damon was the first to speak. "I think they've moved on."

Tess seemed to have regained her composure. Her tears had dried up, her expression was composed.

"Are you from here?" Yelka asked her.

"No, we came all the way from the West."

"That's funny," Yelka grinned, "so did we."

"Well," Damon interrupted them, "the three of them are from the West, I'm actually from Berlin."

"Your sister's name is Vivian, right? And what's your other friend's name?"

"Exactly. My friend's name is Zander. He's not my boyfriend, though, we've known each other since we were kids."

Tess smiled. "An interesting name."

"Yeah, an exceptional guy, too," Damon cut in again. "What were you doing here?"

"Photos," Tess replied with a smile.

"Photos? Are you a model?" Damon's interest was piqued.

"No way." Tess's eyes twinkled. "Do I look like one?"

Damon eyed her and let his gaze wander over her body, but the darkness concealed her. "I'm confident." Damon winked at her. For a moment, the grimness of the situation was forgotten.

"At least there are three of us now," Yelka interrupted the budding flirtation, "We're going to find your friend Nela as well as our friends, and then we'll get out of here together."

"Mmm," Tess nodded with encouragement. "Sounds like a good plan."

Damon leaned over to Tess and wiped the tears from her face. "Hey, starlet, it will be okay."

For decades, the old open-air swimming pool in the middle of the forest had had no guests. Ivy had overgrown the ticket booth, hiding it under its leaves in the moonlight. The starting blocks at the swimmer's pool were covered with moss, barely visible in the dark. Birch trees had grown around the pool, their roots breaking through the tiles. The pool's light blue plates alone were bright enough to break up the darkness of the night.

Through rust and dirt, they looked like a broken mirror reflecting the light of the moon. Hard winters and hot summers had cracked the tiles. At the end of the basin, a little water pooled. It was dark and brackish. Grass and shrubs were growing there, turning the once smooth and clean surface into dirt and mud.

Between the swimmer's pool and the wading area was the lifeguard's seat, located at the edge of the outdoor pool. Just like on the first day, the steel of the railing still shone and gleamed in the light of the night.

Dave had turned Vivian's arm behind her back and was pushing her. Ryder walked beside him, his dog tightly on a leash, pointing to the life-guard's former seat. With determined faces, the rest of the gang followed them.

"Go on, over there," Ryder commanded. "Let's see what you brought us."

"At least I wasn't as incompetent as you!" Dave grinned derisively. "Next time, don't trip over your own feet."

Ryder joined in his laughter. "That's a lot of booty, my boy." He let the sentence sink in, then continued. "Not bad, considering you were trying to fuck off earlier." Jesse, Mike, and Mousey silently grinned.

"Exactly, because otherwise you would be lost in the forest right now."

Vivian stood with her back to the railing, the dark forest behind her was. Bluntly, the group stared at her. She was trembling and had lowered her view.

"Now, before you run your mouth like that," Ryder snapped at him, "what does that girl have with her? Anything worthy?"

Dave grabbed Vivian and turned her around so that Ryder could examine her from all sides.

"Nothing" he hissed, "except those ugly flip-flops."

"Purse? Money? Cell phone? Anything?" Ryder was impatient.

Dave grabbed her butt, feeling her back pockets. "She's got nothing on her."

With a firm grip, Ryder pulled Vivian's chin up. "Hey, is anybody home?" He gazed at her. When their eyes met, Vivian gushed.

"You must be out of your minds," she scolded. Vivian wanted to gesture, but Dave held her tight. "Do you actually know who I am? And what kind of trouble you're getting into right now?"

Astonished, Ryder let go of her chin. "She can talk" he laughed mockingly.

"You bet I can! My name is Vivian Donahue and I will give you hell!"

"Now I recognize her!" Ryder laughed enthusiastically. "This is today's afternoon model!" Delighted, he turned to his gang. "Where's the rest of you?"

"They've already gone to the police," she sneered, "and they'll show up here any minute!"

Ryder examined her from top to bottom. "You had such expensive equipment with you. Where is it now?"

"If I knew, I wouldn't tell you."

"Don't be sassy, bitch!" Dave grabbed her hair and yanked her head back.

"Ahhhhhhh!" Vivian tried desperately to fight back, but she was no match for the boy.

"I bet your manager takes care of the camera and your photos, am I right?" Vivian was silent.

"Bitch," Jesse now interfered, "tell us where your stuff is."

"Yeah, come on, ugly cunt!" Mike scoffed and Mousey laughed.

"Yeah, bitch, don't act like that." Tami spat out.

Ryder let his gaze wander over Vivian's body. Her long legs ended in skimpy denim shorts, above them a trained belly. Just below her tits was the end of her top. Dave had a grip on her neck, her long blonde hair wavy hanging back. In daylight, she would certainly be a treat. Ryder reached into her hair and pulled out a pair of gold-framed sunglasses. He turned the frames in the moonlight. Surely, they had been expensive.

"That's a start," he said with satisfaction. Vivian didn't reply, Dave's grip hurt too much. "Dave, what do you think? Will she stop bitching if we accommodate her a little?"

"Most definitely." Ryder watched Dave loosen his grip. With his other hand, he stroked Vivian's bottom, sliding down the back of her thigh. Their eyes met. Ryder and Dave glanced at each other for a moment.

"So, now you tell us where your shit is stored!" Jesse took a step towards Vivian.

She pinched her lips together and shook her head. Pain had broken her anger.

"Suddenly, she is all hat and no more cattle!" Tami pulled out her cell phone. She took a picture of humiliated Vivian. "Well, how do you like that? Want me to share it on Insta?"

It was Mousey who laughed the loudest. "Yeah, hashtag 'stupid bitch crying'!" He took his stick and waved it in front of Vivian's face. The others laughed briefly, Mousey turning to Tami. "See, I'll shut her up!" He tried to push the branch into her mouth, but he didn't succeed.

"Shove that stick between that bitch's legs!"

Tami shuttered and Mousey laughed. He enjoyed having the girl's attention for the first time. He did not exist as far as Tami was concerned. The way she smiled at him, with that wicked expression on her face, left him speechless.

"Yeah!" he shouted enthusiastically and reached out to touch Vivian's private parts. But a hearty kick threw him back.

"Fuck off, brat!" she firmly hissed.

Ryder and Dave grinned at each other, while Mousey jumped backwards, startled. Angrily, he waved the stick in the air, but he didn't dare approach Vivian again.

"Hey, hey, hey, easy!" Dave pulled Vivian back and wrapped one arm around her belly to prevent her from further attacks.

"Leave me alone!" she hissed softly, but that half-hearted resistance was useless.

"Come on, let's be clear about it," Jesse demanded. "Where's your stuff? We want money!"

"Where did you hide it?" Mike brandished his steel pipe, threateningly. "Come on!"

Vivian was desperate, her courage gone. Whereas before she had relied on Damon to free her, now she doubted her manager. Where was he? Why didn't anyone come to her aid? What if they really hurt her? What kind of people were they anyway?

Ryder raised his eyes, watching Mike's angry face. "I'll slap you!" he shouted; his face contorted with rage. "Fucking whore!"

Opening her eyes, Vivian screamed in terror so loudly that Dave had to shut her mouth. She jerked around under his hold and swung her head.

"Hey," Ryder whispered to Mike, "don't!"

He looked at his boss in irritation. What now? Why not? Was he too tough? But somehow, they had to get the group's money and equipment.

"You're scared, beautiful model?" he cynically asked. "Maybe your friends will come to rescue you."

Vivian crouched, frozen in Dave's grip. Tears came to her eyes.

"Hey, we got your bitch here! Bring money and you'll get her back!" Mike yelled through the night.
"Are you nuts? Shut the fuck up!" Ryder snapped at Mike.

He paused in his position and looked at Ryder in amazement.

"Yeah, man! Shut up!" Jesse agreed with Ryder.

Silence suddenly fell over the old pool. They were all waiting for Ryder to say something. He looked at Vivian and then turned to his gang.

"You" he pointed at Jesse, "go with Mike and the little fellow and look out for those assholes." He watched the boys. Jesse stood with his head held high, nodding proudly. Mike was as tense as ever, and Mousey looked sadly at the ground. "Hey, Mousey!"

Looking up, the boy was expectant. "You take Gazoo with you. You'll find them easier then." The youngest gang member's eyes lit up. "But always keep him on a leash. If the dog goes nuts, there will be a bloodbath." He winked at Mousey.

"Yes, I will!" Mousey nodded his head several times.

"I'm counting on you!" Turning to everyone else, he said, "If you find them, you bring them here. But," he continued, "if you haven't found them in an hour, come back. Understand?"

"Yes, all right!" — "Come on, let's go!"

Tami stumbled. "In an hour? What will they spend an hour looking for?"

Ryder looked her up and down and grinned. "Who knows? Maybe they'll be looking for their balls."

"What about me?"

But Ryder had already turned away and was staring at Vivian. "Do whatever you like, girl."

Once again, Dave's and his eyes met.

He pursed his lips and smiled viciously.

When the shouts of the gang had faded away, silence rose around Zander. No animal gave a sound, the wind had died down, and the trees no longer rustled. Zander was alone with himself and his demons. Slowly, he slid his back down the tree trunk behind which he had previously hidden. He felt dizzy. The attack and the shock had been too much for him, his body gave in to the strain.

He sat on the cold forest floor, legs spread. After inhaling and exhaling a few times, Zander took off his gloves. He felt his crotch with one hand. To make sure he wasn't just imagining the mishap, his fingertips felt over the inside of his thigh. The cotton fabric felt clammy and damp. He rubbed the liquid between his thumb and forefinger. Zander closed his eyes and brought his hand to his nose, smelling his finger. He thought he smelled a faint odor of hay.

Zander hadn't peed his pants in years. The last time it happened was in high school. He had woken up in the morning and immediately felt that damp cold on his bottom. Whenever that happened, he sat up and paused for a moment with that wet feeling on him. He then pushed the blanket aside and glanced down at himself. Usually, the dark spot was large and fresh, but every so often it was small and already dried around the edges. He then got up and let his mother know. "Mom, it happened again!"

She frequently got upset, especially since she had bought a new mattress every now and then. "Are you kidding me?" she shook her head. "This must stop. Even at your age."

Zander wasn't embarrassed by his bed-wetting until he hit puberty.

Before that, it had been quite normal for him. Later, this feeling passed. The more upset his mother got, the less he cared. Of course, no one had ever known this, certainly not Yelka. Zander was all the more surprised that it was happening again. Smiling, he imagined how upset his mother would be right now. Actually, it wasn't all that bad. He was alone and it was dark. No one would see the stain on his black pants anyway. That was the advantage of wearing all-black clothes like he did. Yelka chided him for always sporting black. Zander smiled …

He slowly stood up again and peered around the tree. No one was there anymore. He had survived the danger. Actually, he could move freely now. In the darkness, only his face would be visible. But if he … Zander knelt on the ground once more. With both hands, he reached into the earth and ran them wildly over his head until it was completely rubbed with dirt. The ground smelled unpleasant, but he didn't care. He was now covered in disguise. Like a soldier, a lone wolf. Now, whatever may come, could happen!

Straightening up, he left his hiding place. He was one with the night. Like he was wearing a magic cloak that made him invisible to the enemy. Courage drove him forward, and so without hesitation he ran in the same direction in which the gang had disappeared.

He avoided making loud noises and hasty movements, and paid attention to his steps again. After all, they had a dog with them that could scent him even without sight. Why did he actually go in that direction instead of getting back to safety anyway? Zander felt crazy.

After a few minutes, he reached the edge of a clearing. From his position, the outlines of people in pale torchlight were visible. The ground beneath them was partially tiled. Zander guessed an empty pool next to them. This had to be the outdoor swimming pool. His heart beat faster. Normally trespassing was exciting enough, but this situation pushed him to his limits. His instincts drove him to flee, but something inside kept him there.

As a black figure, he stood upright among the trees and watched the outdoor pool. The gang was up to something, but he couldn't see what it was. Slowly, seemingly on his own, his hand reached into his pocket. The knife was still there. He produced it and unfolded the blade. Bright metal glinted in the moonlight. Zander felt a certain kind of security emanating from the cold steel. The knife can be both a tool and a weapon. Zander would stay right here.

He didn't know what drove him—was it the abandoned place he wanted to see so badly? Did he want to save his friends? Or was it simply danger that drove him?

He remained in a crouched position, attempting to get closer to the group. There were three or four people there, Zander couldn't tell for sure. Just a little further out of the forest and behind the bush, and he would be as close to them as possible.

At that moment, the person standing closest to him turned in his direction. By a hair's breadth, the glow of a flashlight shone on Sander.

Even his perfect camouflage would not have saved him, though. But he was lucky and remained undiscovered.

Now he realized who was lighting a cigarette at the edge of the pool. It was the only girl from the group. In the dim light, he saw her face and parts of her upper body. Dark blond hair, slender features, full lips, and a hard look that was atypical of most girls he knew. Her body was in good shape, not as well-toned as Vivian's, but by all means attractive. She was pretty and had a charisma that captivated Zander.

Something that Yelka and Vivian did not carry with them. Zander sensed something in her that reminded him of a former classmate. Her name had been Kimberly, and she was small, petite, and dark-haired, not necessarily a beauty. But when she moved, when she spoke to you or simply just looked at you, it no longer mattered. Kimberly had never had a boyfriend, but she dated countless guys. The next day, if one of his classmates had dated Kimberly, he would be standing in a group of boys in the schoolyard, and they would be whispering and laughing. For Zander, Kimberly had always been an unattainable dream, but he had always longed for her. The girl over there in the dark was just like her.

When the lighter went out, she took a drag on the cigarette and gazed in his direction. Without knowing it, their eyes met. She then turned around, and the flashlight fell on a second person. It was the guy with the red t-shirt, wearing heavy gold chains. Like frozen, he stared into the light. Zander saw his eyes twinkling maliciously. Evil seemed to be staring right back at him.

Like spellbound, he remained in his place. Now, Zander would stay.

Tess could not be too far away. Most likely, she hadn't run into the forest at all, but had hidden in one of the buildings. Probably in that little supermarket where they had taken pictures earlier in the afternoon. Of course. Moreover, that would explain why Tess had not answered when Nela called for her.

She held on to the pepper spray tightly and walked slowly but surely back to the settlement. Branches cracked under their steps, but regardless, the gang had disappeared in the opposite direction. Basically, she was safe. Still, Nelas senses were more alert. Unable to see much in the darkness, she listened intently and turned her head slightly to the side to avoid being surprised by an ambush.

What the heck were those guys anyway? The red-shirted guy seemed to be the shot caller. He had the dog on a leash and was giving commands. She had only seen the rest of the gang from a distance when Tess and Nela had watched them from the apartment building. One of the boys seemed a little younger, so there were three other boys and the girl.

She thought back to her childhood and the neighborhood bullies. When there was trouble, her mother had always told Nela to run away as fast as she could, but her father had taken her aside one day and told her otherwise. She should always go for the biggest and strongest person in the group, he said, if there was no other way. That one would not expect to be attacked by a girl, and certainly not to be defeated. If she beat him, the others would fear her. It had never come to that, but Nela had taken up martial arts as a teenager to feel safer. She had never thought she would need both her father's lessons and the training.

In her mind, she went through her strategy. She would start by disabling the dog with the pepper spray, then spray the rest of the bottle onto the guys, and then go after the leader. She would punch him in the lower jaw, then she would have him in a choke hold and be able to overpower him. And then … yes, and then she would scream and lash out wildly until everyone had fled the scene.

Nela fervently hoped that this situation would never come to pass.

Even though she thought the danger was over, she kept thinking about it and every noise made her feel scared. Nela chewed frantically on her lip and had to pause briefly to regain her composure. She took two deep breaths and let her arms hang down. When she had herself relaxed, she whistled in the dark.

"Oh no, not I, I will survive. Oh, as long as I know how to love, I know I'll stay alive. I've got all my life to live, and I've got all my love to give, and I'll survive, I will survive!"

The music made it better, and Nela was able to put aside the gloomy thoughts. Anyway, she would soon arrive at the settlement and could leave the darkness of the forest behind her. Everything would be all right. Once she found Tess, they could make a run for it as quickly as possible. But they would still have to get their equipment…

The beam of a flashlight blinded Nela.

It was on! Screaming, Nela threw her arms up. The pepper spray shot out of the can, spraying in a semicircle around her. Further forward, right at the leader. He coughed, staggered. The light slid to the floor.

Nela held her breath and struck. The first hit shot into the air, but the second hit its target. The edge of her fist had caught his neck. He tumbled, covering his burning eyes. Nela could feel the gas in her face.

Tears ran down her cheeks. Don't give up, keep at it. She was on the verge of victory. The flashlight had fallen, shining into the forest. In the dark, Nela didn't see where she hit him. Just keep on punching with full force. Under her blows she felt something, maybe his back. She wanted to grab his neck, cut off his air until he passed out. She would kneel on him and...
But Nela's legs were torn away.

A kick to the back of the knee knocked her off balance. Nela stumbled, yet caught herself again. She tried to make out from what direction the attacker had come. Where was he?

Nela was pushed to the ground. Someone was lying on top of her and had pulled both of her arms away, pressing a knee into her back. She felt a hand on the back of her head, pinning her down. Another one twisted her arm in the back.
Nela was defenseless. Her plan had not worked. Now God help her...

But then she heard a gentle voice whispering in her ear. "Calm down, young lady. I don't intend to hurt you."

"Your sister Vivian, what kind of person is she?"

"Oh, she's an exceptional person. Vivian is my younger sister. You know, I always wanted a little sister. She could not yet walk properly, when I wanted to take her to the sandbox."

Tess laughed. "Sounds like an exciting childhood."

"Oh yeah. But Vivian is stubborn. Even back then, I always had to force her to be happy. If she didn't want to go to the playground, I just grabbed and carried her. Then she would cry and scream."

"Pooh, sounds a lot like authoritarian parenting."

"Oh well, when we were finally there and played, everything was forgotten. She then grinned like a Cheshire cat."

"She's still good at that today," Damon interjected. "Vivian is incredibly good at posing. Every facial expression, every movement, is just right with her."

Yelka agreed with him. "Oh yes, it must have been passed down from our mother. She was an actress." She paused. "I take it after our dad. He was a cameraman and filmed her."

They laughed. For a moment, the serious situation was forgotten. With the three of them, the darkness of the forest and the threat of the gang was easier to displace. They were finding each other, opening up and for the first time, something like lightness came up.

"She looks a lot like you." Yelka smiled at Tess. "You and Vivian have a lot in common."

"Is she pretty?"

"Vivian is extremely attractive," Damon said. "So are you."

"But that's about it in terms of similarities." Embarrassed, Tess looked down at the floor. "Gosh, no one would have to urge me to be happy. I would appreciate it with arms wide open. But somehow, sadly, there is no one to force me." With feigned sadness, she looked at them both. "Please, I am here! Push me real bad!"

Yelka laughed. "I'm sure you'll get your chance."

Damon looked at her seriously. "I am," he finally said, "by the way, Vivian's manager."

"Oh, is that true?" Tess doubted, "Really?"

"Yes, he cares about Vivian's career" confirmed Yelka.

"We've only known each other for a few months," Damon said, "but since she signed with Duke Executives, her recognition has grown exponentially."

"What Damon is trying to say is that Vivian's Instagram is through the roof."

"You're kidding" Tess doubted.

"Quite the opposite. Tonight, we'll share the photos from the shoot, so we'll have about 30,000 followers. This will allow for the first small-scale collaborations."

"Unbelievable."

"In the long term, I'm planning to get her first advertising contract in six months. Then, she'll be able to live off her beauty alone." He paused and eyed Tess. "More than just good."

Tess felt dizzy. Hadn't Damon just said that he found her attractive? Those had been his words, after all. Would it be possible for him to care about her career, too? She was breathless. Maybe this trip with all its hardships would be useful in the end!

"Yes, but first we have to find her" Abruptly, Yelka snapped her out of her reverie.

"Absolutely," Damon agreed. "That should be our top priority."

Tess gathered herself. "Um, yeah. Sure."

"The gang went that way."

"Then maybe we shouldn't go there."

"I think we should at least …"

Loud barking silenced their conversation.

"Get down!" hissed Damon, pulling the two women down with him.

Tess had put her hands over her mouth and was staring into the forest. Yelka had crouched down and held her breath. A few moments later, barely ten feet away, several young men passed by, that terrible dog on a leash. Their mood seemed tense, and they talked in short, curt sentences.

Yelka crept forward a few inches. She wanted to find out who was walking through the forest. But most of all, she wanted to hear what the gang was talking about.

"What are you doing?" hissed Damon. "Stay here."

"Shhh …" She put her finger to her lips and looked back at him. Snippets of sentences came to her.

"… do we need to search for that long?"

"I'm sure they just want to have fun with her."

"Shut the fuck up, bubs. You don't know about that yet."

"Never will."

Their last sentence made Yelka's blood run cold.

"They're gonna bang that blonde whore big time."

There was a fine line between the fear of behaving against valid norms and values and the fascination with archaic violence. Most people became intoxicated with it through simulations. They release endorphins by watching scary movies or roller coaster rides. Few people were able to cross the red line and put themselves in situations that threatened their lives. Or even that of other people. Most people, however, followed their conscience.

Yet, the girl Zander had named Kimberly was not exactly a symbol of ethics or a clear conscience. She aroused desires within him that had been denied to him all his life. He watched her every move, soaking up her charisma. Kimberly's posture was not marked by grace and elegance, as was the case with Vivian or Yelka. Rather, there was something feline about her as she slunk around the gang's leader. Her fingers touched him as if by chance, posing coquettishly as soon as she caught his gaze.

Zander knew what Yelka called such girls: cheap. And maybe Kimberly was just that. But at least she seemed attainable to him—in contrast to Yelka, who had never shared his longings. Kimberly would be his half loaf before he could even think of the bread. Wouldn't he give his right arm to have another chance with Kimberly?

For that, he would probably have to become like this guy in the red shirt. Kimberly seemed to admire him deeply.

What qualities made him so appealing? Well, he was big and strong, hung with heavy chains. His dog Gazoo seemed to be a beast. In addition, he commanded a gang of hoodlums and drove them to commit crimes.

Zander understood what Kimberly liked about him. He was the strongest among all the predators. As long as he was with her, no one could harm Kimberly. Unfortunately, Zander's chances of winning her affection were nil as long as the guy was around. However, maybe he could learn something from him.

Perhaps he could become a little like him.

Zander watched them playing that game of approach and rejection. Whenever she threw herself at him, he pushed Kimberly away. But she didn't let him discourage her and kept looking for physical contact. Occasionally, it became more intense. He, on the other hand, was really not interested in her.

Undefinable words came to him, too quietly for Zander to understand. They sounded harsh and abrupt. In the dark, there seemed to be something else that obviously interested him more than Kimberly's pandering.

Zander sharpened his gaze and recognized two more people at the back of the outdoor pool. A dark-haired boy and a blond girl. Would that be Yelka? Or Vivian? Had the gang caught them? What would happen next?

Zander became restless. He wanted to get closer to the group. Had to see what was going on. Wanted to know what they were doing.

Carefully, he felt around for the knife in his pocket. That steel felt good, cold, and sharp. It gave him a sense of security, making him a monster. Like Black Death out of the forest. He favored that. Leaving norms and values behind, he would cross that fine line.

He left the cover of darkness and ventured from bush to bush on the grounds of the old swimming pool. His heart raced. Like a wolf, he stalked his prey. The pack was busy with itself. Two boys had set up in front of the blonde girl, Kimberly stood a little apart. Zander hid behind the high seat at the edge of the pool. Adrenaline shot into his system. He was very close now.

"Ryder, honey, why don't you come over here? We were supposed to go to the playground, just the two of us."

So, Ryder was his name.

"Yeah, go ahead." Laughter.

Wow, Ryder had no respect for anything or anyone. Zander wanted to be like him. Everything would be more bearable if only he were like Ryder. All the humiliations, the rebukes, and insults he had experienced were back in his mind. Guys like Damon Duke had always managed to make him look ridiculous in front of everyone.

Ryder, whom Kimberly admired so much, would not have put up with Damon's humiliations. He would have finished him off! Moreover, the relationship with Yelka would have been different if he had been like this guy. If so, he would not care about a woman who was more interested in the satisfaction of her selfish sister than in the man who sincerely loved her, anyway.

Zander was now standing right behind Kimberly. He thought he could feel her skin–all he had to do was reach out to her. The half loaf was within reach. Zander was trembling with excitement. His blood was throbbing with adrenaline. He could easily take her. Ryder would just take her.

"Don't be a douche. I'll bang you tomorrow."

Yet, Ryder didn't want her anymore.

When the boys at his school had stopped talking about Kimberly, she no longer had been interesting anymore, either. After everyone had had it, she simply disappeared. No one wanted her anymore, though. The guys were now more into girls who had called Kimberly cheap. They had only had their first experiences with he–thereafter, she was worthless. Nobody wanted a slut for a girlfriend anyway.

Zander calmed down. The trembling passed. Obviously, Ryder now had a girl who outranked Kimberly. He wanted to see her, wanted to know who was prettier and more desirable than Kimberly. And most of all, he wanted to know what Ryder would do with her.

He crept around the high seat, pressing himself into the shadows of the moonlight. Only a tiny shrub now separated him from Ryder. He saw his tense muscles, the flashing gold chains, heard his breathing. Across from him stood another boy from the gang. Black parted hair, steely earrings and a three-day beard, piercing eyes. Zander could sense the aggression and violence emanating from them, even as they only stood there.

Then he saw which girl he was holding.
His heart leapt.
It was Vivian.

The youngest member of the gang was constantly both scared and fascinated by his friends. Watching them assault, chase, and ravish put fear into him. The only way he could turn off that fear was to get recognition, preferably Tami's or Ryder's. Yet, these moments were rare. Usually, he was busy enough, not drawing any negative attention to himself.

Mousey had trouble keeping Gazoo under control. The dog was just as excited as he was. However, he did not have the same instincts as the animal. He stumbled in the dark, lurching from obstacle to obstacle, always trying not to let go of Gazoo.

"Can't we just turn on the flashlights?"

Jesse and Mike walked in front of him, scanning the darkness.

"You stupid, douche? Want them to see us?"

"Nothing yet to worry about. Keep walking in the dark."

Mousey silently followed their instructions.

"But honestly, I don't understand why Ryder bawled at me like that."
Angrily, Mike slammed the steel pipe into the void. "That's how we could
have lured them out of hiding."

Jesse laughed maliciously. "You really don't get it, do you?"

"Shut the fuck up! What am I missing?"

"Ryder doesn't give a shit about the booty," Jesse claimed. "He wants
the bitch all to himself."

"But he's with Tami," Mousey snapped.

The two older boys laughed.

"You think?"

"Yeah right. Didn't you see the way he looked at her?"

"If so, then Dave, not Ryder" Mousey interfered again.

"Oh, you've got a crush on that girl, huh?"

"Yeah, everybody noticed that." Jesse laughed. "You'd love to stick
your little willy into Tami, huh?"

"Are your little balls even hairy yet?"

In shame, Mousey looked down at the ground. He felt his ears getting hot, his head glowing. It was true, he would have done anything for
a kiss from Tami.

"Hey, bubs, do you ever jerk off to her?" They laughed like they had
made the best joke ever.

"If you keep being so loud, we might as well turn on the flashlights" he grumbled. "Besides, I think Dave is going to lay her. Not Ryder."

"Did you just say 'lay'?" Jesse laughed.

"I think so too," Mike agreed with him. "Dave will do the girl."

"Don't bullshit me, man."

"Yes, he will."

"We go right here" Jesse decided abruptly.

"Why? Why do you want to go down here? That's where we'll get to the exit."

"That's precisely why. Come on, down the hill."

"Do not be a jerk," Mike said. "You're not the boss!"

"As long as I have to think for you, I'll be in charge."

"Boy, don't push it!" Mike tightly clasped his steel pipe.

"Or else what?"

Mousey was afraid. He would rather not be there when Jesse and Mike were beating the shit out of each other in the dark. It wouldn't be the first time that the gang fought among themselves, though. Mike was quick to fly off the handle, but Jesse was not to be trifled with either. Mousey knew he had a criminal record for assault.

Furthermore, he would not be Ryder's best friend if he were a stranger to violence.

"I think Gazoo found something" he interrupted them, pointing down the slope. "Down there."

In fact, the dog moved in the direction that Jesse had suggested.

Jesse grinned. "Look, even the dog agrees with me."

"Fuck you!"

But Jesse only laughed. "No kidding, guys," he relented. "Wanna know why Ryder is gonna fuck that bitch?"

"Go ahead."

"I was in foster care with Ryder, you know."

"Right, you look like a freaking orphan."

Jesse, however, ignored Mike's provocation. "We were maybe fifteen or sixteen, had our first girlfriends. In our clique, there was a girl our age, though. Carrol was her name. You know what I mean, one of those special chicks. A chick who thought she was better than us. Never put out with anyone."

He caught Mike and Mousey's attention, and they were captivated.

"We all had met our girls downtown that day. They were alert about Carrol, probably afraid that we would cheat on them with her. They were really going off the deep end, and picked on her. We were turned off by that, but Ryder got crazy."

Slowly, they went further down the slope. Mousey and Mike had turned their heads to Jesse.

"When we got home, he waited until the hacks left, then went to Carrol's room."

"Then, what?"

"I don't know, but it was an hour before he returned. We were all listening at the door. Now and then, there was a humming noise, and one could hear strange bellows as well. But he didn't say anything. Just grinned all night."

"Damn."

"Yeah, the next morning they had to break down the door, you know. Carrol just wouldn't come out. She had locked herself in. When they found her, she was crouched on the bed crying, bruises all over her body. She was transferred straight away, never came back from the hospital."

"And what happened to Ryder?"

"Nothing."

"What do you mean by 'nothing'?"

"Carrol never told what happened to her that night."

"Damn."

"Rumor had it Ryder's big brother paid her visit."

"Henry?"

"Yes."

"Holy shit…", Mike finally muttered.

Silently, they continued walking toward the exit. Mousey was trembling. He didn't want to go back to the old pool, didn't want to know what Ryder was doing to that poor girl.

Maybe it would be good if they found the others. Surely, Ryder would let her go, be content with the prey.

Jesse suddenly said, "Look at this!"

Mousey looked at the dirt road, in the direction Jesse was pointing.

Was anyone else here?

"So, our little teenage boy can prove himself now." Jesse grabbed Mousey by the neck. "Fucking wreck it. Smash everything!"

Yet, that was simply not done. Hopefully, they would give him credit if he did. Because he was afraid.

After all, he knew Mr. Marshall.

Dave was standing behind Vivian with an arm around her waist. He had his face hidden deep within her hair, inhaling her scent. Damn, she smelled so good. His lips touched her neck, tasted Vivian's skin. Dave wanted to bite her. She was so extremely delicious. His other hand moved up, touching the metal bar of her brassiere.

Her trembling and sobbing did not change his enthusiasm for the pretty girl. She felt stunningly good, her blonde hair shining in the moonlight. This slut was way classier than Ryder's Tami, that little whore. And she was all his, for he had captured her. Now she was his property.

"Hey, Tami! What do you think of this girl? Isn't she a hottie?"

Dave pushed Vivian's top up and her shorts down enough to show her panties. She resisted, trying to push his arms away, but Vivian lacked strength. Instead, the first tears ran down her cheeks.

"Now that's a yummy body, isn't it? Huh? Any thoughts, Tami?"

But Tami did not reply. She was staring at the floor with her hands in her pockets. Out of the corner of her eye, she watched Ryder. She paid no attention to that blond skunk. He, however, had such a dirty grin on his face, and he wasn't giving her any look at all. Tami knew Ryder. He gazed at the blonde chick the same way he had eyed her on the swing this afternoon. She wanted to go back there with him. The others should come back here quickly, so they could go home.

"Ryder, I'm cold," she whispered in a shaky voice.

But he did not respond. It was Dave who answered.

"Ryder, your little girl is cold. Why don't you take care of her for once." His dirty grin screamed with mockery.

Ryder gave Tami a sideways glance. "Down the pool, get the fire going. You'll be warm." He pointed to the fire pit in the non-swimmer area, which had been lit quite a few times. Dave laughed derisively.

"But …"

"Shut your mouth and do as I tell you."

Without contradiction, Tami disappeared into the dark pool. She knew that he would bitch slap her if she did not hurry.

Ryder was fascinated by the blonde bitch. She was a bombshell, a yummy mommy sex kitten. Oh yeah, he dug her.

"I guess your girlfriend doesn't like my baby mama too much, does she?" Dave was no longer grinning. His stare was challenging. "I can well understand that. Her ass could use one less candy bar, though. Compared to this one, it's a fatty." He pinched Vivian's butt.

"Ouch, please let …" As she tried to squirm out of Dave's grip, he grabbed her chin and yanked it upward, covering her mouth. Her tears ran down his hand, her sobs were stifled under his grip.

"And she doesn't talk back, either."

Ryder stood in front of him, a wolfish smile on his face, head slightly cocked to the side. He breathed in and out deeply, Dave could feel his energy.

"Look at those gorgeous tits," Dave continued, ripping the spaghetti-strap top off her shoulders, so she was standing in front of them wearing just her thin bra.

Vivian whimpered, but her resistance was broken. "Aren't those really nice, firm, big tits? Huh?" Provocatively, he stared at Ryder. "Better than those little kid titties," he murmured, nodding over to Tami. "But you know what's best?" Vivian cried out as he yanked her back by the hair and put an arm around her neck. "She's my girl, she's fucking mine now."

Ryder raised his eyebrows with a smile. "Oh yeah, who said that? Huh?"

"I'll say this," Dave hissed. "Caught her, keep her."

"Oh, our hunter caught himself a deer. Sweet!"

Dave had anger on his face. "First, Big Daddy sent his bitch away, and only then he dares to speak up."

"Big Daddy wants his share, sucker," Ryder whispered.

He had averted his eyes from Dave and was leering at Vivian. His hand stroked over her belly, wandering upward.

"Get your hands off her!" Dave tore Vivian away from Ryder.

"What are you doing?" Tami threw in, outraged.

Out of nowhere, he slapped her face with the flat of his hand. The ringing hit knocked her unbalanced, causing her to fall to the floor. His hand raised, he stood above Tami, glaring angrily at her. "Don't you dare do that again. Never ever!" Cowering on the dirty tiles, Tami held her cheek, whimpering.

Hand still raised to strike, he turned to Dave. "Want some, too, punk?"

For a moment, time seemed to stand still. Dave stared indecisively at Ryder, Tami knelt silently on the floor, and Vivian's breath caught in her throat.

Then finally, and it seemed like an eternity to them, Ryder lowered his hand and placed it on Vivian's hip. He slowly pulled her to him as he positioned himself between her legs.

"Let's do the deer together," he urged Dave, grabbing Vivian between the legs. "Right here, right now."

The old man sitting on Nela was soaked in tears and had mucus running down his shiny red face. His eyes were swollen, his nose running. Every sentence he uttered made him cough. And yet, he had such a tight grip on Nela that she couldn't fight back. Despite all this, he seemed to mean well for her.

"Calm down, young lady. It is not my intention to hurt you," he claimed with a runny nose.

Nela couldn't help but laugh. This sentence from the older gentleman, who was obviously in a bad position, seemed just too bizarre.

"You should blow your nose first. And then, please get off from me."
"If you promise to behave. Then I'll let you go." The man was a tough cookie. "Promise faithfully!"

With a quick movement, Ben Marshall rolled off Nela and helped her to her feet. Only then did he take off his polo shirt and wipe his face. Turning his back to Nela, he spat out, letting the tears wash the burning spray from his eyes.

"Dear girl, what's wrong with you? Just walking through the forest and attacking people."
"I'm sorry about that. If we find my belongings, I could help you out with water." Nela's mirth gave way to a rising sense of shame. She'd given the guy a pretty bad time. "I'm sorry," she said sincerely. "My friend and I were attacked a few minutes ago. We lost each other, and I thought you were one of them."

Ben squeezed his eyes shut and opened them again to stimulate the flow of tears. Resting his arms on his knees, he asked, "Who were you attacked by?"
"A gang of young men with a dog, that's all I can say. They must have been about five to six people."
Ben spat out. "So, they have a dog with them?"

"Yeah, right! A nasty, big mutt."

Ben took a deep breath. It had to be Ryder and his gang. He had feared this. These good-for-nothings meant trouble!

"Your friend, where could she be?"

"I don't know. We were just in that building back there when they were going to jump us. And all of a sudden, she was gone."

"What does that mean, 'they were going to jump you'?" Ben bristled. Her phrasing sounded strange.

"It means just that. They sneaked up on us, sicced their dog on us, beat us with clubs and yelled."

With an appraising eye, Ben looked at her. The girl didn't seem to be exaggerating, and made a matter-of-fact, objective impression. "Did they take your things?"

Nela hesitated. "I think so. At least they have my friend's equipment. I was able to save mine but lost it on the run."

Ben reviewed the facts of the case in his mind. Armed robbery. Attempted aggravated assault. Trespassing. He breathed heavily. They were kids, he knew the gang. But it was pointless. They would have to call for backup.

"Okay, we're going to go back to my car now and call the police," Ben said firmly. "After that, we will look for your friend."

"Hm …" Nela pressed. "I wonder if the police were a good idea. After all, Tess and I had also been trespassing."

"Don't worry about it, you won't get into trouble." Now it was his turn to smile. "Well, I already know what you were doing here. You're Urbexers, aren't you? Wanted to spend some exciting time here. Take pictures and get a little spooky sensation."

Astonished, Nela nodded. "Yes, that's right. We're taking pictures here for my senior thesis."

"That's what I thought. My name is Ben, by the way. Ben Marshall." Conciliatory, he held out his hand to her.

"My name is Nela Dubois."

"Nice to meet you, Nela Dubois. Let's go then, we have no time to waste."

Ben seemed to have recovered. In the light of the flashlight, his face still shone red, but the irritation had subsided. Nela estimated the man to be in his mid or late 50s, but he was in good shape, seemed athletic and fairly fit. He probably worked for the local security service.

"Have you guys been here on the grounds for long?"

"No," Nela replied, "we just arrived this afternoon. Actually, we wanted to spend the night in the old settlement and explore the rest tomorrow."

"Well, that's not going to happen now," Ben stated factually. "I hope you were able to take enough pictures."

"Well, I'll see if I can find my camera again." Nela was dismayed.

"It'll turn up," Ben assured her. "Tomorrow, at daylight, the world will be a different place." After a small pause, he continued. "You're not the only ones who have strayed here." He squinted an eye at her. "But most of them have only discovered the old soldiers' settlement. Very few make it as far as the barracks. These, in turn, are secured by a fence. And certainly no one ever made it to the old hospital. Do not enter there, as it may collapse."

"Thank you for pointing that out." Nela smiled. She wasn't going to let that stop her. "That gang, do they hang around here sometimes?"

"Frankly, I've never seen them here before. The area is well secured, and it's a few miles to the city."

"So, they're from here?"

"Yes. I guess every tree grows some bad apples. But I don't think they're going to cause much trouble. They're just kids, really."

Inwardly, Nela laughed sarcastically. My ass.

"What do you think they're looking for here?"

"I don't know what they are doing out here. The kids are probably having a ball here, breaking windows and letting the dog chase around."

"Right, makes sense," Nela remarked.

"The police will take care of it. We'll be at my car soon, then we able to make immediate contact through the CB radio."

Heavy barking startled them. Where Ben's car had been, there was only a wreck left. The windows had been smashed, the tires and seats slashed. The doors hung loosely on their hinges, the radio had been ripped out, the antenna snapped off. Three young boys lurked there, sitting on the roof. One of them kept the dog on a leash. The tallest of them grinned maliciously.

"Look, Mousey. There's Grandpa Marshall. He's probably mad because you broke his old car."

Ben was stunned.

Zander staggered backward against the high seat, holding on to the cold metal. He retreated into the darkness of the night, groping his way backward, foot by foot, with one hand pressed over his mouth. However, his emotions had gotten the better of him. His boldness collapsed like a house of cards, giving way to a wave of dizziness and confusion.

Seeing Vivian in the grip of the gang tore his fantasies apart. Zander had to sort himself out, become master of his very own emotions again. He slipped back into the darkness of the forest, hearing Vivian sobbing and crying. He wasn't close enough to realize what was happening to her. In a strange, macabre way, this reassured him. It would go away if he didn't see it.

Still, he didn't know these violent emotions. Zander couldn't tell if it was fear or disgust that had driven him. It was an overwhelming feeling that had completely consumed him.

After all, Vivian was the sister of his love, Yelka. If something bad happened to her, Yelka would be devastated. She would never be happy again; Zander was aware of that. He chewed on his lip, and let his thoughts sink in.

But basically, it didn't change anything for himself. His chances with Yelka would neither increase nor decrease because they were simply non-existent. And hadn't she always preferred Vivian over him? Where had she been when they decided which route they should take back?

She had sided with Vivian and Damon. After all, it was her fault. They would not have fallen into the clutches of this gang had they followed him in the first place. Anyway, Yelka was no longer an option. He would have Kimberly, who she would consider cheap anyway. Zander would not have to think about Yelka again until after Kimberly. Whatever this meant...

However, it wasn't fear that was in him. Zander hated Vivian with all his heart. Her haughtiness and condescending sayings flashed through his mind. She was arrogant and selfish and ruined his plans and wishes. Lasciviously, she staged herself in front of him, teased him and finally made him look stupid. She was able to turn her sister against him. He knew all too well what they called him behind his back—they called him 'freak'.

A fire slowly lit up in the pool. Kimberly had apparently gathered plenty of wood and lit a large pyre in the back of the basin. Warm, yellow light illuminated the scene. In the glow of the fire, he saw Kimberly sitting at the edge of the pool. She was staring into the flames, ignoring what was happening behind her. As Vivian sobbed loudly, she lit a cigarette.

Ryder had a real grip on his girl. This was the way it had to be. Men like him were born to put the haughty Vivians of this world in their place.

The fire was getting bigger. In the flickering light, he saw Ryder pressed against Vivian. Behind him, the other guy had his arms wrapped around Yelka's sister. Her head turned from left to right, trying to avoid Ryder's approach. Tears ran down her cheeks, mascara left black marks on her face.

Zander remembered something he had seen a few days ago. It had been in a movie. One of those flicks he had hidden deep in the subfolders of his hard drive. Where no one would be able to find it. It was a fetish movie. For over three hours, two muscle-bound men and a petite, surely underage girl had had sex.

They tied her up, beat her, humiliated her, and abused her over and over again. Occasionally, the girl liked it, but every so often it went too far. She screamed and cried. Just like Vivian over there. Usually, Zander deleted these kinds of movies when he had watched them, but this one was special. He had kept it.

The clearing of the old outdoor pool was brightly lit by now. Ryder had a firm grip on Vivian's chin, she didn't move anymore. He grabbed Vivian's bustier and ripped it off. Vivian wanted to scream, but Ryder pressed her mouth shut.

Zander tried to make out her tits, but Ryder covered them with his back. He crept a little to the right to get another angle, and Ryder stepped back from her. For a tiny moment, Zander was able to catch his eye on Vivian's breasts. They were heavy and plump, leaving him open-mouthed.

But immediately after, Ryder stepped between Zander and her again. He seemed to be fiddling with her, lowering his gaze downward. Vivian squealed in panic, flailing her arms. She screamed for help! But Ryder just slapped her face. His hand flew past her, stopped in midair, and hit her again. Saliva flew through the air; Vivian's eyes fell shut.

Oh yes, Zander now understood that this intense feeling deep inside him was not fear. Quite the opposite. When Ryder pulled down her shorts, he got an erection.

Ben and Nela did not have to figure out their feelings at all. Their hopes for a quick end to the night had been dashed and had turned into a nightmare. It seemed like a prank from naughty boys at first, but they're now being slapped with the real thing. They were cut off from civilization, could expect no help, and had to fight for their lives.

Ben's car was in ruins, nothing could have been saved. The windows were shattered, the tires slashed, the seats ripped open, and technology destroyed. The car was a wreck. He would not be able to save it, not with all the tools in the world. Those brats had done an impressive job!

Ben couldn't believe that the guys who had known him for years had done this. He looked at their cheeky, smiling faces. Jesse Raffensberger, Mike Zimmermann and little Mousey Gilman were taunting him and his companion. Mousey had a big dog on a leash who growled at the two of them. It was a miracle that the boy could hold the animal at all. It was Ryder Sherwin's dog. If he was around, Dave Sloan and Tami Butcher certainly weren't missing either.

As soon as they were back in town, Ben would make sure their parents taught them a lesson!

"Have you guys gone insane?" Ben gazed at the boys. "You're freaked out off your minds!"

"I told you," Jesse laughed at Mousey, "Grandpa Marshall is so angry with you."

"He's about to poop his pants."

Mousey looked down at the floor, holding Gazoo with both arms.

"Boy, can't you look into my eyes?" Ben approached Mousey.

Nela had stood next to her new friend. She knew disaster was coming.

"Yo, leave our friend alone, old man!" Mike reared up full width in front of Ben.

"Yeah, man! Don't act the big shot, grams!" Jesse swung the steel pipe and let it clap in his hand.

"You guys take it down a notch," Ben instructed the two older boys.

"Or else?"

Ben saw the fire in the thug's eyes. No empty words behind their threats. They stared at him, waiting for an opportunity to attack. Jesse approached from the left, Mike from the right. Ben reached behind him and held one arm in front of Nela, while the other hand held the flashlight.

"Calm down, nobody's been hurt yet. We can all just go home and forget about this."

Mike spat out. "The fuck we can. Unpack your wallet!"

"You too, cunt!" Jesse pointed at Nela.

"Or else we'll smash you like your car, Grandpa!"

Threateningly, Mike raised his steel pipe, but Ben held his flashlight out to him.

"Roll the riches, bitch!" Jesse roared, swinging his club at Ben. At the last moment, Nela pulled him aside and the steel rod whizzed through the air past his shoulder. Mike went on the attack, sending the pipe hurtling at Ben. But he struck at it, deflecting the direction of the weapon away from him. A kick to the thigh stopped him, and Ben went after Jesse. His massive flashlight struck Jesse's forearm, disarming the boy.

Jesse cried out. He was holding his arm; the steel pipe lay on the floor in front of him. Mike paused, perplexed.

"Back off, boy, or you'll get some too!"

Indecisive, Mike stood next to Jesse, having lost the courage to continue fighting alone, but not yet completely. While Jesse held his bleeding gash, he looked for a hole in Ben's cover.

"Hit it, man! Smash it!"

"Ha!" Mike feinted a blow, but Ben rammed the end of the lamp against his torso. He staggered back, holding his chest in pain.

"Let go of Gazoo! Mousey! Now!" Jesse was beside himself, the dog barking madly. Drool flew from his mouth, his claws digging deep furrows.

"Mousey, I'm going to beat that dog to death," Ben said in a calm voice.

"You better not. I mean it!"

Alternately, Mousey looked at Jesse and Ben.

"You'd better do what he says" Nela intervened. "Better believe me, this won't end well."

Mousey pulled the aggressive dog back to him. Jesse cursed.

"Come on, back to poolside. We'll get the others and then, God may have mercy on you!" he angrily hissed.

"Scram!" shouted Ben confidently. When the three boys had disappeared, he and Nela ran in the opposite direction, back to the abandoned settlement.

"And the three of them were actually just kids?" asked Nela wryly.

"I know these guys. They're good-for-nothings and troublemakers. But I didn't expect anything like this from them."

"Do you finally believe me that they were going to rob us?"

Ben nodded. "Their boss is Ryder Sherwin, and he owns that dog, too."

"Gazoo? What kind of name is that?"

"Ryder is crazy. But he's nothing compared to his older brother Henry."

"There's also a next-level version of this one?"

"The Sherwin brothers grew up in foster care," Ben told her. "Their parents were murdered when the boys were nine and twelve years old. The perpetrators stabbed their mother and father to death while they slept. They have never been found until now."

Nela whistled softly through her teeth.

"The boys went to foster homes and became problem children. Henry served several years in prison for aggravated assault, and Ryder still has that coming. But Henry is by far the more dangerous one."

"Nice guys."

They had almost reached the block. In the pale moonlight, it had lost all beauty and seemed more than threatening. The summer night had lost its warmth, damp cold came up.

"If these two have Tess, we should get help as soon as possible."

Nela looked at Ben. "What's that supposed to mean?" Her eyes locked onto his.

Ben took a deep breath. "It means we should hurry."

"No," Nela snapped at him. "I'll tell you what now. We're going to get Tess first. There's no way I'm leaving her alone with those psychos."

Ben put a hand on her shoulder. "That's far too dangerous, you've seen what they're capable of…"

Nela wiped his hand off, "I'm going with or without you. Your choice."

Determined, she went back into the forest.

Yelka's heart was racing. They had got Vivian! Her sister was in the hands of these disgusting pigs. And not only that, but they were also about to rape her.

They had to act quickly!

Yelka quietly crept back to Damon and Tess. They remained motionless in their position. Damon wrapped his arm around Tess, who was trembling with fear. "Everything will be all right, the boys will be gone in a minute," he whispered to her reassuringly.

"Damon," Yelka radioed in, "they have Vivian."

"Are you kidding?"

"I just heard them, they're holding her."

"Oh my God. This can't be true."

"We should go in the direction these guys came from."

Her voice sounded dull as she put on a washed-out smile. "Yeah, let's go."

Damon reached out to Tess and helped her up. "Don't worry about anything. I got you."

"We should arm ourselves," Yelka suggested. "Let's find something to hit with."

"Yeah, sounds like a plan."

Damon stopped and watched Yelka, who was searching for solid branches in the dark. The day was turning into a disaster. His schedule had been awfully dismantled by that freak Zander; photo retouching and editorial schedule were pushed back and to top it all off, some redneck was about to deface his pick of the bunch. As if that weren't enough, he was in the middle of nowhere and couldn't do anything about it. He simply lacked options. He looked at Tess.

"Hey, I think two of us fighting is enough." Damon swung a sturdy branch and winked at her. "It would be good if you secured the way back."

Tess looked up and smiled in surprise. "You think?"

"Yeah, just stay behind me and warn me in case anyone comes up behind us."

"Okay, I can do that."

"We'll be out of here faster than you think," Damon promised, "and then we'll see what we can do about your career, starlet." Tess's unease had faded. She laughed at him confidently.

"Come on, let's go," Yelka shouted. She ran ahead, carrying a heavy club.

They walked through the forest in a crouched posture, carefully watching their steps. The silence was eerie, broken only by the call of an owl. However, as they progressed, other sounds began to get louder. From between the trees, voices filtered through to them. They were isolated sentences, shouts, and screams. But they were too far away to understand anything.

It lightened further, the closer they got to the voices. The trees were bathed in yellow, flickering light. A clearing opened in front of them. The area where a large campfire burned in the middle used to be an outdoor swimming pool. For a moment, Yelka was enchanted by the sight. Light blue, cracked tiles, a deep pool. Starting blocks overgrown with moss. An entire ticket booth overgrown by nature. What a stunning image this was. Except for the fire in the basin, there was little damage done. This had to be the open-air pool that Zander had talked about. Good him. Where could he just be?

However, Yelka noticed several people behind the fire, who must have been the source of the shouts and screams. Oh, dear God, that had to be Vivian, being approached by those boys!

"That's Vivian over there," Yelka whispered to Damon and Tess. "We'll go around the house to the left. From up there, we'll have a better view."

"Hey, careful." Damon put a hand on her shoulder. "Someone's sitting by the fire."

"That's the girl from the gang." Yelka recognized the only female member.

"They have women in their gang?" Tess was confused. "Why isn't she doing anything?"

"Just because she's a girl," Yelka said angrily, "doesn't mean she has character."

Tess looked at her in wonder, but Damon interrupted Yelka. "Yes, and she's not pretty either. But it's not worth it, let's move on."

In the shade of the forest, the three of them stooped down to the little house that stood away from the swimming area. The entrance to the house was open. From here, they could observe the action without being seen.

Equipment was stored here, the water was filtered, and the supply was regulated. Yelka knew the facility's function because she had already seen many abandoned pools. Since the municipalities cut the funding, they had closed them down one by one.

The window provided a view of the shady scenery between the swimmers and non-swimmer basin. Two men held Vivian down in front of the old lifeguard's chair. She screamed, trying to resist, while her top and brassiere were torn from her body. The dark-haired man held her from behind while Vivian screamed and cried. Tears and makeup rushed down her face into a dirty liquid. Another man had built up in front of her. It was the dog-owning leader of the gang, sporting a red t-shirt. He stood close to her, unzipped her shorts, and pulled down her pants. Vivian fell silent. Her body tensed.

"Oh my God!" Panic seized Yelka. "They're raping her!"

Tess gagged. She leaned forward and threw up.

Damon stared blankly at the window, looking over at his model. This wasn't really happening right now. It was just a hallucination. A bad, very realistic dream. These guys were ruining both his model and his hard work.

Yelka sighed. She cried, "We have to do something! Damon, we have to help her!"

When Vivian's sister shook him, he regained consciousness. Oh yes, they would have to do something. But what? Damon's weapon was the word, not the fist. The boys would finish them off, beat them up. They would be worse off than before. "Yes, we have to do something," he whispered quietly.

Tess puked her guts out. Mucus ran out of her nose, tears down her face. She was shaking all over. "What's happening?"

"Don't look." Damon took her in his arms and closed his eyes. "Just don't look, starlet."

Outside, Ryder had grabbed Vivian's legs and ripped off her pants. His victim did not make a sound anymore. She howled softly to herself as she lay naked and defenseless in her torturers' arms. Vivian did not notice that Dave was licking her face, and that Ryder had opened his pants. She did not hear the grunts of the men, closed her eyes and blanked out everything around her. Just like Tami, she simply pretended that none of this was happening.

"Come on, get to the pump!" Yelka tore Damon away from Tess and pushed him toward the pump basin, where old brackish water had accumulated.

Damon was overwhelmed, Tess sobbed out. "What are you going to do?"

Yelka now also grabbed Tess and pushed her rudely to the other side of the pump.

At that time, the pump was operated manually so that they would not lose water in the event of a power outage. "You go to the left side, and you go to the right. Hurry!"

Confused, Damon and Tess grabbed the levers and stared at Yelka.

"When I'm outside, I run at those pigs, hose in my hand, roaring. Then, pump as hard as you can."

"Okay!" Tess hastily nodded her head.

"All right," Damon said.

'And God grant that the pump still works,' Yelka added quietly in thought. Quickly, she left the house and unrolled the old hose. Over the years, it had gotten brittle and rotten, but it could be pulled off the reel without any problem. Determined, with the club in one hand and the hose in the other, Yelka walked around the house. She took a deep breath, preparing for her attack, when more voices interrupted her plan. The rest of the gang was coming back from the forest!

Damn it, this couldn't be happening! Three more boys and the dog appeared in the light of the fire. Yelka's gaze wandered back and forth between Vivian and the other group. For a brief moment, the rapists paused, looking over to the edge of the forest. When they caught sight of their cronies, they grinned and turned back to their victim.

Yelka took a deep breath, swallowed. Damon and Tess were in their position, obviously hadn't seen the three newcomers yet.

She closed her eyes and sent a push prayer to heaven.

Yelka tensed her body and silently counted down. "Three, two, one…"

"Where could they be going?" In the dark forest, Nela saw the gang a few yards ahead of her.

"They're on their way to the old pool," Ben answered confidently. "Or to the forest stage, but we'll see."

"If they're holding Tess over there, it would be beneficial if we arrived sooner than the three of them."

"Girl, in the first place, you should know what to do when we get there, though."

Nela waved it off. "We'll see about that. Come on, we'll pass them on the right."

Ben shook his head. The girl looked sweet, but inside she was savage. If she was as smart as she was stubborn, they might be able to free her friend. But it could just as easily go wrong. He now understood what these kids were capable of. Words would no longer be able to calm them down.

In a stooped posture, they crept past the three. Branches cracked under their steps. The dog barked. Damn it, Nela, not so fast! But Ben had to stop himself. Any word out of her mouth would have blown her cover.

Ben picked up speed, walking beside Nela. He pointed to a hill on her right. They would reach the outdoor pool soon. Flickering light filtered through the trees to them. Apparently, the gang had lit a fire there.

As they walked up the slope, the view of the old pool became clear. A magical place that, under other circumstances, Nela would have loved to photograph. However, by the light of the bonfire, she spotted two boys abducting a blonde girl. Tess!

Nela clenched her fists when she saw what was happening to her friend. Ben grabbed her shoulder, holding her back. It was horrible. His breath caught. Ben knew Ryder was a fiend, but this was clearly going too far. They were about to rape Nela's friend. The poor girl was almost naked and hanging lethargically in the arms of Ryder and Dave.

"That bitch sits idle and doesn't do anything" Nela added angrily, pointing to Tami. "Let's go down and free her."

But Ben held her back. "In a few moments there'll be six of them, and two of us won't stand a chance against the gang."

"Then we stir up trouble," she suggested. "Distract them, drive them apart. You go from the left; I attack from the right." Nela's body quivered. She could hardly be stopped.

Ben nodded in agreement. "Up there," he pointed to the hill, "forestry work is taking place. Due to bark beetles, the forest is being thinned. If we let one or more of the cut trees roll down the hill, it will panic them."

"Okay, up the hill," Nela agreed.

They were taking full risks as they ran up the slope from cover. Whatever happened now was beyond their control.

The last few yards were steep and made it difficult for the two to climb. Yet, Nela knew that this would make the logs roll all the faster. The old man behind her was breathing heavily, his condition was no longer the best. Arriving at the top, he leaned forward, propped himself up on his knees, and breathed heavily. Nela saw the piled logs lying in front of her. They were an arm's length across, the bark almost completely gone. If they could push the top one down, it would roll like a wheel.

"Come on, we don't have any time to waste!" She grabbed Ben by the arm and pulled him behind her.

"Careful, girl," he hissed. "You would rather not hurt yourself in the last few feet."

But Nela had already climbed the first trunks of the pyramid, looking for a firm foothold. "Come on, let's go!"

Ben puffed, pulling himself up trunk by trunk. The wood was light, the little remaining bark eaten away by beetles. The trunks were short; they must have been younger trees. Ben knelt forward, propping himself up with his right foot. He wondered if they could get this log to move. "Come on, together!"

Nela put her weight against the top trunk, pressing as hard as she could. Ben tensed his arms and with a jerk let himself fall forward. The tree came a little bit.

"Again," Ben called out to her. "This time with more pressure."

Nela did the same, gritted her teeth and threw herself against the trunk. It tipped forward, but their efforts were not strong enough, the tree rolled back into position.

"Again!" shouted Nela. "This time, don't stop, follow through!"
Ben smiled. Really? "Okay, young lady!"

Together they went back, put their hands on the wood and threw themselves forward one more time. Every muscle in Nela's body threatened to burst as she pushed the log forward. It toppled over again. "Keep going!" she hissed tensely. She could feel the tree wanting to move back into position, but this time they would make it. Nela looked at Ben, who was groaning under the weight of the tree. Slowly, very slowly, he moved forward. Soon, he would... and suddenly the resistance broke, and the trunk rolled down.

Ben and Nela fell forward, lying with their upper bodies on the wood-pile, watching the rolling log.

It bounced against the lower tree trunks, jumped onto the slope, and rolled down the former bathing meadow. It increased speed, jumping up and down, burying bushes and shrubs beneath it. The gang looked in horror at the approaching disaster.

"Come on, down the hill, right now!" shouted Nela. Dropping all caution, she jumped down the woodpile.
Ben hurried after her as best he could. Screams emanated from the below pool. Horrified, the gang had jumped apart.

Ben jumped after Nela, who was already starting to climb down the slope. Then, with a loud crash, the roar stopped. Astonished, they stopped and looked down at what was happening.

Several bushes and shrubs had slowed down the log and caused it to hit the starting blocks at the edge of the pool at a moderate speed. The gang stood startled between the swimming areas or had taken refuge in the empty basins. But none of them had fled or panicked. Only the dog barked like crazy, tugging at the leash.

Nela clenched her fists and cursed softly. That moment of surprise was gone. Ben stood on the slope, clutching the heavy flashlight. Time to fight!

But then all hell broke loose.

Whenever Ryder did something Tami disliked, she just tuned it out. She would fantasize about other things and imagine what it would be like when they were both older. Maybe one day they will have children and a house.

Often, though, she found it hard to turn a blind eye to Ryder's behavior. Especially when he made out with other girls. Like he did right now with the blonde chick. She didn't need to cry and complain in the first place. She had made her guy hot, after all. And now she regretted it. Tami was envious of the bird, though. Ryder could screw her more frequently. She was tired of constantly making him jealous with Dave just to get him to fuck her. She was aware that the other guys were hot for her as well. And if Ryder kept cheating on her, then she would just fuck Dave. Yet, one day he would realize that she was the right pick for him.

Tami wondered if he would be done with the blonde one soon. She couldn't hear her howling anymore. Maybe they had let the skunk go? Anyway, Tami didn't feel like staring into the fire alone anymore. She wondered if she should try Jesse? Or Mike? Ryder would get jealous really bad if she made out with him. She stood up and flicked her cigarette into the embers as the noise began.

A massive log came rolling down from the hill above the meadow. Startled, she jumped up and called for Ryder. However, he was standing pants down in front of that girl. His bulging erection stood far from his belly. With wide eyes, he saw the log coming. Dave had dropped the chick and jumped into the basin. She lay on the ground and whimpered.

Tami looked at her. She didn't look pretty at all anymore. The make-up was smeared, her hair ruined. Her magnificent tits were scratched, and her body was battered. She lay wailing on the floor, the splintered tiles and dirt carving small wounds into her skin. That's what she got from her haughtiness!

Motionless, Tami stood and watched as Jesse and Mike jumped into the empty pool. The furious dog dragged Mousey to the ground, and Ryder frantically tightened his pants. He watched helplessly as the tree approached faster and faster. But then, it finally slammed against the old, weathered starting blocks at the edge of the pool and came to rest.

That damn bastard! Ryder could still have saved her. Yet, he would simply have stood there and watched the tree roll over everyone. If he hadn't been busy with that tramp, he would have seen the tree coming sooner. Tami was beyond disappointment with her lover. However, she was even more angry with the blonde bitch who had seduced him. She would teach this whore manners.

The gang had just caught themselves, coming back from their hiding places when a bloodcurdling scream startled them.

"Uhhhhhhhhhh!"

At the same time, all heads moved back, looking toward the old pump house. Tami could not believe her eyes. Out of the darkness, an angry blonde came rushing toward them. Her mouth and eyes were wide open, screaming like a banshee. In one hand, she held a club above her head, in the other a hose. What the hell was going on?

Dave was the first to jump out of the pool, Ryder got into a fighting position. When water sprayed from the hose, Jesse and Mike were caught in a sudden flood of stinking water.

Ryder was next to be splashed, and then Dave got sprayed back into the basin. The water smelled absolutely disgusting. Tami gagged. Jesse and Mike kept their distance. Ryder roared with rage, but he did not move out of the way. As the hose-carrying savage approached, he ducked away from the jet of fetid brackish water. Then, vicious blows from the wooden club struck him on the head and upper body. Ryder had no choice but to flee to Dave in the pool.

"You fucking pigs!" the girl roared. She continued to let the jet sweep from left to right, like shooting bullets. Only when all the men had ducked away did she throw the hose from her and help the blonde up on her feet. "If you come after us, we'll kill you!" Limping but briskly, the two had disappeared into the woods.

What in the world was that? In less than a minute, chaos had descended upon them. The only one still standing was Tami.

ESCAPE PATHS

After his body processed the shock of the cold shower, Ryder noticed the foul smell of stale, brackish water. He stretched his arms and stared at himself, his eyes wide. Soaked in dark water, the stench of rot and decay made him retch. His stomach began to cramp. Bending over, he threw up where his victim had just been lying. Tears and mucus ran down his cheeks and mouth, but the nausea didn't subside until his senses had adjusted to the stench. Using his right arm, he wiped the remains from his face and took a look. The rest of the gang stood behind him, staring in bewilderment. The only one hit as badly as him was Dave, standing next to him, getting rid of his stinky T-shirt. He, too, fought nausea, spitting and blowing his nose. However, Dave had moved to safety, giving up his prey without a fight.

"Where is that bitch?" Ryder yelled at Dave. "Where is she?"

Dave looked at Ryder and rubbed his eyes. Now, what did he want from him? They had been robbed, though.

"You just let that skunk do that, you shitbag cunt of a coward!"
Dave held his wet, disgusting smelling shirt in his hand like a weapon. "So what? You didn't stop them either!"
"You're just a little wanker, showing off, acting like a boss. But when

it comes to it, you pull your pants up."

"Shut the fuck up!" countered Dave angrily. "The bitch was mine anyway. You rather fuck your little whore" he hissed, pointing to Tami.

Ryder's fist struck Dave unexpectedly. The force of the blow threw his head back. It hit the tiled edge of the basin with a crashing sound, sending Dave to the floor. For a moment, he lay unconscious in a puddle of brackish water, then slowly regained consciousness.

Ryder stood over him, his fist raised.

"Want some more, punk?" But Dave had had enough. His leader's sudden outburst of violence had put him in his place. "I'm going to take what is mine. Remember that."

As he relaxed and glanced at his gang, there was Tami standing over him on the edge of the pool. She was shaking and sobbing, but her gaze was steady. "You're such a pig," she whispered.

Tami took a deep breath and said louder, "Just a disgusting bastard, you are!" Her tears stopped running, her body tensed. "What kind of man are you anyway?" Her hands clenched into fists, and she shook her head. "You have affairs with other women. You cheat on me with other women, fucking those sluts behind my back. Even when I'm standing next to it, you cop off with another one!"

For a moment, Ryder was overwhelmed with Tami's emotional outburst. Silently, he lowered his fist.

"Do you know how that makes me feel? What did she have that you couldn't get from me?"

Ryder did not answer her. With a quick leap, he had jumped out of the basin and was now standing in front of her.

"But that's okay," Tami continued with mock resignation, "then I'll just find another guy." Provocatively, she looked around. "Mike, what's up with you? Do you feel like …"

That was as far as Tami got. Ryder slapped her two times. Her head flew from left to right, she staggered.

"Who do you think you are, little skunk?" Ryder grabbed her by the neck and drove her in front of him. "Ever looked in the mirror? Have you ever done so? Who do you think you are anyway? Strutting around like a top model, trying to tell me what to do?"

Tami tried to get away from Ryder, but he wouldn't let go. She gasped for air.
"You're nothing more than a cheap slut." Ryder let go of Tami's neck. "Now fuck off!"
Stunned, she stared at him. "But…"
"Ain't no 'but'! Get out of here!" Ryder shoved her off him, kicked her in the butt, "Get out!"

He chased her to the edge of the forest and waited there until she disappeared into the night, sobbing.

"Does anyone else have an issue with me?" Ryder spread his arms provocatively, scanning the area. "If so, feel free to go after the little girl."

He waited for a moment, then called his dog to him. "Gazoo, come to your master!" The animal joyfully ran toward him, and Ryder embraced it with a grin.

The balance of power was restored.

"What do we do now?" Jesse was the first to reply.

"Yeah, man! We can't let that slide!" Mike added.

Looking down, Dave said, "Yes, we can't let that happen to us." His voice sounded quiet and controlled.

Appeasing, Ryder put his arm around him. "I'll tell you what we're going to do. They fled to the barracks down south. Probably the rest of those fuckers were with them, too. We're going to split up and hunt them down!"

He looked at serious faces. They nodded, ready.

"Jesse and I go to the rolling gate. Dave and Mike go further down to where the hole in the fence is located. We'll round them up from both directions."

"Good point, Ryder," Dave said, still quiet and controlled. "But what if they get through to the barracks?"

"Then we'll chase them all the way to the old hospital if we have to." Ryder's expression was petrified.

The gang did not say a word, but instead stared at the ground.

Mousey was the first to speak up again. "But we're not allowed to go there." He raised his eyes and looked at Ryder with fear. "What if Henry finds us?"

"Then God help us," he replied curtly.

Mike swallowed; Jesse put on a determined expression. Dave kept his jaw clenched and remained silent.

"Come on, let's not waste time." Gazoo immediately barked at the gang. As they started to move, Mousey asked, "Where do you want me to go?"

Ryder grinned. "You will look after Tami. You're just too tied on her apron strings anyways."

Laughing, the gang disappeared into the darkness.

Tess and Damon had been pushing the pump up and down frantically. The dark water in the pump basin was sloshed back and forth. It smelled terrible. But they ignored it and kept pumping. Their bodies were dripping with sweat. Outside, they heard Yelka yelling and screaming. They looked into each other's eyes, listened to the noises. A short fight must have taken place. The shouts and aggression died down, and the stream of water sounded monotonous. It seemed to flow in one direction, the hose had hose stopped moving. Silence.

Tess and Damon paused for a moment and lowered their breath. Had

Yelka and Vivian managed to escape? How come everything was so quiet all of a sudden? Tess was trembling. Uncertainty sent her into a state of panic. The urge to flee overwhelmed her. She felt her heart beating faster. Tess thought she could no longer breathe. She inhaled and exhaled deeply before turning and heading for the door.

At the very same moment, roaring started outside. The gang seemed to be going at each other. The voices were animalistic, the words vulgar. They acted like wild animals. A fight appeared to be brewing.

Tess stood at the door. Damon yanked her back. She screamed in pain as he twisted her arm.

"Are you crazy?" he hissed urgently. "You can't go out there right now."

"I want to get out of here, I want to get out of here," Tess sobbed desperately. "I just want to get out of here."

"Hey," he whispered patiently, "wait a little longer. They'll take us outside. In here, we're still safe."

Tess closed her eyes and swayed back and forth. "Okay, okay, okay…" she finally replied in desperation.

Damon smiled at her, wrapped an arm around Tess. He stroked her hair and pressed her against him.

"Starlet, calm down. You're with me, you're safe."

Carefully, he let go of Tess and took her hand. Gently, he placed it on his chest and breathed in and out. He looked into her eyes as he silently smiled. Damon felt her calmness. Her pulse went down, her breathing slowed. She smiled back at him.

"Are you alright?" She nodded, smiling cautiously. "It appears that they're focusing on Yelka and Vivian now. They don't know anything about us. Therefore, they will not even consider looking for us here. We'll just wait and see."

"Yes," Tess reluctantly agreed, "but shouldn't we be with Yelka and Tess?"

"You're absolutely right, starlet."

Questioningly, Tess looked at him.

"But if we are all on the run together, they will get us much easier. We are louder together, attract more attention. Separately, our chances are much higher."

Tess thought about Damon's arguments and found them convincing.

"You'll be fine, I'm sure of it." Damon squeezed her hand.

"But," Tess asked hesitantly, "isn't Vivian your model? Shouldn't you protect her?"

Footsteps approached the pump house.

Tess and Damon froze. Who was coming? Had they been discovered? They crouched down, their heads bent below the window. Carefully, Damon straightened up, so he could look outside. In the flickering light of the flames, he saw a girl approach the house. Blinded by the backlight, he ducked away, leaned against the wall, and looked at Tess. She was wide-eyed, her pupils moving from side to side. The footsteps came closer.

"Come on, next to the door!" hissed Damon. "It's our only chance."

Silently, they crept through the pitch-black room and positioned themselves to the left and right of the entrance door. They heard the footsteps coming closer. The shadow of the girl appeared in the milky windows.

"We overpower her and run straight into the woods."

Tess nodded hastily. Panic was back.
Any moment now, she would walk in.
The door handle was slowly tilted down.
Damon raised his fist to strike.
Tess got ready to jump.

"Hey Tami, wait!" Muffled, they heard the soft voice of another person.
More footsteps approached the door. The handle remained pressed down.
"What do you want from me?" the girl asked gruffly.
"Are you okay?"
"Yeah, I'll be fine. Did Ryder send you? Is he sorry now?"
"No, Ryder didn't send me. I just didn't want to leave you alone."
She gave a short laugh. "Well, well. Wanna be my protector?"

Damon clenched his fists. Tess nervously rocked back and forth.

"Hmm, yeah," the boy stammered softly. "So, what are you going to do now?"

"Actually, I wanted to be alone. Now you're here."

"Mmm, yeah, that's right. Do you want to go to your favorite place?"

"To the theater? What a little romantic you are."

The handle returned to its position.

When the voices ceased, Damon and Tess exhaled deeply. The tension fell away from them.

"Tess, we're going to get help now." Damon was the first to find back his words. "No more experiments. We'll return to the settlement and then back to the wall."

"To the wall? Is there an entrance there? Can we get out that way?"

"Hmm, maybe we can do that, yeah. However, in any case, we will have access to Wi-Fi there."

Tess raised her lower lip and questioningly looked at Damon.

"Then we can call for help. Come on!"

Damon had opened the door quietly and cast a searching glance outside. Silently, he pushed his way out. The coast was clear. He turned to Tess, but she didn't leave the house.

"We have no time to lose, come on!" He was getting impatient. "I promise you that Yelka and Vivian will make it. By the time the cops arrive, the dust will have settled."

"You really think so?"

"Absolutely, starlet."

"And what about Nela?" She frowned and raised her brows. "We have to find Nela first."

Damon closed his eyes and took a deep breath.

The erection in his hand was gone. Zander stood behind a tree and watched stunned as Yelka freed her little sister. For a moment, he was dismayed, remaining motionless in his hiding place. He felt his excitement waning by the second. While Ryder was throwing out, Zander zipped up his pants and stared at the blazing fire.

Despite his initial frustration, Zander now saw more clearly. The most intense feeling he had ever experienced was the lust that had overtaken him when Ryder raped Vivian. It was so strong that it almost made him fall to the ground. Trembling, he leaned against a tree while his own blood pounded in his ears. He felt both hot and cold at the same time.

Everything he had suppressed and failed to get over the past few years channeled into that one moment that unhinged Zander's emotional life. Never again would he indulge in soft feelings like tenderness or romance. At that moment, love seemed so far away to him that he couldn't remember ever feeling it.

His gaze shifted to Kimberly, who had set herself up at the edge of the pool in front of Ryder. Yes, Kimberly at that moment seemed much more attractive to him than Yelka had ever been.

Zander was unable to comprehend what the conversation between her and Ryder was about. Kimberly stood wide-legged; her hands clenched into fists. Ryder lurked in the basin like a predator, waiting for his prey. Zander guessed they must have been arguing. Probably Kimberly had gathered all her courage and frustration and was about to rant and rave. Oh yes, please challenge him. Zander felt nothing more than a desire for more escalation. Please, punish her!

Ryder jumped out of the pool and stood in front of her. From his posture and Kimberly's speaking style, Zander could guess what was about to happen. Show her who's in charge!

With two quick movements, Ryder had slapped her twice. As he had demonstrated earlier, his forehand and backhand had ricocheted through her face.

The excitement that overcame Zander was back again. He already felt his erection returning. His pants bulged out, and he was swept away by waves of heat. Go on, go on! Take it, you've earned it!

And Ryder grabbed his prey. Oh yes, he yanked it from left to right and roared at it. Zander's erection throbbed hard now, his breathing quickening. Eyelids fluttered in approaching ecstasy. Take her right now! What are you waiting for?

But Ryder did not escalate further. He simply chased Kimberly away and kicked her butt. What was that all about?

The stimulation remained absent. Zander felt the excitement fall away from him again. He gritted his teeth and clenched his fist. Now, anger overcame Zander.

"Is there anyone else having a problem with me?"

This time, Zander could hear Ryder's words clearly. Oh yes, I do have a problem with you! Finish it now. He reached for the knife in his pocket. That cold steel soothed him a little.

"You'd better follow her!"

Zander was in a crouched position behind Kimberly, protected by the trees. She circled the fire, casting a long shadow whose tip almost reached Zander. The nearness of Kimberly tickled his euphoria again, as his erection was not yet fully flaccid. Her figure was slim but not athletic, her movement sexy but not erotic. Her hair bounced as she walked, as did her small breasts. However, it no longer mattered whether she was attractive or not. The desire he projected upon her was attractive enough. Zander neither knew what drove him, nor did he search for that reason; mechanically, he followed his urge.

Kimberly had reached the end of the pool and turned right toward the old pump house from which Yelka had appeared. Just a few more yards and she would have disappeared from the gang's sight, leaving into the darkness. Zander sank deeper into the woods, closing in on her. She had arrived at the door and was about to enter the house. His heart pounded faster. She would be there all alone!

"Hey, wait!"

The little blond boy who had carried the dog on a leash had followed her. Damn it, what was that kid doing here? Zander's excitement once again gave way to a pang of anger. Just like a few moments before, the situation was again being destroyed by someone.

They chatted, laughed shyly, and then fled into the darkness of the forest. What was this all about?

He followed them tensely, avoiding every redundant step, moving almost silently. He was now at the back of them. Kimberly had her arm loosely wrapped around the boy's shoulder. Zander watched as the brat buried his hands in the pockets of his pants. He was much too shy to approach Kimberly.

"Is it okay for you like this?" she asked the little one.

"Uh huh …." He was too excited to give a complete sentence.

"Nice. I've never been out here alone at night before."

"Haven't you?" The boy sensed his chance. "I have quite often," he claimed with feigned confidence.

"Aren't you afraid at all?"

"No, never …"

"Phew, I'm reassured, though."

Zander no longer listened to them. Their harmonious behavior frustrated him. He wanted to go back to that Ryder situation. Disillusionment crept into his mind like a winter night's chill. His emotions were frozen, dull. Zander longed for the strong, glaring charms that had enchanted him so badly.

He felt the knife in his pocket, felt the cold metal and finally unfolded the blade. Moonlight reflected in the polished steel. The edge was sharper than ever. Carefully, he placed the tip of the knife on his forearm. Very slowly, he pressed it into his skin. Pain jerked through his body.

The extreme stimuli were back, the drive returned. A tiny drop of blood fell to the forest floor as Zander resumed his pursuit.

After a few minutes, he had caught up with Kimberly and the boy. They walked across a clearing littered with the remains of rotten seats. At their end lay the ruins of a stage. This had to be the abandoned open-air theater.

The place where dramas happened.

Running into the darkness, Yelka had her gaze fixed on the path ahead. Her eyes watered and her lungs burned. Behind her, the gang screamed. She no longer felt anything, neither fear nor panic. She focused completely on her body, on every single move she made—where she was stepping and what lay ahead. Thus, her mind blocked out the terror that haunted her. Yelka blanked out everything. The firm grip on her sister's hand was the only thing that mattered.

Vivian was right behind her, and she heard her panting. Every now and then she would let herself fall back, other times keeping pace with her. Yelka cast a quick glance over her shoulder. Vivian had her eyes closed, her naked upper body bent forward. She staggered from left to right, threatening to trip at any moment.

Yelka slowed down, put an arm around her sister. Vivian sobbed quietly to herself while being completely apathetic.

"Let's stop for a moment," Yelka whispered softly. They took cover behind a fallen tree. Vivian slumped down, crouched in Yelka's arm, crying. "Hey, sis, we're safe." She stroked her hair.

The pale moonlight shone on Vivian's body, revealing sweat and tears. Numerous welts and scratches were silent witnesses to her abuse. She had severe bite marks on her neck, and bruises on her arm. She was in a pitiful condition. Yelka was shocked.

With her thumb, she wiped away Vivian's tears, caressing her cheek. Before taking off her tank top and slipping it over Vivian, she gave her sister a hug. Although it was summer, she immediately felt the cold of the night.

In front of her, Vivian sat silent and impassively. The fact that her nakedness was now covered seemed to be irrelevant to her. Her upper body swayed slightly from left to right.

"Vivian, oh Vivian, what have they done to you?"

Loud voices. The gang approached.

"We have to keep going!" Yelka grabbed Vivian's arm and helped her up. "They're coming."

Vivian's sobs grew louder. Hesitantly she put one leg in front of the other, stumbled forward, only pulled by Yelka. She cried and wailed, her hand resting tightly in Yelka's. If she had loosened her grip, Vivian would have fallen forward, powerless.

But Yelka persevered and did not give up on her. Her senses were focused on the surroundings. Like a cat, she steered around every obstacle, led her sister safely through the dark forest. She listened to the sounds, heard the shouts and the barking behind her. Did the gang know where they were?

The faster they ran, the more unrestrained Vivian cried. In her desperation, she thoroughly ignored the fact that they could hear her. Yelka prayed that they were far enough away not to attract attention!

Abruptly, the forest ended, and they ran into a large clearing, which was only sparsely overgrown with grass and young trees. Yelka let her eyes scan the area. The clearing seemed spacious, was almost rectangular. At the very last moment, they managed to avoid a railing that blocked their way. Yelka had to stop, and Vivian almost ran into her. Although they nearly fell over, Yelka was able to offset her sisters' momentum.

Her cries died away instantly, as shock had taken her by surprise.

Yelka turned around and examined the entire area. Indeed, this had once been a sports field. There was a soccer goal some distance away, with the crossbar falling over. The net was torn to shreds. On the other side of the field, the goal was no longer visible. Surely, it had fallen victim to time and weather. Many years ago, hundreds of people must have gathered here to cheer on the soccer-playing soldiers.

Yet now they had no time for the magic of this place. Vivian was still in shock. Her tears had dried up, and with wide eyes, she looked at her sister. Yelka smiled. She once more gave Vivian a cuddle, but her affection remained unrequited.

"My dear sister, I'm so glad you're with me."

Vivian remained silent.

"You can't imagine the fear I had for you."

Vivian sobbed.

"What did they do to you?" Loosening her embrace, Yelka looked at Vivian. However, Vivian continued to whine without answering.

"Hey, it's all right. You don't have to say anything. Foremost, we will ensure our safety. That is the most important thing."

Vivian took a deep breath. "Isn't Damon with you?" she finally asked, trembling.

Yelka shook her head. "We met another girl who was also attacked by the gang. She and Damon pumped that water I used to free you. They must have fled in another direction."

Vivian started crying again. Her body shook. Yelka hugged her tightly, put a hand on the back of her head.

"Everything will be all right, I'm sure he's safe."

But her sister did not calm down. "Nothing will be all right," she sobbed, "everything is over."

"Hey, you can't give up. We're going to make it out of here."

"No, no, no" Vivian slumped to the floor. "There's no sense anymore …"

From afar, she heard yelling.

The gang was approaching!

Yelka pulled Vivian up and ran. They had to get out of there. The old sports field would be a trap. They could be seen from anywhere around. Back into the forest was the only way out. Past the sports field, further into the unknown, until they had left everything behind.

"Come on!" But Vivian's grip loosened, her hand slipped through Yelka's fingers. Still running, she turned around and saw her little sister sitting on the floor. She gave her a blank stare. Yelka stopped, ran back and took Vivian's hand again.

"Please, Viv, come on! Don't leave me alone." But her sister's gaze was apathetic, disconnected from reality.

Yelka could already hear snippets of a conversation from the forest. The men made no effort to suppress their loudness. They had only a little time left! Yelka crouched down and carefully touched Vivian's chin. She gently kissed her sister and caressed her cheek. "I promise you that we will look for Damon and find him soon as we are safe."

Vivian glanced at her, blinking.

"But for that, you have to get up now and come with me."

She nodded.

Cautiously, Nela and Ben walked down the hill. They were still unable to grasp what had happened moments ago. Their failed rescue was followed by the attack of that unknown girl carrying a hose. They had not yet digested all this when the gang tore each other apart. Nela was already about to chase after the two when the gang set off as well.

The old, abandoned pool lay in front of them. The gang had carelessly left a blazing fire burning in one of the pools. Flickering ghostly, the yellow light reflected off the blue tiles. Nela had forgotten all about the beauty of that abandoned place. She was electrified. Where was Tess, and what had happened to her? That was the only question still on her mind. Despite the warm summer night, it gave Nela a chill. Her nerves seemed to be electrified, her gaze wandered all over the gang's stomping ground.

"It seems they come here frequently." Ben had taken an overview. "This wasn't the first fire they'd started here." He focused his flashlight on more piles of charred branches and ash.

"Strange," Nela replied. "It took us half a day's walk to get here alone. Whatever they're doing out here, they must have a good reason for it."

"So, they'll know their way around here, too."

"They fled in that direction," Nela pointed south. "What is there?"

"Eventually," Ben said, "they'll end up at the fence to the barracks."

"Damn," Nela muttered. "Does that mean they're trapped there?"

"I have no idea," Ben admitted. "I only get to look at the facilities inside twice a year. The fence might be damaged or has holes in it."

With her eyes downcast, Nela walked between the pools. There was dirt smeared on the tiles where Ryder and Dave had abused Tess. Shoe prints and small drops of blood could be found. They appeared to be fresh. When her gaze dropped down, she saw a shirt on the bottom of the pool. She carefully climbed down the ladder and inspected the garment. It was a white spaghetti-strap top.

Obviously, it had been torn from the girl's body because it had rips and fight marks on it. But Tess had been wearing a regular T-shirt. This was not her top. Who was the girl if this hadn't been Tess? And where was Tess?

"Did you find anything?" Ben stepped over her and shone his light down on Nela.

"Yes." Nela was thoughtful. "That wasn't Tess at all. That's not her top."

"Are you certain?"

"You bet. That was someone else."

"Maybe you weren't the only Urbexers around."

"Perhaps." Nela swung out of the basin.

"Be it as it will," Ben said, "we need to get help now."

"I won't leave this place without …"

"I know," he interrupted Nela. "We're not going to leave either."

"But?"

"There is a transmitting station in the old hospital. If we find the emergency generator and turn it on, we can then call for help."

"That run-down hospital you mentioned earlier, is that what you mean?"

"That's right, young lady."

Lowering her head, Nela put her hands in the pockets of her cargo pants.

"You Urbexers are looking for adventure anyway." Ben looked at her in irritation.

"Yes" confirmed Nela, still searching in her pockets. "And I'm not leaving without my girlfriend anyway."

"Well then…"

Finally, she pulled her multifunction tool from her pocket. "This," Nela said, "will be the only tool we have handy in that abandoned, collapsed hospital. Will this be enough?"

"Jeez!" Ben laughed. "We have to get over that fence first, sneak around the gang, and finally into the hospital. Once that is accomplished, we can tackle everything else."

Satisfied, Nela nodded. "Well, so be it, old man."

"Let's get started."

Tess had her arms folded, and her lips pressed together. Seriously, she wanted to find her friend Nela before they sought help. Inside, Damon was seething with anger. Nothing other than the existence of his company was at stake.

"We'll find Nela first!" Tess was about to put her foot down. Her expression revealed a childish rage and stubbornness. "I'm not going anywhere."

Damon closed his eyes and took a deep breath. "Starlet, we will lose valuable time by aimlessly wandering through the forest."

"I don't care at all. , My girlfriend is more important."

More important than what? Damon stared at her. Tess seemed to be serious. At least for the moment. But he knew this kind of woman. Emotionally upset, any discussion was pointless. Withdrawal and change of subject would be his strategy, but currently he lacked alternatives.

"You're right, Tess. We're looking for your friend." Conciliatory, Damon squeezed her hand. "Let's go."

Tess relaxed herself. She instantly lowered her arms and smiled at Damon. She had the handsome guy wrapped around her little finger! Likewise, she knew he found her attractive. His concession proved that, or so she thought.

"Which direction should we look for Nela?"

She had a thought. It would be reasonable to assume that Nela would have walked back to the apartment buildings. After all, they had lost each other there. Hopefully, they would find each other there, too. "I think Nela will be waiting for us at the housing blocks" she finally guessed.

"That's possible. Let's try to go back the way we came."

"Can you still find that one?"

"Pretty sure, Tess."

Quietly and carefully, they walked through the forest, trying to make as little noise as possible. However, the woods absorbed every sound. It was deadly quiet. It was only occasionally that animals called in the darkness. The gang must have left in another direction.

"So, Tess, how are things going? Do you have any plans for the future?" Damon asked casually as he led the way for Tess.

"Well," she hesitated, "I'm definitely planning a career in modeling." It was time to be a little more confident. "Nela and I had a shoot today, which we were actually going to continue tomorrow." She blinked.

"Really?" Damon seemed sincerely amazed.

"Yeah, that's why finding her is so important" she lied.

"Of course, that makes sense. Who would be able to understand that better than I?" Quietly, they laughed together. "So, what are your further plans for the future, Tess?"

"So, my goal," Tess explained, "is definitely Dubai. As soon as it's possible, I would move there."

Tess pulled herself together. For the first time, she was using her acting skills to advance her career. And it seemed that Damon was taking the bait. He turned to her, raised his eyebrows.

"Wow, that sounds promising," he appreciatively said. "Dubai is so impressive. I'd love to be over there more often, but work …" Damon puffed in exhaustion. "I really envy my girls. They have such a wonderful life in the Gulf. Really gorgeous."

Damon let his words sink in. Silently, he counted to three, then asked, "You've probably been there a lot, right?"

The moment was heavy.

Finally, Tess replied, "Well, I'd like to be there more often."

Damon smiled knowingly. "You've likely been to the Burj Khalifa, right? The view from up there is really impressive."

"Oh yeah," she agreed with him. "Really great."

"And surely, you've spent the night at Atlantis, right?"

"Yeah, sure."

"We need to go there together sometime" Damon offered her. "Last time, I went on a private yacht with the girls. Fantastic. Really, really, really great." He was silent for a moment, as if reminiscing. "And afterward, we went shopping at the Dubai Mall. The girls were freaking out."

He laughed. Tess remained silent. The moment was awkward, but then Damon wrapped an arm around Tess's waist.

"Starlet, you should be with me next time."

Tess' heart beat faster. "You think?"

He laughed. "If you don't come, I'll feel deeply insulted."

"I can't answer for that, of course."

Damon stopped and looked at her. His eyes gleamed in the moonlight as he asked Tess, "How do you feel about signing with Duke Executives?"

Tess felt dizzy, her whole body trembling with excitement. Finally, her big dream came true. In the midst of this nightmare, new possibilities suddenly opened up. She could not believe it.

"Oh yes," she stammered uncontrollably, "I do."

He laughed and gave her a hug. "Welcome aboard, starlet. You made the right decision. I'm overjoyed you chose us."

A tear of joy ran down Tess' cheek.

"You'll see, Dubai holds so many possibilities for you." His arm now firmly wrapped around her waist, he kissed Tess gently on the cheek. "Well, let's get going, so we don't waste any time."

Tess was overcome with emotion when Damon said casually, "Oh, then we should change our plan a little and go back to the wall and get help first. Thereafter, we'll get Nela."

"Okay, sure." Tess agreed without any objection.

Damon had achieved his goal. He took Tess' hand and spun her around, laughed victoriously, and gave her another cuddle. She smiled, hugged him again. Damon took a step backward, raised his hands and imitated holding a camera. She posed, smiled, looked serious, and winked at him. Forgotten were the fear of the gang, the search for help, and the worries about Nela.

When they found their way back to the old forest path that led them directly to the settlement, it was more like an unimportant coincidence than it was essential or helpful. The sun would soon rise, and the dangers of the night would be nothing more than a bad dream.

But when the forest opened up and the outline of the old apartment block became visible, they found a black car parked in the dark.

They both stopped and looked at each other questioningly. The vehicle was a van that had recently been parked at the edge of the forest.

Damon crept around the car, taking a searching look inside the empty car.

"Whose car do you think is this?" Tess whispered.

"I have no idea." Damon took a look around, but there was no one to be seen.

"Maybe it's security?" Tess pondered.

"That's a delivery truck. Looks more like craftsmen."

"It's in the middle of the night, though!"

"We should keep moving," Damon decided. "Whoever came out here this late will be trouble."

Hectically, Tess grabbed Damon's hand. Hurriedly, they headed back to the apartment block when they heard a rasping voice from behind.

"Freeze!"

With a jerk, Yelka pulled her sister up, dragging the crying girl behind her. Vivian stumbled and grabbed Yelka at the last second. They increased their speed, ran across the former sports field, dodged young birch trees, hit a snag, and finally disappeared into the woods again. Dogs barked behind them. Men were shouting. Did they see them? It did not matter. Onward, ever so, into the forest. Like sinister shadows, trees flew past Yelka.

The wind blew so hard in her ears that she couldn't hear their hunters' voices. The only thing that counted was her sister's hand in hers.

Her crying finally got through to her. She sobbed loudly and unrestrained, letting herself go. Vivian staggered after her, threatening to stumble at any moment. Yelka stopped, let Vivian run into her. She hugged her sister for a moment. She sighed deeply and felt her racing pulse return to normal.

"I think we lost them." Yelka whispered in her sister's ear.

But her sister did not calm down, still sobbing. Her body rose and fell in Yelka's arms.

"Hey, I think we're safe for now."

"It doesn't matter at all," Vivian said quietly. "It's all over, isn't it?"

"Hell no, why would it be?" Yelka pushed Vivian away and tried to make eye contact. "Nothing is lost, we'll be safe soon."

"Just look at me," her sister whined. "I'm dirty, hurt, and I smell bad."

"Viv, everything will be fine again."

"My manager is with a new model. A prettier one." Vivian interrupted her. "Don't you understand? It's over …"

Yelka gave her a grim look. How could her little sister let herself down like that? She would kick Vivian's butt when they eventually got home. That asshole Damon got over, that was the bitter truth. Yelka was forced to keep her composure and refrain from shouting out loud. She inhaled the cold forest air, held her breath, and exhaled slowly.

"Please listen to me, dear sister. You are in a state of shock right now. That's totally understandable after what you've been through. Tomorrow, though, will be a new day. Until then, however, you must persevere."

Vivian was silent, staring lethargically at the floor.

"Come now, please." She took Vivian's hand and continued walking.

She heard a strangled scream from behind when her sister let go after taking two steps. When she turned around, Vivian was lying on the floor holding her foot. Her sobs had started again, tears running down her cheeks.

"Hey, what happened?"

"I fell over," she whined softly. Fortunately, she had her volume under control.

"Let me see."

Gently, she took Vivian's foot in her hand. Thankfully, she was at least wearing her sneakers. The ankle did not appear to be thick, and her joint could be turned without any issues. It may have been the moment of the fall that felt like physical pain. Yelka gently touched Vivian's leg with her fingertips.

"It's all right, your foot isn't hurt." She squatted down and stretched her arms towards her. "Come on, try to stand up." Vivian looked at her with teary eyes, chewing on her lower lip in a trance-like manner. Taking a deep breath, she reached for Yelkas hands and allowed her to help her stand up again. She carefully shifted her weight to her right leg.

Carefully, she then stepped on her left foot and let the pain come. Tears welled up in her eyes again, but Yelka talked her through it.

"Take it easy, sis. You'll be fine." She clutched her hands tightly, helping her find her balance. "Great. Now let's take a step together." Relieved, she watched as Vivian put one foot in front of the other. Yelka lowered one hand and now walked attentively beside her. Vivian was limping, but they were making progress.

"Great, I'm proud of you."

After a few feet, they finally reached a fence that stood abruptly in front of them. It was a twelve-foot-high dark wire mesh fence, barbed wire coiled on top. It looked imposing, defying any intruder. Still, the fence seemed to withstand wind and weather. Lights were positioned at intervals of a few feet apart, but they had gone off long ago. To the left and right, the fence ran through the forest, finding its end somewhere in the darkness.

For a moment, Yelka was fascinated. This had to be the border of the actual barracks Zander had talked about. Peering through the wire, she saw buildings standing some distance away on the other side. Oh yes, this was the old military installation she had heard so much about. Many Urbexers had talked about it, but few had actually found their way here. It was ironic that Yelka seemed to be the only one of the few who could not enjoy this moment. Clasping her fingers around the wire, she stared into the dark. Vivian had stopped crying, and the forest could now be heard clearly.

The leaves rustled as it crackled between the trees, a bird called. The houses on the other side seemed eerie, as if they were hiding sinister secrets. It was not the same horror they had experienced when being chased by the gang. This was more subtle, creeping silently into their bones. Black figures seemed to be lurking, waiting for the sisters in the darkness. And yet, it was their only way out.

The panic that had been building so slowly and creeping up became real when the gang's voices were heard from the forest. They were breathing down their necks!

"Come on, we gotta go." Hectically, she looked at Vivian. Her sister remained standing there, eyes wide in panic, fingers clenched into fists, tense within. Her breathing became increasingly rapid. She was on the verge of a panic attack, it was obvious.

"Vivian, hey!" Yelka tried to get through to her, but she couldn't. "We have to go," she tried again. But Vivian was breathing harder and harder.

The voices came closer.

Panic seized Yelka, but she breathed in and out calmly while walking towards Vivian. With gentleness, she wrapped her arms around her sister. Yelka remained focused on breathing, refusing to be distracted.

Loud crackling, sounded from the forest, footsteps.

Yelka felt that her sister's fit of panic was over. She loosened her embrace, gazing at Vivian. "We have to go now, Viv. This is important." But she didn't answer, staring blankly through the fence and into the darkness.

Yelka struggled with herself, as she was afraid as well.

"We're out of time! Do you hear me?" Finally, her little sister nodded silently. Yelka reached around Vivian's shoulders and pushed her to the right.

"We're going that way now. Quickly." She then pushed Vivian ahead, forcing her to walk.

"Here's the fence! They can't be far!"

Yelka choked.

Hectically, they ran down the fence, constantly seeking an opportunity to climb through. But the fence was in good condition, offering the sisters no chance to escape. Behind her, Yelka felt the gang approaching. It could not be long before they discovered them. Fear was driving her. Yelka's hand was on Vivian's back, pushing her forward.

But then she stopped abruptly. In front of her lay a field of stinging nettles. They swayed menacingly in the light of the moon, towering waist high. She heard Vivian cry again. Yelka was trembling. Her mouth became dry. This could not happen. Not now.

"There they are!"

Panic spread from Yelka's legs to her stomach. A buzzing reached her ears. She was on the verge of losing consciousness.

"No!" she cried aloud. "No, no!"

Yelka shook her head, shooing away the fear. Determined, she went ahead, clawing her hands into Vivian's forearms. Her sister cried in pain, as Yelka pulled her forward into the field of stinging nettles.

As best she could, she kicked the plants aside. Her long pants kept the painful leaves off her skin. However, Vivian screamed her head off behind her.

"I'm sorry, I'm sorry, I'm sorry...", Yelka whispered to herself like a mantra. The painful path seemed never-ending.

"Fucking cunts, we'll get you."

The gang must have been standing at the edge of the field. They hesitated, just as Yelka had done. But she did not look around. Keep going, keep going.

Stumbling already, she noticed something at the fence.

At the level of their heads, a large hole opened up the fence.

They were blinded by the flashlight's glow. Damon held his hands in front of his face, while Tess was hiding behind his back. Tromping, the man approached, cracking branches cracked under his feet. When he finally lowered the light, their eyes needed a moment to adjust to the darkness again.

Although it was a balmy summer night, the man in front of them was dressed darkly, wearing a black flight jacket. It was hard to tell how old he was, but his hairstyle seemed old-fashioned, like it was from the 90s. He had his hair parted in the middle and cut short on the sides. A bushy mustache grew under his hooked nose, making him appear older than he was. With a cold stare, he gazed at them.

"What are you doing out here?" There was something threatening in his voice. Like it was not about the reason for their stay, but about the punishment for it.

Damon slowly lowered his arms. "We're on our way home," he finally replied evasively. "If you don't mind me asking, who are you, though?"

"Security," the man replied with utter superiority. "This is a restricted area." He shone a light on Tess's face. When she closed her eyes, he pointed the glow at Damon until he, too, shut his eyes again. "How did you get in here?"

Damon averted his eyes and defensively held his hand between himself and the man. "I apologize, would you mind not shining that light on me? You seem to be blinding me."

The glow of the lamp moved downward, just enough for Damon to see again.

"Thank you. And I think we need to clear up a misunderstanding here," Damon remarked. "My name is Duke. Damon Duke, CEO of Duke Executives." He lifted his chin and let the words sink in, as if they would impress the sinister fellow. "We rented this location today for a photo shoot." He pointed to Tess, who was standing behind him. "Here's Tess Walker, one of our main models, known as Com-Tessa."

Damon waited a moment. The flashlight's glow traveled over to Tess, lingered on her torso, slid down her legs and back up. Eventually, he shone it into her eyes again until she turned away. His gaze remained emotionless, no expression stirring on his face.

"We did the first shots for the centerfold today. The entire shoot was incredibly energy-consuming, and we were already behind schedule. So, it would be beneficial if we could continue undisturbed, Mr. ...?"

Damon was hit directly by a light from the man as he took a step toward him.

"Don't fuck with me. What are you doing here, boy?"

Tess immediately backed away, and Damon also became defensive. "Listen, everything is correct. I would appreciate it if you could contact Mr. Wilbanks from the city administration. He will confirm my statement."

For the first time, the man with the cold eyes smiled. But he didn't smile honestly; he just lifted the edges of his lips. The gaze, however, remained cold and penetrating.

"So, Mr. Wilbanks is the person who gave you the permit?"

"That's what I'm saying."

"And you've been to a photo shoot, Damon Duke and Tess Walker?"

"That's precisely how it is," Damon confirmed. Tess nodded eagerly.

"That's all well and good," he lashed out, "but where's your equipment? You probably need cameras and stuff like that."

"All gone already," Damon replied curtly, "the other team has already left."

Thoughtfully, the man nodded, looking up at the starry sky above them. "Yeah, sure. Sounds valid." Then he lowered his gaze and looked Damon straight in the eye. "But there's no Mr. Wilbanks working for the city, you lying son of a bitch. Nobody at the fucking city administration gives a damn shit about anything out here." His eyes lit up angrily. "It's only you phonies and me." He took another step toward Damon. When he tilted his head, they almost touched. The flashlight was pointed downwards with a firm grip on the handle. "Time and again, good-for-nothings stray out here. Troublemakers, hobos, and cable thieves. Rats."

Damon could smell his breath, that's how close the guy was to him.

"I should slap you to the floor and get you hog-cuffed."

Tess got scared. She immediately wanted to run. Always following the path until she got to her car. Just away from here.

"Well," Damon suddenly blurted out. "You're right, we don't have a permit and I lied to you. I want to apologize for that."

The man raised his eyebrows and nodded appreciatively. "I just believe the first part, boy."

"But the rest is true as well. We were here for a photo shoot."

"Is that true? Then, where are the rest of you kids?"

"We have been assaulted by a criminal gang. They robbed us. Our friends are on the run somewhere in the forest."

"What are you saying?" The man wrinkled his forehead. "You've been attacked?"

"Yes, it is true."

"My friend is still somewhere out here." For the first time, Tess spoke up.

"All right, got you. But first things first now. What happened?"

"A couple of youths approached us at the old settlement. They said they were security. When we were already on our way back later in the evening, accosting us was no longer enough. They sicced their dog on us, beat us with clubs. One of us was kidnapped and abused. We don't know where they are now."

The man exhaled slowly. "They had a dog with them?"

"Yeah, that's right. A pretty big one."

"And how many attackers were there?"

"Six," Tess exclaimed, "five boys and a girl."

"Uh-huh, all right."

"Do you know these people?"

"It's possible."

"So could you," Damon asked, "give us a ride into town, so we can call the police?"

"No," the man promptly replied.

In one instance, he struck Damon with his fist.

Faintness. He was surrounded by darkness.

Dogs barking. Yelling. Branches cracked.

In front of them, the gang ran through the forest.

Nela and Ben followed them in a crouched position. From behind the trees, they could see two people. One of them was holding that dog on a leash.

Nela's heart pounded in her chest. They were so close that one small mistake would have been enough to have given them away.

Ben crouched in front of her, dropping for cover against a tree. Nela followed his example. Carefully, she peeked over Ben's shoulder. The guys had stopped, gazing around. The dog growled loudly, then barked.

Nela's mood swung between courage and panic. This was damn serious. For the first time, she was glad to have the old man with her.

"We have to outrun them," Ben whispered, as quietly as he could. "We'll go that way." He pointed to the left.

"What's there?"

"We'll hit the fence soon," he murmured to Nela. "It will take us some time to climb over it. Therefore, we need to put some distance between us and them."

Nela nodded. She glanced over Ben's shoulder. The men had started moving again. Their voices were no longer audible, presumably they had become aware that they could be heard. "They're moving on."

"Come on, we have to hurry."

They headed through the forest with quick but careful steps, careful to make as little noise as possible. But Ben was rushing. He moved off with a firm step, holding on to his heavy flashlight. Shortly afterward, the black shadows had disappeared into the darkness of the forest, their voices and sounds fading. Again and again, he glanced behind him to check on Nela.

"We're here," he finally said, as the forest ahead of them ended at a high fence. Heavy concrete pillars with wire mesh stretched between them. At a height of about twelve feet, barbed wire towered over them. This military barrier had defiantly withstood the ravages of time.

Nela placed her fingers in the wire and gently shook it. The metal seemed solid, but could it withstand her weight? A weathered sign warned of the use of firearms for trespassing.

"Ain't there a main entrance?" Nela doubted that she could climb the fence.
"Yes, there is," Ben said, "but that's where the gang is headed.
"Couldn't we just slip under the fence somewhere?"
"Brilliant idea, young lady. But everything here is overgrown. The Allies haven't paid the gardener in a couple of years."

Nela glanced down at the fence. Sure enough, there were weeds and grass growing underneath it. The wire mesh had grown in with nature. "We should look for trees close to the fence. We might be able to get across better that way."
"Indeed, we should consider that."

Nela was the first to go. She hurried along the fence, Ben behind her. Again and again, she glanced at the other side. In the darkness, there were rows of large buildings. It had to be the barracks Ben had talked about. This looked both interesting and frightening at the same time. Decades ago, soldiers had prepared for war in this place. Troops had been marching up and down. Shots were fired and orders were shouted. Now it was quiet and eerie. Were the buildings waiting for the screams and fears to come back?

"Let's try here." Ben gently touched her shoulder.

A birch tree grew next to the fence, with its crown towering over the fence by about nine feet. Branches were growing through the wire mesh.

"I'll go first" Nela determined.

She was able to quickly climb onto the trunk and pull herself up from the branches. Climbing the tree was no challenge, after a few minutes she had reached the top of the fence. Nela reached out her hand and pulled the birch tree over to the fence. She used her free hand to feel over the rusted barbed wire. The tips had gotten dull, but the coiled wire had to give way, or she wouldn't be able to climb the fence. She looked for that tool in her pants. There were pliers or scissors in it, Nela knew.

Carefully, she checked the utensils in the moonlight.

In fact, the tool had pliers she could use to loosen the barbed wire. While the summer wind gently cradled her, Nela placed the pliers around the wire and snipped it off.

"How's it going up there?" Ben's voice came to her quietly.
"Ready within a minute," she whispered.

From up there, Nela felt like the whole world could hear her.

She took a deep breath as the barbed wire dropped to the right. Nela then put her tool back into her pants pocket. With her right hand, she reached into the wire mesh for a firm grip. Nela swallowed. If she let go, she had to be held by the fence. Otherwise, she would fall twelve feet down.

Nela closed her eyes and quietly counted down to three. Then she let herself fall.

Behind her, the birch tree rocked back. She immediately looked for a foothold as her body fell against the fence.

Relieve. The fence held her weight. The only thing she would have to do now is pull herself up and climb down the other side. Screws cracked, bolts came loose, wire broke as Nela moved up and down. The rusty fence threatened to collapse under her every step, menacingly swaying back and forth.

After what felt like an eternity, she finally found solid ground under her feet. Nela gazed around. In contrast to the other side of the fence, she felt unsafe here. The protection of the trees was missing, the open area of the barracks grounds offered no protection.

"Well done," Ben murmured to her.

His closeness, although separated by the fence, reassured her. Still, Nela thought she heard voices from the forest. She had no protection here. They would have to go on.

"You go," she excitedly whispered. "At the top, hold on tightly. Then, you simply drop against the fence."

He nodded with a smile.

"After that, you simply climb over, and the rest will happen on your own volition," she claimed.

"See you soon, if that's what you're saying."

Nela watched as Ben pulled himself up from branch to branch. The old man was strong. She smiled resolutely, clenching her fists. Hopefully, all was going well. Ben was the only one she could count on. She would be lost out here if she were alone. When Ben reached the top, he held on with both hands and pulled himself up against the concrete pillar before swinging onto the edge of the fence. The wire mesh shook violently. Nela could see Ben clinging to the concrete pillar. The man was heavier than she was, pushing the fence down.

When the vibration had calmed, Ben carefully moved his other leg over the fence and released one hand from the post. His feet attempted to find support in the mesh, but it broke.

Ben fell.

His fingers gripped the fence in panic, searching for a foothold. The wire cut his skin; blood gushed out. Under his weight, the fence collapsed. With a thud, Ben fell to the floor. Only a second later, he started to scream.

"No!" Nela bit her fist immediately. Damn it, this wasn't supposed to happen.

She jumped on Ben and clamped his mouth shut. "I'm sorry," she whispered tersely. "If they hear us, we're screwed."

Ben closed his eyes, reared up. The pain was unbearable, but Nela did not let go. When he stopped screaming and his movements became calmer, she took her hands off his mouth. "I'm sorry," she whispered again.

"My leg," he hissed in agony.

Nela turned and glanced at his legs. "Which one?"

"This."

Nela opened the left boot and immediately noticed a red swelling. "That's not good."

Ben sat up straight and examined his leg. "That's one hell of a bruise. Son of a bitch!"

"You need to get medical help."

"Even more reason to visit the hospital."

When Ben attempted to stand up, he was forced to suppress another cry of pain. "I need a moment, please."

Dogs barking. Screams.

"We need to move on."

Vivian cried. The pain must have been unbearable. In the moonlight, her legs looked red, and she had wealts all over her skin. Her fingernails dug into her arms as she rocked back and forth, crying.

However, to escape the clutches of the gang, Yelka had to block out her sister's suffering at that moment. When they saw the silhouettes of the men approaching in the shadow of the fence, they realized they had no more time to waste.

The hole in the fence was just big enough to allow them to squeeze through one by one. The wire was rusty, the fence brittle. If it didn't hold their weight, they would fall to the ground from about six feet. And then the hole would be so big that the gang could follow them without hesitation.

"You have to listen to me now, Vivian." Yelka grabbed her sister by the shoulders and turned her around to face her. When she didn't respond, she gently pushed Vivian's chin-up, so she could look into her eyes. "We're going to climb through this hole now, do you hear me?"

Vivian looked at her sister silently. The tears had drained, but she was unable to answer.

"Dear sister, can you do it?"

Eventually, she shrugged her shoulders and nodded imperceptibly.

"I'll give you a boost," Yelka explained. "I'll lean against the fence, and you use my hands to climb up. Okay?"

Vivian's upper body swayed. Her lips were pressed together tightly, her gaze fluttered.

Yelka had to pull herself together to control her emotions. She had never seen her sister in this heartbreaking state. Those bastards must have done unspeakable things to her. When this night was over, they would bring the gang to justice!

Still, she missed Vivian's fighting spirit, which would have made their escape much easier. Damn it, sis, pull yourself together. For your love!

"Come on, Viv, you can do it!" Yelka leaned against the fence. Behind her, the weathered wire gave way, groaning under her body's pressure. Bracing herself on both legs, she squatted and clasped her fingers.

Vivian hesitated before taking a tentative step toward supporting her sister.

"Go ahead, prop yourself up with both hands on my shoulders, and I'll push you up."

Vivian sobbed again, but still followed Yelka's instruction. Eyes squinted, every muscle in her body tensed, Yelka pushed her sisters up. Her back ached, and her hands threatened to give way. Vivian hung on her shoulders like a wet sack, barely helping.

"Pull yourself up now, Viv! Put your arms through the hole!"

Turning her gaze up to her sister, she could observe how Vivian had at least put her hands around the hole. However, she couldn't reach the other side on her own.

Damn it, Vivian, come on!

"Stand on my shoulders" she finally hissed as her hands ran out of strength. Slowly and wearily, Vivian placed one foot after the other on her sister's shoulders. Relieved, she lowered her hands. Blood flowed through her fingers again, tingling. Using all her strength, Yelka pushed her sister up.

"Our sweet princesses, there they are!"

They came!

"Vivian, you must go through the hole now. Please!" Yelka's voice trembled.

"I can't …" were the only words Vivian uttered.

"Please, please, sister. You must. Go!"

"I don't know how …"

"Just pull yourself through. You'll be fine."

The night sky and her sister's legs were all that Yelka could see now. Looking to her right, she could see the shadows of the attackers approaching. Panic overwhelmed her. Yelka grabbed Vivian's leg with both hands and pushed her up.

Vivian cried out loudly. An open wire end had pierced her upper arm and tore the skin open. But Yelka could no longer take her sister into consideration. She was pushing Vivian's legs up as hard as she could.

"I'm bleeding…" sobbed Vivian.

She hung out of the fence with her upper body on the other side and her legs on Yelka's side. Vivian had to do the rest; it was out of Yelka's hands now.

"Please, please, you have to jump!"

Yelka now looked desperate at her pursuers, eye to eye. At the edge of the stinging nettles, they raised their steel pipes.

Yelka jumped up, reached into the fence, and gave her sister one last push. Head over heels, Vivian fell forward, her hands stretched far from her.

"I'm sorry," Yelka whispered.

With a dull thud, Vivian hit the other side.
Immediately, her screams broke out. The pain made her voice explode. Vivian lay on the floor in agony, whimpering and sobbing. Then she huddled together like a dying insect. She cried so hard that her body jerked in spasms.

"We're coming over, darling!"

They used their bludgeons to cut through the brush like they were scythed. The nettles flew to the left and right, clearing the way in an instance.

Yelka grabbed the fence quickly, pulling herself up as fast as she could. Pieces of wire snapped, drawing blood across her hands and arms. Desperately, she climbed upwards, faster, and faster. She was already pushing her head through the hole, turning her upper body to hold on to the other side when the pursuers came up. At breakneck speed, they had crossed the field of nettles. Yelka felt a steel pipe bang against the fence.

"Stay here, bitch!"

She had just pulled herself up when someone grabbed her by the ankle. The size of her safety shoes caused the grip to be less firm than planned. Yelka stepped on the attacker's hand as hard as she could. A short scream, his grip loosened. Eventfully, Yelka pulled herself to the other side.

She had no time, she simply let go and fell backwards into the darkness. Knowing that she would not fall deeply, she attempted to cushion the fall. But her body was exhausted, everything was happening too fast. She fell hard. For a moment, she lost her breath.

She groaned and got back to her feet.

Their attacker was already climbing the fence, following them. Yelka recognized him. It was one of the two guys who had been preying on Vivian. Another man glared at her with a predator's grin, exposing his teeth. All humanity had vanished from the men's grimaces.

"Hi there, beauties!" the guy called, poking his head through the hole in the fence. "Miss us yet?"

Yelka was still struggling with her breath; Vivian lay sobbing at her feet. Soon, they would be there.

"No!" shouted Yelka with a strangled cry. She jumped up, clawed at the fence and, with all her might, punched the guy in the face.

Surprised by the attack's pain, he fell back on his crony.

They could only watch as the two women escaped into the dark.

The old theater looked like something out of a fairy tale. The branches and bushes had grown together, forming a natural roof above the stage. Rotting and weathered over the years, hundreds of seats sat on the clearing. Between them, ferns, bushes, and small trees had sprouted.

Once upon a time, this place must have been imposing, like an island in a sea of trees. Today, however, the forest had reclaimed the theater. In a few years, eventually, the stage would be swallowed up by nature, and even the last remnants of it would have been destroyed. But for now, the old open-air theater seemed like a magical place from a fantastic world.

Zander felt the aura shift to him. Blood was still dripping from his hand, where he cut himself. Theater blood…

In the shade of the trees, he crept up to Mousey and Kimberly. She had settled on the stage, her legs drawn up to her chest. Inconclusively,

Mousey remained seated under the podium. Snippets of conversation softly drifted over to Zander.

"...look at all the candles."
"So, why don't you light them?"

A yellow light flickered on. Mousey lit each candle one at a time. There must have been ten or fifteen, now burning with a small flame. The light seemed weaker than the glow of the fire at the swimming pool. It burned more quietly, giving the place a mysterious atmosphere.

From his hiding place, Zander looked at Kimberly. In the candlelight, her face had a dreamy look. Her arms were wrapped around her knees. On her legs, her naked skin was visible.

Again and again, he clenched his fist. Each time, a little pain twitched through his hand. Zander's desire had not faded.

"I wonder who owns all those candles?" Mousey had crouched down on the floor in front of the stage.
She glanced at him from above. Her eyes were half closed. A faint smile played around her lips. "Who do you think put them here?"
"I don't know," Mousey shrugged. "Maybe some Satanists or something."
She laughed. "Ain't no Satanists around here."
"How would you know? It could be!"

For a moment, they were silent. Mousey was uncertain, Tami enjoyed the silence.

"It's a beautiful place, isn't it?" she finally asked.

"Hm … Yes, it is." Mousey was obviously overwhelmed by that emotional question.

"Imagine how hundreds of spectators used to sit here. And how they cheered the actors on."

Tami leaned back and looked up at the sky, smiling. Finally, she jumped up and paced dramatically. She put her hands on her hips and gave Mousey a beguiling look. "Believe me, when something is too good to be true, there is often evil behind it."

"Um…" Mousey stuttered quietly.

Tami threw her head back, her hair flying through the air. She paused for a moment, tightening up. "Don't you feel that I deserve applause?" She laughed.

Oh yes, Zander would have gladly served her the applause she deserved. He wouldn't have been as shy as that little brat. Yeah, he would like to be alone with Kimberly now!

Quietly, Mousey began to clap. When Tami bowed down, he got louder and louder. Together, they laughed.

"What piece was that from?" he finally asked.

"I don't know, just some horror movie I saw the other day."

"That was, of course, good."

"You think so?"

"Yes, absolutely. Why don't you actually do some acting?"

She laughed. "Yeah, right."

"Why not?"

Tami was overcome with embarrassment. She shrugged, her smile ebbing. "Where am I going to perform?"

"I don't know, maybe …"

"Nobody wants me anyway except Ryder" she interrupted Mousey. "I'm just a cheap slut to everyone else anyways."

Mousey shook his head frantically. "Not to me, not at all!"

Tami waved it off. "I get it…" she mumbled.

"I think you're great, really."

"Come on, gimme a break!"

Zander's eyelid twitched. That little dumb train kissed Kimberly's ass like the submissive puppy he was. What was he thinking? That she would let him have it if he just begged for it, like 'please, please'? No, no, no. The kid should fuck off!

"Do you think that girl is alright?" asked Mousey after a short pause.

"I don't know. Maybe."

"What they did was wrong."

"I don't know, I don't care." She shrugged her shoulders.

Mousey frowned. "Didn't you think it was bad that Ryder…?"

"If you thought it was all so bad, then why didn't you help her?" She gazed at him with anger. "You were an enthusiastic participant in the beginning, weren't you?"

"It's true, though …"

"There you go."

"But actually," Mousey stuttered, "I just hang out with the gang because I don't have any other friends." He took a deep breath and bowed his head. This was a deeply sad truth he spoke for the first time.

"I know that feeling," Tami agreed with him. "It's just you guys, too."

Mousey raised his head and looked at her. Tami smiled. It was the most honest smile Mousey had ever seen on her face.

This god-damn harmony paralyzed Zander. What the fuck just happened? This little shitbag robbed him of his kick! Zander pressed his thumb into the wound on his left hand until the pain returned with arousal.

"And you seem to be the only one who really likes me" Tami surmised, still smiling.

"Well, sure, but you don't believe me."

"You're just trying to suck up." She winked at him.

Zander's breathing sped up. He kneaded his bleeding fist, opening and closing it repeatedly.

"Not true at all!" Mousey lowered his head, he blushed.

"Are you ashamed?"

"No, nonsense!" Mousey stood up and took a deep breath. Leaning on the edge of the stage with both hands, he swung himself up and climbed onto the stage.

Zander slowly disengaged from his position.

"Hey, what are you doing?" asked Tami as Mousey sat down next to her. "Don't exaggerate now. Just because we're alone, that doesn't mean we're making out." She glared at the blond boy.

Ashamed, he turned away. Tami's direct manner overwhelmed him.

Zander's chest rose and fell, he felt sweat on his face. Something within him prompted him to act.

Mousey remained silent, unable to utter a word. He had a bright red head and a racing heart. In fact, he was unsure of what he was about to do. But sure enough, he just wanted to be close to Tami.

Zander felt for the knife in his pocket.

Mousey gathered all his courage and looked deep into Tami's eyes. "Can I just give you a hug?"

Before she could answer, she was splashed with blood.

Zander had rammed his knife into Mousey's neck.

Jens Boele

THE BARRACKS

A bloodcurdling scream echoed across the barracks yard. Ryder and Jesse paused briefly, listening to the night, but it remained silent. The boys looked at each other, smiling darkly. Whoever had been hurt, it was certainly not one of them.

"That came from inside" Ryder guessed, rattling the gate of the fence. "They somehow made it to the barracks."

"Son of a bitch!" Ryder pulled angrily on Gazoo's leash. "We have to get in there, too." He rattled the fence again, but the gate didn't open.

Around the gate of the fence was a thick chain secured with a massive padlock. The yellow metal reflected the moonlight. Jesse held it while he examined it.

"This is still brand new," he muttered.

"Yes, I realize that too," hissed Ryder angrily.

"Your brother will kill us if we just break this up."

"Henry's going to bust our asses when he finds out what's going on." Nervously, Jesse chewed on his lower lip.

"Come on, do it now! Hurry the fuck up."

"Okay …" Jesse raised his steel pipe and struck the lock with a tentative strike.

"Harder!"

Uncontrolled, powerful blows crashed down onto the chain and lock.

"Fuck that shit up!" Gazoo angrily barked at Jesse.

Jesse was sweating as he continued the beatings. When his strength was almost gone, he staggered back and lowered the metal club. With a sudden slide, the chain sank to the ground in front of the gate.

"Well done!" With a push, Ryder opened the gate and stepped into the yard. Jesse followed him silently.

With a certain awe, the two cronies walked across the square. They were forbidden to enter this area of the compound. Never before had they entered the parade ground or seen the barracks buildings up close. The exposed concrete slabs were overgrown with grass that had turned yellow due to the summer heat.

The long stalks were blown gently back and forth by the night wind. Trees that had not existed a quarter-century ago now towered over the barracks roofs. The old, two-story structures looked eerie in the dark of night. Peeling plaster, missing windowpanes and crumbling bricks were hidden in the darkness. They looked huge and still seemed to have a sense of authority and power. Behind the barracks was the old military hospital, towering over the treetops.

Ryder strolled across the parade ground with a broad, swelling chest, while Jesse still let his gaze wander. He had a connection to this place right away. Power and strength, still wrapped up here, gave him a chill.

"Where do you think they are?" asked Jesse finally.

"Somewhere in the dark …" Ryder had turned his attention to the fence.

"We better find them soon."

"Have a look over there." Ryder pointed into the darkness near the fence. "I think something's moving."

"I don't see anything."

But at that moment they saw shadowy figures running from the fence to the barracks. Gazoo barked, a voice called over to them. "There they are!"

It was Dave and Mike who were climbing through a hole in the fence.

"Go!" Ryder ran after the fleeing girls, Gazoo pulling on the leash.

A large building was in front of them, apparently the main house of the barracks complex. Massive columns surrounded the entrance area, a long staircase led up to the entrance area. The dark windows looked like eyes watching the visitor, empty and sinister.

The two girls ran up the stairs, tripping over the broken steps. Ryder and Jesse were about twenty yards away from their prey. Mike and Dave came running from the right side. Ryder's pulse was racing, they had to get those girls. No matter the cost!

They were only ten yards apart when the two disappeared into the house.

"Dave, Mike! Go to the right! Block the exits!" Ryder paused. "They're not getting out of here! It's the end of the season!"

"We should split up," suggested Jesse.

"Fucking A." He gave Jesse a thoughtful pat on the shoulder. "Make sure you have the whole backside in view! We're gonna smoke the rats out of their holes!" Turning to Jesse, he said, "There's no other exit. See, all the lower windows are boarded up. Either they'll jump from the second floor or come out front. Either way, we'll get them."

"Yeah, man!"

From the bottom of the stairs, Ryder focused his gaze on the front door. In there, Yelka and Vivian had disappeared a few moments ago.

"We're coming in now!" roared Ryder, grinning.

Ryder strode up the steps to the main entrance, Gazoo by his side. From close up, the building looked ramshackle. Numerous cracks in the steps made the ascent a shaky affair. The large columns looked dilapidated, plaster had peeled off and revealed weathered bricks. The large double door of solid, dark wood had lost its luster. Moisture and sun had weathered the wood. However, Ryder's grip was not strong enough to open the door. Obviously, it had been locked from the inside.

"Jesse, open the door!"

His crony kicked the wood twice, but nothing happened. "There's something in the way from the inside" he guessed. "Come on, gimme a hand!"

Ryder and Jesse now kicked the door simultaneously. The hinges groaned; the wood trembled. However, the door did not give way yet.

"Let's fucking ram it!"

"One, two …"

"… Three!"

When the two men pushed against the door with their weight, it finally gave way. With a crash, it flew off its hinges. They immediately stumbled into the dark room. In the pale moonlight, Ryder and Jesse realized that they were in an entry hall. The room was devoid of furniture or pictures on the walls.

Only the cold concrete was left over from the occupants. To the left and right of the house were corridors that led to the wings, and in front of them was a wide staircase that led up to the second floor.

"You go right, I'll search to the left," Ryder instructed his crony. He quickly walked into the darkness, entering a long hallway that must have been light flooded back in the day. However, the hallway was covered in darkness by the boarded-up windows. Ryder tried to adjust to the darkness for a moment, but he was unsuccessful. He listened but could hear no sounds coming from the girls. Ryder turned around and went back into the entrance hall.

"I can't see anything." Jesse was already waiting for him. "Even with my cell phone I can't see anything" he justified himself.

"They're not down here either," Ryder guessed, pointing up the stairs. "They can't see anything down here as well. The windows aren't boarded up upstairs, so it's brighter there."

"True, you're right."

"Always am."

"Let's go, let's find them," urged Jesse.

A diabolical grin appeared on Ryder's face. "Someone else will do that for us."

He crouched down and untied his dog's leash.

"Go, Gazoo! Get them bitches!"

He seemed to be floating above the stage. Zander could see himself pulling the blade from the boy's neck. It was simple, two shorthand movements—in and out. Still, it felt weird. It appeared that someone else had guided his hand. He thought back to the time when he had smoked joints alone behind the schoolyard. Back then, he felt like he was wrapped in cotton and saw his surroundings through a soft veil. He smiled and let the effect wear off. Then, he usually returned home. But today he couldn't enjoy that feeling.

Zander shook his head to get rid of the dizziness. It was, however, the screams of the girl who brought him back to reality. She had jumped up and was yelling in shrill, almost painful tones. He stared at the bloodstained knife in his hand. There were red splatters all over his arms and hands.

In front of him lay the blond boy. Blood splashed from the open wound. He stared at Zander with his wide eyes, unable to say a word. He was pale as a ghost. Life had drained from his body.

Stunned by what he had done, Zander stood over the corpse. Tami screamed at the top of her lungs, backing away from him. From Zander's belly, a soft laugh escaped, worked its way up to his throat, and then turned into resounding laughter. Zander was overcome with himself, laughing at Tami.

What was he really feeling, though? Was it triumph or panic? Fear or a thirst for action? Despite his exuberant laughter, he was in a state of emotional turmoil. Never before had he done physical harm to another person. Although he had wished it countless times, he had never opposed his tormentors with violence. His sleepless nights were filled with fantasies about what he would do to the boys in his school if only he could. Those who had dated Kimberly, were also the ones who had bullied him. He would have liked to beat them up, rape them, and burn them to death. Their names would be forgotten. However, his desire for revenge dried up after the school days.

Zander's heart was racing. On his forehead, beads of sweat formed. He felt dizzy. While Tami watched him laughing like a maniac, Zander knew he had to make a decision. He could cry and ask God for forgiveness. By now, the boy was dead and had bled out within seconds. Nothing could save him anymore.

He could also enjoy his belated triumph and now take what he always desired.

When the laughter ceased, he looked at Tami with seriousness. Her screams had stopped, as his laughter had. Eye to eye, they gazed at each other. Tami was trembling. The dark forest behind her, the madman in front of her.

Zander wrapped his thumb and forefinger around the blade, wiping away the blood. The knife gleamed in the moonlight. Zander rubbed his left hand until the blood on his fingers had dried. He then grinned at Tami again. This time it didn't come from his belly.

"Ryder couldn't have done that, could he?" Lurking, Zander searched for emotion in Tami's face. "All he could do was slapping. Right?"

Tami's breathing sped up. Hectically, she inhaled and fought her fear. She said tonelessly, "You killed him." Her voice was soft as she spoke. "You just killed him."

"Oh, yes. You got that right. Did you like the little one?"

"You'll pay for that, bastard."

"Really? And who's going to hold me accountable?" Zander laughed victoriously. "Your friend Ryder, will he?"

Tami continued to back away from Zander, silently shaking her head.

"Ryder can't hold a candle to me," Zander asserted. "I'll gut him like a fish!"

"Ryder's brother will be here any minute," Tami whispered.

"Oh, the big brother. I'm getting scared."

"Henry will break your neck" she continued, unperturbed. "He's even crazier than you are, believe me."

"Tell me more."

"They call him 'Psycho Henry', and that's exactly what he is. He's completely insane, and he's beaten someone into a coma before, and he's going to do the same to you!" she whispered, her eyes lowered. "And then he will snap your neck, you're gonna die."

When Tami looked at him, there was a conviction in her gaze, which made Zander realize that she believed what she was saying. But unlike her conviction, it did not frighten him. Her thirst for revenge, her fear, and her threats excited him. The feeling he had experienced in the outdoor pool, watching Vivian be abused, returned. Her threats were going nowhere. Zander was the danger, he was the killer. Nobody could ever intimidate him again–neither Damon nor Ryder nor Henry.

What was wrong with her? Couldn't she see that he was the one who decided who lived and who died? He would show her in detail what he did when he was threatened.

"Would you like that, Kimberly? Would you like to see more dead people?"

Tami's mouth opened, and she incredulously looked at him. "My name is not Kimberly! What's wrong with you, you freak!"

Zander clenched his fist and pointed the knife at her. "What did you just call me?" His confident grin was gone; anger took over.

"Freak, freak, freak! Fucking freak!" Tami screamed at him, fury driving away her fear.

That good tingling had disappeared from his stomach. Zander was overcome with hate. His left eyelid twitched in uncontrollable ways. He had to punish her. But how? How did one punish a woman? Ryder had to help. Ryder knew how to deal with rebellious females. He thought back to the situation at the poolside. Yes, that was the way to do it.

Zander slapped her twice. Her head flew from left to right, and Tami staggered.

Stunned, she stood before him, holding her aching cheeks.

"Who do you think you are, you little bitch?" Zander grabbed her by the throat and held the knife to her face. "You call me a freak? Who do you think you are?"

Tami had both hands around Zander's arm, but she could not escape his grip. Hoarsely, she struggled for breath.

"You're nothing more than a cheap fuck."

Zander imitated Ryder's every word, even adopting the same posture. But now he had to do better than his role model. He was not allowed to become as soft as Ryder. Yeah, Kimberly would realize that he was not to be trifled with. With a jerk, he hurled her to the ground. Struck, she fell to the ground and cried out in pain. Zander bent over her.

Tami squealed in panic, flailing her arms. She screamed for help! With his palm, Zander hit her in the face. His arm flew past her, stopped in midair, and went back again. A second time now, his backhand slapped against her other cheek. Mascara ran down her face, leaving black streaks on her face. She wailed and sobbed.

Just like Vivian.

Vivian…

Tess was shocked to see what was happening right in front of her. With one blow, the security guard had knocked Damon to the ground. He fell and lost consciousness immediately. Tess wanted to scream, but she couldn't. Silently, she covered her mouth with her hands, and stared at the burly guy as he bent over Damon and continued to beat him. Slowly, she backed away. The man appeared to act mechanically, no anger or fury was visible on his face. It seemed like he was just doing a job he did every day anyway.

A soft scream finally appeared from Tess' throat. Damon was bleeding from the nose and his eye was swollen when the man stopped his blows. Stunned, she watched as the burly guy grabbed Damon by the collar, lifting him up with just a single hand. He turned his attention to Tess and took a step toward her, dragging Damon behind him.

Tess was now screaming loudly. Her hands were stretched forward in defense. Blindly, she slowly backed away, avoiding him. The man approached with firm steps. He dragged Damon behind him just like a shopping bag. He seemed to have powers that were not visible when you looked at him. Like a machine, he came closer and closer.

"Stop right there!" he finally ordered Tess.

His harsh words snapped Tess out of her swoon. She turned on her heel and ran off into the forest. The darkness seemed to her like a saving refuge where she could find protection from the creepy guy. Tess, however, had lost all orientation, simply running in the direction that led away from the attacker.

"Help!" she cried at the top of her lungs. "Heeelp!"

She had forgotten all the protective measures. She no longer thought about the fact that there was no one left who could have helped her. That was because Tess was afraid. More than that, she was downright panicked. That night, for the first time, she felt completely alone and defenseless. First Nela had left her, now Damon. Tears ran down her cheeks. It felt like a nightmare that she had to wake up from. But Tess didn't. She kept running and running into the forest's darkness. Her calls faded further with each step.

Exhausted, she looked down and recognized a path. This must have been the old path between the open-air swimming pool and the settlement, which they had walked before that night. Was she on the right path? Was she walking back to the settlement or further into the area? Her pace slowed, finally she just trotted, daring a glance over her shoulder.

The path behind her was empty; she had escaped the man. Relief came over Tess. Resting her hands on her knees, she took a deep breath. Only now did she realize how frantically her breathing still went. Her heart was racing. She had overcome the exertion of running, but not the strain of panic. As her body relaxed, the thoughts came back. Where was she?

How would she get back home? Fear paralyzed her muscles. Tess sank to her knees, squatting on the floor. What was going on? Was this real at all?

She then thought back to her first day as a waitress. She had taken over the evening shift and had to fill in for a sick colleague right away. The guests were getting drunker by the hour and chased her back and forth. In the end, she had been desperate, working duly and mechanically one order after the other. That was how the day had passed. Tess Walker had passed her baptism of fire. And that's precisely how she would do it now. She regained her composure, stood up with a jerk, and raised her chin.

She would have to return to the settlement, as that was the only option she had. From there, she knew the way back to the car. She would drive into town, inform the police, and then return with the cavalry and rescue Damon. And Nela. She just shouldn't run into that creepy security guard on the way. But wouldn't that be precisely the direction she had come from?

Tess remembered his dead eyes staring at her with piercing intensity. His whole aura radiated something threatening. Perhaps it would be better if Tess first crept quietly past him through the forest and thence to the settlement.

"Stop right there!"

Suddenly, he was back. Unperturbed, unstoppable, he came toward Tess, still dragging Damon by the collar. This time, Tess was overcome by unexpected panic. A shrill scream of fear rang through the night. Without a second's hesitation, Tess continued running straight down the path, away from the man.

From the settlement, further into the unknown. Trees and bushes flew past her, Tess just kept running. A root that arched up the sidewalk knocked her off her feet. In a high arc, Tess flew through the air, landing belly-up on the damp forest floor. But she felt no pain, just picked herself up, and kept running. Panic took away her sense of hurt, driving her onward.

Finally, she dashed into a fence that suddenly appeared before her. Tess bounced in the mesh of the fence and was thrown back. Panic-stricken, she looked for a way out, not daring to glance back. From there, the man who relentlessly chased her would come closer. The fence seemed to be impossible to climb, as it towered into the night sky. Barbed wire flashed from above.

Tess tried her hardest to shake the fence, but it refused to give way. There was only one way out, and it was along the fence. Tess only saw darkness in both directions, left and right.

"You stop fucking now!"

There he was again, closer than ever. Tess ran to the left, right along the fence. Concrete pillars and old lights flew past her. She hoped she wouldn't run into an obstacle.

But then, suddenly, she stood at an open gate. The path would lead her further into the facility's darkness. Tess didn't look back; she knew he was behind her.

She ran off, through the gate into the unknown.

With all she had, Yelka had closed the door behind them. Now, they were in complete darkness. Silence. The smell of mold and lime hung in the air. It took them a moment to get used to the darkness. Apathetically, her sister Vivian stood beside her, staring into the dark like a ghost. Her breathing was frantic. She seemed eerie, like possessed.

The suffering she had endured must have been terrible. Nevertheless, her apathy frightened Yelka. Vivian had begun to become self-destructive and fatalistic. She did not know her sister like that. Vivian seemed to have become a different person. It increasingly frightened Yelka, more than the gang out there. She realized that Vivian not only didn't care about herself, but that she had just as little interest in her sister's life anymore. Chills ran down her spine.

"We're coming in now!"

There, they were. In front of the door. Yelka looked around the entrance hall. To the left and right, dark hallways led into the wings of the building. The windows to the outside were boarded up, with little light coming in.

Here, they would have to walk slowly to avoid crashing and being helpless against the gang. Ahead of them was a wide staircase that led them to the second floor. Yelka remembered that the upper windows were free of plywood panels. Here, at least a little moonlight would guide their way. But the stairs looked ramshackle. The wood was old and certainly rotten. They would have to be careful, but it was their only chance to escape the gang.

"Darling sis, we have to go." Carefully, Yelka approached Vivian. She put a hand on her shoulder, gently stroking her hair. "Will you come with me?" She took Vivian's hand and took a step forward. "Please?"

Wordlessly, her younger sister started moving, following Yelka hesitantly and reluctantly. Yelka kept close to the left side of the stairs. This is where it would still be the most stable. The railing appeared solid but wobbled a little under her grip. Glancing to the right, it was clear that the staircase was in serious danger of collapsing. In the middle, where people had most frequently walked, there appeared gaps and holes. The wood was rotten and had collapsed. With a little luck, that would stop their pursuers.

Yelka glanced over her shoulder, but Vivian followed in her wake. Her head was lowered, her shoulders hung forward, powerlessly. Yelka squeezed her hand. Please don't let me down, dear sister.

Through a large window, cold moonlight shone onto the second floor. The walls and ceilings were damp, plaster was peeling. In the middle of the room, the ceiling had collapsed, letting in the rain. The window sashes were open, moving slightly in the night breeze. A soft squeaking sounded, from below they heard the gang bawling.

To the left and right, just as on the first floor, corridors led off, leading into the outgoing wings of the house. Yelka pressed along the outer edge of the floor to the left corridor. Just one wrong step would have caused the ceiling to collapse beneath them.

The hallway in front of them, however, looked even worse. Large holes gaped in the floor, revealing the rooms below. Going there would have been suicide. Yelka turned around and gazed at her sister. Silently, her upper body was swaying back and forth.

"We have to go the other way, Viv. We can't go any further on this side." Yelka forced herself to smile.

This time her younger sister replied. "I don't feel like it anymore."

Again, chills ran down Yelka's spine. Vivian's voice was ice-cold. She had to pull herself together not to lose her composure. "Please don't let me down now. We have to keep going."

"We won't be able to save ourselves anyway," she asserted in a sepulchral voice.

"Yes, we will," Yelka drove at her with suppressed anger, "and you're coming with me now."

Yelka grabbed Vivian hard, passed her with firm steps and pulled Vivian behind her. She pushed past the window front and went down the stairs. Under her, the floor creaked menacingly. But Yelka would not be deterred. She would not be infected by her sister's fatalism. Determined, she entered the right hallway and was relieved. Decay hadn't reached this wing yet; at least the floor had not completely collapsed. Pressing her back against the wall, she walked on, roughly dragging Vivian behind her.

There were rooms to the left and right, but they would be a trap. They would not be able to hide there for long. Yelka hoped for another staircase at the end of the hallway, through which they could leave the building unnoticed.

A loud clanging sound reached them from the lower floor. The gang tried to break down the entry. It couldn't be long before the weathered lock gave way. Yelka ran faster, glancing back at her sister. Stay with me!

The door on the first floor shattered with a loud bang.

The exit at the end of the hallway was only a few feet away. Yelka heard the gang kicking the door over and over again. Now, she wasn't worried about the floor anymore. She ran, pushed down the door handle and was relieved to find that it was not locked. Ignoring all caution, she rushed through, pulling Vivian inside and locking the door behind her. A brief moment of relief came over Yelka. They had made it unharmed! Yet, the joy did not last for long. Contrary to her assumption, this was not another stairwell, but a locked room with only one exit. A massive desk stood in front of them, a multitude of old floor lamps had been placed in a corner. A rotary dial telephone was hanging from a cable in the wall. They were trapped!

The echo of loud footsteps reverberated through the building.

In panic, Yelka glanced out the window. Below, members of the gang were waiting for them to come out. The swiveling of their steel pipes elicited a sarcastic, evil expression. They had to get out of here, that room was a death trap!

"Come on, we have to get out of here!" Yelka grabbed Vivian's hand, but she refused.

"I told you it was too late."

"Vivian, sister, we can't give up now!" She pulled on her sister's hand. "Come on!"

But Vivian remained stubborn. A cynical smile played around her lips. "They'll get us, believe me." Vivian slightly nodded.

Yelka could no longer bear her sister's words. They were in vain, she had to act. She opened the door and was about to pull Vivian behind her again, when she heard the thugs coming up the stairs. She didn't have much time left, so Yelka would have to …

Out of the darkness, the dog hurtled toward them!

The bestial growl made her blood run cold. Panicked, she slammed the door shut again, throwing herself against it. Yelka's heart raced. What could they do now? The desk!

"Vivian, help me! We'll push the desk against the door."

But Vivian made no effort to help her sister. She watched impassively as Yelka fought to save both their lives.

"Come on, please! I can't do this alone."

However, Vivian just stared at her silently, not responding. While Yelka braced her back against the heavy table, she realized that she could no longer expect any help from Vivian. Her gaze drifted ahead to the wall, where an open shaft led downward.

When she took a peek inside, she found that it led downward, into complete darkness. Crouching backwards in front of it, she inserted one leg into the hole and felt no resistance. Nothing but uncertainty lay beneath.

"Vivian, come to me, this way down!"

The dog scratched at the door, barking at the top of his lungs.

Vivian did not move.

"Vivian, please!"

With a crash, the door flew open. She looked at her attackers' faces, smiling like demons.

"Viviiiiiian!"

Vivian, oh, Vivian. Zander experienced a feeling like he had never sensed before. Triumph, excitement, and invincibility blended into a drug that unleashed an unprecedented state of euphoria in Zander. His body tingled; his blood raced. That fear in Tami's eyes both amazed and overwhelmed him.

When she bumped into Mousey's lifeless body, she cried out, turned to the side and got back on her feet.

The sight of her friend's dead body made Tami sob, cry, and scream. Pure, naked desperation tightened her throat. She saw death coming, and she knew what was going to happen.

Yet, she had nothing more to offer her attacker than anger and pain. So, she howled and screamed at the same time, insulted Zander with all the words in the book. Piece of shit, scumbag, bastard, wanker, son of a bitch … Tears of panic stifled her words, but Tami did not stop.

Zander, however, was no longer responsive to her insults. Her desperation and hatred tickled his emotions, driving him further on. The knife ready for attack, Zander followed her every move. He laughed, circled her. The knife shot up, piercing the air next to Tami. Panicked, she jumped away, stumbling across the stage.

"Are you scared, Vivian? Fuck, are you scared?" He laughed in a frenzy.
Tami's panic grew beyond belief. "Jeez!" Why was he calling her Vivian? How insane was he?

Zander mimicked her. "Jeez! Aren't you understanding me? Are you stupid?" His blade shot out in front of her, slicing the air in front of Tami's face.

Protectively, she raised her arms, lifted her shoulders and lowered her head. She quietly sobbed, continuing to back away. Somehow, she believed she was just caught in a dark, bad dream. She wanted to break out, to wake up. This couldn't be real.

But she did not wake up at all. Punches brought her back to reality. Zander slapped her arms and head.

"Hey, Vivian, how do you like that?" He gave her a good punch to the ribs. "Still think I'm a freak?" He struck her again, passing through her guard right into her face. "I should have done that to you a long time ago."

Staggered, Tami lowered her arms. Her upper body swayed from left to right. A thin trail of blood ran from her nose. She gave Zander a blank stare. Tami did not utter a sound; her tears had dried up.

"You're just insane," she muttered, "You really are."

"Haven't you figured it out yet?" Zander slapped her face again, guffawing. "You never call me a freak again, Vivian!"

Tami's cheek was glowing, but she didn't react. Tired, she looked at him, forcing a smile. "Okay ..." she murmured softly. As she stood there like that–her guard down, motionless–he paused.

"What's that supposed to mean?" He raised the knife, hissing, "Do you want me to carve it under your skin?"

"Go ahead ..." Tami shrugged her shoulders.

What was wrong with her? Why was she behaving like this? Again, Vivian was supposed to sob and cry, was supposed to cower in fear of him. Her apathy took away his excitement. That tingling subsided, the rush dried up. Damn, Vivian should function again! At least now, after all the years of humiliation, in the face of his dominance and superiority, she was to give him what he demanded!

Vivian, however, remained motionless, head tilted to the side, staring silently at Zander. A smile curled her lips.

Was it necessary for her to treat him with such disregard and contempt? Even at the moment of her total defeat? Zander's frenzy seemed to be ebbing. Within seconds, he would return to being the scared, introverted boy who had peed his pants. No way would that ever happen again!

Zander yanked the knife up and ran it across the inside of his left hand. The wound, not yet completely healed, tore open, sending jolts of pain through Zander's body. Oh yes, he was back!

With his bleeding hand, he grabbed Vivian by the neck and slapped her face with his other hand. The blade of the knife drew bloody marks across her cheek and forehead. Vivian cried out. Yes! Finally! That bitch was doing what she was supposed to do!

Blood ran from her nose and mouth as Zander threw her to the floor. She hit her back, her head banging on the old stage's wooden floor. The pain made her cry out again. When Zander kicked her in the ribs, she cried out again in pain.

She crawled backward, kicking at him. That was how it was supposed to be. Zander wanted to subdue her bit by bit, humiliate her until all his shame would be erased. Like in a frenzy, that little fury kicked and punched at him.

But that did her no good. Zander jumped on top of her and sat on her belly. He pushed her chin back with his left hand, so he could see her neck. When he put the blade to her throat, she stiffened. Slowly, he pressed the tip into her skin until blood gushed out. Only breathing shallowly, she no longer resisted.

Zander let the knife travel down her neck until it reached her cleavage. With one quick cut, he parted her top and the bra underneath.

His excitement had returned with full force.

Zander opened his pants.

With a crash, the door flung off its hinges. Ryder knew his prey was trapped. Gazoo shot into the room like a torpedo, growling and barking. Motionless, that blond sweetheart stood in the middle of the room, not moving an inch.

The other bitch had taken refuge behind the big desk. With slow, swaying steps, Ryder walked around the table to the left, Jesse circling her from the right. She screamed and yelled her sister's name at the top of her lungs.

"Viviiiiian!" But Vivian did not listen to her.

Ryder grinned. "Come to Daddy, kiddo."

"We fancy you, too."

But she did not react. Slowly, her body disappeared into an opening in the wall. "Vivian, hold on. I'm going to get you out of here ..."

And then she was gone.

Gazoo was excited. He jumped up and down on Vivian, barked like crazy. Yet, the girl didn't seem to care. Emotionless, she let the animal have its way. She seemed utterly impassive.

"Hey, you're a good boy. Come here!"

Jesse took a peek down the shaft. "Cunt's gonna rot down there anyway."

"She asked for it," Ryder smiled. "With us, she would have had endless fun."

Jesse sneered. "Oh yeah!"

They had built up around Vivian. Ryder lustfully stroked her hair. "You appreciate our closeness, don't you, sweetie?"

Jesse put his hands around her hips. "You look like shit, but you're still hot."

"All that jelly and no toast."

"Got some clothes on, huh?" Ryder tugged on Vivian's top. "Show some skin again, girl."

"We were having such a good time just before this little fury showed up."

Ryder put his hand on her breast and kissed Vivian on the lips. "You've lost your zest, haven't you? Your kisses taste bland." He eyed her from top to bottom. "Come on, let's go downstairs. Dave and Mike are waiting. We should get out of here as fast as we can before Henry shows up."

Jesse went ahead, Vivian apathetically following him in front of Ryder. When they reached the hallway, she stumbled into the corridor, almost losing her balance and slipping through the rotten floor.

"Watch it, stupid!"

"Put your ass to the wall."

She staggered in front of Ryder, tipped her shoulder against the wall and stopped every so often. Ryder was losing patience with the girl. If she didn't pull herself together, they wouldn't be back at the poolside before sunrise. The walk back down the hallway turned out to be an obstacle course. Refusing where she could, Vivian deliberately walked down the middle of the hallway several times. Ryder had to pull her back harshly, losing his patience with her.

"Believe me, honey, the more you bitch now, the harder I'll bang you later."

Jesse laughed. Ryder knew how much he admired him. He was an idol for the boy. Due also to his big brother's bad reputation. Jesse was the most loyal in his gang. Quite unlike Dave, who constantly challenged him. It was time to teach that loudmouth some manners. Tonight, he would show him who was calling the shots. After that, he would leave Tami to him, that little slut. That blonde chick was way hotter than little cheap Tami. Dave could even share the skank with little Mousey. Ryder laughed hoarsely to himself.

Upon reaching the stairs, he pressed Vivian tightly against his body.

He held the banister of the stairs with his free hand. "Stay with me, I don't want you to hurt yourself," he whispered into her ear.

Silence reigned outside. The moon cast its pale light through the open front door. The planks of the old house creaked under their heavy steps. When they opened the door, they looked down from the stairs onto the parade ground. It was a majestic sight the officers must have enjoyed at the time. In the dark of night, he saw his boys standing in the middle of the square. Quickly, he ran down the stairs. Let's get out of here, back to the old pool.

"We've got them, let's go!" Ryder shouted. But his gang remained motionless. In the darkness, Ryder couldn't make out who was there, waiting for him. They were three boys. Dave, Mike and certainly Mousey, who had caught up with them. But as he got closer, he saw something between the three of them.

There was an unconscious person lying on the ground. Ryder knew the face. It was that braggart Duke from the other group. Why was he lying there? He glanced at his gang's faces. Dave and Mike looked to the ground in dismay. However, it was not Mousey standing in their midst, but his brother Henry.

"What the hell are you little fuckers doing out here?" Henry's eyes were wide open. "Are you fucked in the head?" His carotid artery throbbed, thick as a thumb. With a wide stride, he stepped over Damon and walked toward Ryder. "You're supposed to be watching the barracks, not letting anyone into my place. That's your job!" Ryder had lowered his head, looking down at the ground, resigned to his fate. "You're supposed to not ask questions, shut the fuck up, and keep the fucking tourists out of here." With his left, he grabbed Ryder by the collar. "And now I come here and meet strangers all over the place, hanging around unmolested. I find my new lock broken. Can you explain that to me, little brother?"

Shaking his head, Ryder continued to stare at the floor. "I'm sorry."

A searing slap hit his face, nearly knocking him off his feet.

"I don't give a fuck whether you're sorry or not. Are you a fucking faggot or something?" Henry turned around, looking at the rest of the gang. "Are you a bunch of faggots? Are you fucking each other's little asses out here?"

No one dared to look at Henry. Let alone give any resistance. He walked past them with slow steps, waiting for a sign of rebellion, his fist ready to strike.

"I can't have any confidants and witnesses. Don't you understand that? Can't you get that through your little degenerate brains?"

Finally, he stopped in front of Vivian. "And who is this young lady?" Roughly, he grabbed her chin, examining her like a horse at an auction.

"I'm ..." Damon had awakened from unconsciousness and reared up. "... Damon Duke."

When she saw her manager, emotions burst out of Vivian. Her lethargy was wiped away. Panic and fear shot up inside her. Vivian began to scream. Tears of fear ran down her face. She sobbed and cried, screaming like a wounded animal.

Henry threw her to the ground and walked back to Damon.

"Let us … go," he demanded. "This will get you at least ten years in prison, if not …"

A hard blow sent him back into darkness. Damon collapsed unconscious. Vivian screamed and cried, but Henry was not deterred. He kicked Damon's head with full force. Muffled sounds accompanied the following kicks. From above, Henry stomped on Damon like he was exterminating a pesky insect. His expression was cold and emotionless, his kicks not losing their force and intensity. Damon's head bobbed slightly back and forth.

"Let …" Jesse took a step toward Henry, but Ryder held him back. "Don't." Decisively, he shook his head.

Vivian was cowering on the floor, still screaming and sobbing, when Henry finally let go of her manager. He turned around and cast a cold glance at the gang. No one doubted that they had just witnessed Henry kill a human being. Damon's body lay motionless in their midst, with Henry standing over him. They avoided his gaze, staring at the ground. Henry lurked like an animal, searching their faces for weakness.

Finally, he walked over to Vivian and slapped her face. "Shut the fuck up, you're getting on my nerves!" Vivian's cheek glowed, she had almost lost consciousness. Then he turned around and punched Mike in the face. "Something wrong with you?" He staggered, bracing himself against Dave. Then Henry hit Jesse's chin with his fist. Ryder's friend went to the ground, remained there in shock.

Henry reared up in front of Dave, raised his hand to strike, but he gazed into his eyes without any fear.

"Remember, you brought this all on yourselves, morons!"

"Henry, we get it, that's enough. It will not happen again before …"

Henry bitch slapped him, knocking Ryder to the ground. Again, blows pelted his little brother. Dave smiled silently as Henry grabbed Ryder by the collar and yanked him back to his feet.

"Who do you think you are? Do you think you could raise your voice against me just because we share the same blood?"

Ryder remained silent, wordlessly shaking his head. He understood.

"I get it," Henry said in a conciliatory tone. "You've been partying out here, letting your hair down."

Ryder looked up, gazed into his big brother's face.

"It happens." He spat out. "But it is not supposed to."

Ryder nodded. "You're right."

"That's it. We'll fix it."

"Yeah, right. We'll fix that."

"I knew you would, little brother. Can I count on you?"

"Yes. Of course."

Henry patted his cheek, nodded at Damon.

"Then take care of your bitch now."

Zander rolled down from Tami's body. He was sweating and breathing hard. Lying on his back next to her, he closed his eyes, smiling. Gradually, his pulse slowed and he came down. His first time had been wonderful! After he had cut her clothes off, everything went by itself. She hadn't even resisted. That hot feeling when he had penetrated her had completely robbed him of his senses. It had been the climax of his intoxication.

Desire, drive, and dominance combined to create the ultimate sensation, the fulfillment of all his dreams. A tear ran down Zander's cheek.

The tingling subsided, the dizziness of intoxication faded as his breathing returned to normal, and he slowly slipped into a state of calm. He hadn't felt anything like this in a long time. It was a state of heavenly contentment in which Zander swam between reality and dream. Complete composure and calm surrounded him. He felt a sense of security and safety that was all his own. Zander was at ease with himself. There was nothing more beautiful he could have imagined in this wonderful moment. This old, abandoned place with its magic—wasn't that why he had come here in the first place?

Slowly everything came back—the trip, the barracks, the photos, his clique. Well, perhaps the word 'clique' was exaggerated. Basically, it was just him and Yelka who had taken Vivian and Damon along. Yet, as a little sister, Vivian was probably part of it somehow. Regardless, he now realized that the way to Yelkas heart led past Vivian.

Without her sister, Yelka just didn't exist. Maybe it was time to act like a man and break out of this friend mode that had gone on for far too long. Zander had to admit that he had always acted like a nerd, too; like a loser waiting to be loved. He laughed as he thought back to how he had made a fool of himself in his few advances. The flowers he had given her to confess his love and then hadn't dared. The candlelit dinners where he was unable to express his feelings. Zander was pretty sure that Yelka knew of his love for her but thought of him merely as a friend. That would change now!

Perhaps he should actually make friends with Vivian. Not so much with Damon, whom he would have to put in his place. A little meeting in private with the blade at his neck would clarify the situation, once and for all. And if Damon showed him respect, Vivian would automatically be kind to him. Zander would forgive her, make a fresh start. After all, he was a man now. Nothing would stand between him and Yelka anymore. He could finally have what he longed for so long. And then …

"You lousy piece of shit!"

Tami had regained consciousness. Fear and despair were gone from her voice, only anger and hatred remained. She gathered her torn clothes and crouched down next to Zander, pulling her legs and arms close to her.

"You dirty motherfucker. If Ryder and Henry get a hold of you, God help you. You don't know what you've done."

Tami talked herself into strength, the threats brought energy back to her.

"They're going to find you and fuck you up, bastard. You'll wish you were never born, you sick fuck."

Zander took a deep breath and let her talk. Tami reminded him of an over-excited Vivian when she picked on him. He would let her have her way for now, until she calmed down.

But Tami was far from moderating. "Henry is going to slice you open like a fish and rip your guts out!" From the side, she spat in Zander's face.

His pulse shot up. Her shrill, hysterical voice made his nerves tingle. Zander's eyelid twitched.

"You fucking freak! Freak! Freak!"

Zander's hand clenched around the knife.

"Fucking pisspants!"

His arm shot up and blindly drove down on Tami. Blood spurted; he must have hit her in a sensitive spot. Tami cried out, gurgled.

Zander, still lying on his back, stared up at the sky, as more and more blood rained down on him.

But Tami was not dead. She continued to rant and roar.

"You smell like piss! That's right! You stink like piss! Like you pissed yourself! Fucking freak!"

Zander didn't want that slut to tear him out of his calm, his equilibrium. For that was precisely what she was, a slut. He now understood why the other guys had lost their lust for Kimberly. After all, she was just a slut who became hysterical and vulgar when they stopped fucking her.

"Pisspants! Fucking pisspants!"

Again, Zander rammed the knife into Tami lying next to him, this time a little higher. He felt a brief resistance, then it stuck. Hesitantly, he loosened his grip around the shaft, finally letting go completely. The knife stuck, Tami's roar was silenced. A soft gurgle entered his ear, then she was quiet. It took a moment for Zander to calm down again, for the nervousness to disappear from his body.

He took one last deep breath and then slowly stood up. He zipped up his pants and turned to Tami. The knife had pierced her cheeks and nailed her tongue to the wooden floor. The first stab had severed her carotid artery. Tami had bled to death in a short time. His gaze fell on the empty, weathered seats in front of the old forest stage.

Applause, applause!

The drama was over.

So, that was it. Tami's death had no longer caused that rush he had felt just a few minutes ago when he murdered the boy. It no longer made any difference. Zander smiled rapturously. He had become a wolf.

He wiped the knife on his pants and jumped off the stage. As he strode through the rows, he gazed up at the sky. The full moon shone bright and cold.

Zander howled into the night sky. "Awooooo!"

It was open season, and the time of the wolf had come!

Ryder's gaze wandered back and forth between Henry and Vivian. His brother's stare was cold and unyielding. Ryder looked down at the lifeless body of the young man. Was he supposed to do the same to Vivian? Was he serious? She was cowering on the floor, crying in despair.

Nevertheless, she still looked pretty. More beautiful than the girls he knew, anyway. Having her by his side would lift Ryder up. He knew that she would do anything he asked of her, broken as she was. But Ryder didn't want to break her. He wanted to adorn himself with Vivian. Hashtag Violet-D. As her stud, he'd be a social media star, just like her.

"Don't be a coward. Get to the point."

Henry's words were soft yet demanding. No one dared to question his authority. Not even Ryder. Reluctantly, he walked toward Vivian. She dropped back, staring at him in fear. Her crying turned into frantic, shaky breathing. Ryder pulled himself together. Don't go soft. He grabbed her by the hair, yanked her head toward him.

"No," she stammered, "please don't."

Ryder felt like everyone was watching him. He felt sick. Slowly he raised his fist, inhaled and exhaled.

"Please, please ..."

He couldn't force himself to do it. Ryder was unable to hit her. He closed his eyes, breathed fast, tried to build up anger—but it didn't work.

"Ryder, don't let that bimbo soften you up. She's no good."

Henry's words encircled him, like hands tightening around his neck. Ryder felt paralyzed.

"We can't have any witnesses. Not you, not you, and certainly not me." Henry now positioned himself close behind Ryder, his hands clasped behind his back like a spit. "You've had your fun, gone a little overboard. Got a little crazy. Swung the steel pipes too hard." His gaze swept over the group's faces. "And you let them come to my camp." His hand settled on the back of Ryder's neck. "What's happening now is your very own fault. You brought this shit on yourselves, now you're going to sweep up the mess and dispose of it."

Henry let go and bent down to Gazoo. He stroked the dog's back.

"Come on, little brother. Be a good leader and do the deed."

Ryder had still raised his fist to strike. But Henry's words only made him feel worried and scared.

"Yeah, man. Your brother's right."

Dave sensed his chance. Ryder started to feel hatred again. He averted his eyes from Vivian, gazed into the night. Come on, just beat her. But something in him still resisted.

Then there was a moment of silence. Henry was quiet, no one from the group said anything. The longer this moment lasted, the harder it became for Ryder. Finally, Henry continued his talk. His tone became harsher.

"What do you think is going to happen? Do you believe she will return to her home and pretend that this incident never occurred? Your little adventures with those Urbexers?"

Ryder swallowed.

"Or maybe you seriously believe that she will one day be your girlfriend?"

He heard soft giggling. Surely, it was Dave or Mike. Not Jesse, he was loyal.

"The old lady is ruined, look at her. You guys fucked her up really bad." Henry gazed at the gang. "Or do any of you still want her?"

Ryder released his gaze from the darkness, looked into the faces of his cronies. They shook their heads, grinning in amusement. Dave spat out in disgust. "Fuck, no!"

"Your boss, it seems, sees it differently. He digs that broken skunk."

They laughed. They laughed at him. Ryder was seething. His fist came down on Vivian. Muffled, his blows pelted her face. One, two, three. Fainted, she fell to the floor. His face distorted with rage; Ryder stood over her. His chest rose and fell. He clenched his fists and stared at Henry.

The laughter had stopped, all eyes rested on him. Henry's gaze became curious, he tilted his head.

"That was a good start, little brother."

Ryder did not move.

"You need to finish the job, though," Henry urged him, amused. "Bring it to an end."

Ryder, however, no longer knew at whom his anger was directed. His brother, the gang, or Vivian. Seething inside, he stared at Henry.

"You can't do it, can you? You're too soft for that!" Henry's eyes widened. "You want me to show you again? Just like this!" Again, he stepped on Damon's head. "Go on, do it!"

While Ryder was still standing over Vivian, Dave stepped out of the group. "I'll do it."

Henry looked at Dave from every angle. "Did you hear that, little brother? He wants to help you out."

Dave lifted his chin and gave him a hard stare.

"Kid has grit. He may also have what it takes to see things through." Henry picked up a club. "Could be, he knows how to swing a steel pipe like that." Henry put an arm around Dave, but never took his eyes off Ryder. "Do you have the confidence to get it right?"

"Sure thing." Dave had put on his most arrogant tone. His stare was arrogant. See, your brother values me more than you!

Henry thrust the baton into his hand. "Get on with it, then."

With swaying steps, Dave walked toward Ryder, holding the steel pipe in his hand. They looked into each other's eyes. Dave lowered the metal rod, sliding it over Vivian's body. "Take a last look at her, she is about to be whacked."

He tried to lunge, but Ryder stood in his way.

"Step aside, homes." They glanced at each other challengingly. "And show me some respect for doing your dirty work."

Ryder noticed the outraged faces of his gang. Even Jesse had his eyes on the floor and was restless.

"What now?"

Ryder was about to explode. Cold rage flooded him. No weakness, no forgiveness.

"Shut the fuck up, bastard. Respect is what I'll stick up your ass."

Ryder grabbed Dave's ear, twisted it around, and then ripped the steel pipe from his hand. Frenzy overcame him when he heard his rival squeal.

"It took you a long time, brother. Show them what blood you are."

When she let go, everything seemed to end. Her life flashed before her eyes. Images from happy childhood days with her parents, the birth of her little sister. School, friends, vacations. She and her sister at the Pacific Ocean. Los Angeles, the Mojave Desert. Photography. Abandoned places. Passion. Freedom. Yelka fell and fell and fell. An infinity seemed to pass. With every second of her fall, reality blurred more and more. Memories were the only things left. It was over.

Impact. Water. Cold. Pain.

With a thud, Yelka woke up. She had landed in cold, stinking water, sunk to the bottom and hit the soft ground. Pain shot through her body like lightning. Yelka wanted to catch a breath, to scream, yet she was still underwater. Panic-stricken, she shot upward, reached the surface, and gasped for air. Her feet barely touched the bottom of the water, it was dark around her. Hastily, she breathed in and out. Slowly, the pain passed.

In the dark, Yelka could see nothing. Where was she? The only recognizable feature was the shadow of the walls. There was an unpleasant smell of mold and rot. Somewhere close to her, something was moving in the water. Were there animals here? Rats? Or even fish?

Yelka swam on the spot, turning her head in all directions, yet all she could surmise was being in a passageway or some sort of sewer. From a distance, she heard a dog barking. The gang must have been around. Yelka tried to figure out where the sounds came from. They came from above her, not far away at all. Voices mingled with the barking. Screams. A man was yelling. There was then a moment of silence. Yelka held her breath. She felt a sense of restlessness rising. It felt as if something horrible was about to occur.

When the screaming started, she burst into tears.

However, Yelka had to cry even more when it stopped.

She had bailed on her baby sister Vivian and left her to her killers. Yelka screamed and cried, covering her eyes. The pain was so overwhelming she was unable to overcome it. She would rather not live anymore–not with this guilt she had brought upon herself. Without thinking, Yelka dropped back into the water, waiting for death to embrace her.

Darkness surrounded her like a harbinger of the afterlife. She would simply have to open her mouth and flood her lungs with water. It would be a moment of overcoming. Just an instance, and she would be united with Vivian. Slowly, she opened her mouth, tasting the stale water. Her mind wanted to inhale, but her body resisted. She counted down from three. Two. One. But when she tasted the foul liquid, nausea set in. Severe coughing finally caused her to gasp for air. Hectically, Yelka rowed her arms. Her mind was turned off, survival instinct took over. Coughing and spitting, she came back to the surface, panting.

Groaning, she floated on the surface, her head thrown back, her gaze fixated on the gloomy ceiling. Slowly, her body calmed down again, and her mind was back in control.

Having Vivian as a baby sister had been wonderful. She still remembered how excited she had been when the day of her birth arrived. Vivian did not quite see daylight yet when Yelka wanted to take her to the sandbox. She had become very fond of the family's youngest member. Together, they had built sandcastles, learned to ride a bike, and went to the same kindergarten. Whatever Yelka had done, Vivian was eager to be there. She wanted to do the same thing, too.

There were few things the two sisters had done apart from each other. It wasn't until she was a teenager that Vivian began to change. She quickly noticed that she was pretty, and boys fought over her. But they had never lost touch with each other. When she broke up with her first boyfriend, Vivian let her whole family in on it.

She became a real drama queen. But that faded more and more with each new boyfriend. Despite being only 18 years old, Vivian already had more friends than her older sister Yelka. Finally, her little sister had comforted her when she had her first heartbreak.

From Vivian, she had learned that everything was not as bad as it seemed, and her soul could get back to feeling good after a while.

Furious, Yelka hit the surface. She would not seek death in this stinking sewer. She would rather make these pigs pay.

Her eyes had slowly adjusted to the darkness. Rough concrete walls shimmered in dark light. Yelka suddenly knew where she was. This must have been one of those underground channels that connected all the buildings. Obviously, she was in one of the escape tunnels the Allies had built in case of an attack. Therefore, there had to be a way out of here.

Yelka tried to orient herself. The tunnel led from north to south, if she remembered the layout of the houses and the place from which the voices had come correctly. To the north, there was the old apartment block. More forest and unknown terrain were to the south. If she managed to find an exit in the north, Yelka would be able to escape.

With powerful strokes, she swam further into the darkness, spreading her arms wide to spot potential obstacles early. Her hands brushed over craggy concrete, felt garbage floating in the water. Occasionally, she would brush against something that seemed to swim past her. Yelka did not think about what that might have been. She swam straight ahead, stubbornly. But the further she got, the darker it became. She found it increasingly difficult to breathe.

The ceiling came closer and closer. The tunnel got smaller. Panic overcame Yelka again. Yet then she understood. Here, the tunnel would have run deeper downhill, further into the ground. It had been flooded.

Damn. What was she supposed to do now? She tried to remember what

Zander had said. Where did these tunnels lead? Was it possible it led to the hospital in the south?

If that was the case, it was her only chance to find a way out of this tunnel. She turned around and swam back to the place where she had fallen into the tunnel, determined to get out. Off she went into the unknown.

After a few moves, Yelka found solid ground beneath her feet.

"We need to take a break," Ben murmured to Nela. "If we keep running, I'm going to start screaming right away." In fact, the old man's running style had visibly changed into a bouncing motion. It was hard for him to step up with his left foot.

"Just a few more feet. We need a place to hide." Nela supported Ben as he walked, wrapping an arm around his shoulder. "There's a shack up ahead. We can rest there."

The dilapidated, weathered building apparently once housed a large workroom. Shards and debris covered the floor. Maintenance pits were the last witnesses to repairs that had been made to vehicles.

Not far from them, voices rang out. Men were talking, shouting at each other. A woman screamed.

"Show your foot again," Nela prompted Ben.

Carefully, she opened his boot and pulled the shoe off. A low moan escaped from his mouth. The pain seemed to be great. In fact, the ankle was swollen and red. Nela swallowed.

"Maybe it's actually best to get to the hospital quickly."

"I love your optimism, girl." He smiled grimly.

"In all seriousness, this doesn't look good, Ben."

"Oh, come on," he blocked. "It's a sprained ligament at best. It'll be fine."

"Are you going to make it to the hospital?"

Nela was sincerely concerned about the old man. On the one hand, she had no one left but him, and on the other, she felt great affection for him. He radiated a warm-hearted calm, but at the same time was determined and disciplined. She would have liked to have someone like him as a mentor at university. Or as the grandfather she never had.

"Don't you worry about that, young lady. We'll find our way together, I promise."

Nela squeezed his hand. "Put your leg up for a few minutes, meanwhile I'll check the situation."

She carefully slipped out of the cover, hiding behind a piece of crumbling wall. Her gaze strayed across a large square surrounded by barracks buildings. Back then, there must have been parades and marches here. Nela could hear boots pounding the asphalt, and officers yelling instructions.

Yet now, dark figures were standing at a distance. Four men were gathered there, arguing intensely. Unfortunately, she couldn't hear what they were saying. Nela was sure they were the guys from the outdoor pool. And they had the blonde girl with them that Nela had first thought was Tess. Their argument seemed to be about her. A little guy from their midst pushed the blonde to the ground. Then, they started to argue loudly.

"What's going on there?" Ben murmured from behind.

"I have no idea. They seem to be arguing."

"Is that Ryder and his gang?"

"I can't make them out. But I think it is them. And they have the blonde girl in their power as well."

"Is the other one there, too?"

"I can only see her."

"Maybe she was able to escape."

"It may sound heartless," Nela whispered, "but I'm glad Tess isn't in their grip."

"That's perfectly fine, girl. Don't worry about it, it's okay."

Nela glanced over at Ben. She was glad that he was with her. However, when she looked back at the square, her blood was running cold. One of the men raised a club and beat the girl. Nela had to cover her mouth to keep from crying out in horror.

"What's going on?"

But Nela could not answer. Horror rendered her paralyzed. The thug continued to beat the girl, roaring like mad. Yet, the worst part was not the blows or his frenzy. It was the muffled sounds she heard with each blow that really disturbed her.

Clang, clang, clang. Like a hammer hitting wood.

Nela was trembling. She wanted to scream but forced herself to be quiet.

"Nela, what's happening?"
"We have to get out of here," she finally replied tonelessly. "Quickly."
"Nela, what's going on?" Ben became restless.

She looked at him with a calm expression. "They are starting to kill people. And when they find us, they will murder us, too." Her chin trembled; her voice quivered. "We have to leave. Now."

She could literally see what was going on behind Ben's facade. He immediately understood how serious the situation was. Yet, he remained calm, disciplined. "Put my shoe back on, please. Then close it loosely, not too tightly."

While Nela complied with Ben's request, he pushed himself against the wall, shifting his weight to his right leg. When Nela had laced his boot up, she took his hands and helped him stand up. At the same moment, blood rushed to his leg. Pain returned like a thousand pinpricks all at once. Ben clenched his teeth and hissed out a silent cry of pain.

"We're all okay, this is going to be over very soon. Take a deep breath."

Nela squeezed his hands as tightly as she could to distract him from the hurt in his leg. Ben pulled himself together, wrapped an arm around Nela, and let her help him find his balance. He took a deep breath and exhaled, letting the pain go, then carefully moved forward.

"All right, carefully and slowly."
"One step at a time."
"That's it. You're doing great."

Ben paused. Gradually, it got better.

"Okay, young lady. I can walk on my own from here."
"Are you sure?"
"You bet."

Nela let go of him and with both feet, Ben stood firmly on the ground.

"All right. Let's get out of here."

With a loud crack, Ben crushed a shard of glass. They stared at each other, horrified.

At that moment, the barking began.

So, the darkness of the night hid what had happened on the old parade ground. Silence fell, even the owls remained still. Foxes and badgers had taken flight. They smelled cruelty. The aura of abomination drove all life away from this place. Envy, greed, pride and sadism emanated from the event like a poisonous cloud, corrupting everything around it. The smell of fresh blood was in the cold night air.

After Ryder had bashed her head in with the steel pipe, Vivian had not moved anymore. The grace of unconsciousness had accompanied her from life to death, taking away the pain. She didn't feel the countless blows that came at her anymore. She no longer felt her bones breaking and splintering. Neither how she lost her sight nor how her jaw broke. She didn't hear Ryder's screams. Death had saved Vivian from that terrible fate.

Exhausted, he stood over her, baton raised above his head. A single drop of blood dripped onto his head, running further down his neck and chest. Screaming in frenzy, he gazed at his gang with a crazed stare–madness and barbarism reflecting from his face.

Mike bent over, throwing out. Dave stared at him, stunned and distraught. Jesse had closed his eyes and kept nodding in silence.

"I knew we were cast in the same mold, brother." Appreciatively, Henry put his hand on Ryder's shoulder. "You didn't let down on me."

As the tension drained from his body, Ryder slowly lowered the steel. He had crossed that red line. With a casual wave of his hand, he dropped the club to the floor. Now, he was a murderer. Something inside him had died and vanished forever. Just like that dead girl at his feet. Ryder would kill again and again. He glared at Henry with a cold stare. Suddenly, it was there; the connection between the brothers. They were bound by death.

Ryder eyed his gang with a fixed glare. His cronies were broken, no one would dare to rise against him anymore. When he stared at Dave, he recognized his submission. Like a whipped dog, he backed away.

"Any more of them around?" Henry's question broke the deadly silence. "Before I came here, I was actually hunting down a blonde chick."

Jesse opened his eyes, nodding frantically.

"Two of them left. A girl and a dude." Ryder's voice sounded hard and emotionless. "The girl should be dead by now. The boy has disappeared without a trace."

"And Mr. Marshall is out there, too," Jesse interjected.

"Fucking what? Old Marshall is kicking it here?"

"Where did you see him?" Ryder stood up in front of Jesse.

"When we were roaming the woods. His car was there."

"Just his car, or was he there as well?"

"We were fucking the car up. Ain't going nowhere, right? And then suddenly, he and a girl showed up.

"So?"

"We were going to waste them."

"Yes, but they were able to escape." Mike had regained his composure.

"Why are you telling me this just now?"

Mike ducked away. "It all happened so fast. When we got back, chaos had already broken out at the poolside."

Ryder took a deep breath. "We will find them all and hunt them down."

For the first time that night, Henry smiled. "Each of you will be able to make your bones." His gaze glowered. "Are you ready?"

No one dared to contradict Henry or Ryder. Silently, they nodded, staring at the floor. "Yes," Jesse murmured softly.

"I can't hear you!" Henry shouted.

Gazoo jumped up and barked.

The dog was excited, looking toward the old shack at the edge of the square. Ryder grabbed his collar. "Easy, boy!"
When Gazoo stopped barking, they heard crunching and rumbling. Hasty footsteps. Someone was running away.

"That's coming from over there!" Jesse pointed to the barracks. "Come on, let's get them!"

Henry walked ahead with firm steps, Ryder following him. The rest of the gang caught up, glad to leave the scene of horror, plunging from one disaster to the next.
In the shadow of the lapsed barracks, they chased after the noises. Then, a field opened up in front of them. It was lined with spruce forest. Underneath the field, there used to be a road that led to a big, dark building. In the distance, two people were walking through the knee-high grass. One limped, the other walked beside him.

Henry rumbled. "They won't reach the hospital."
"You heard it," Ryder shouted. "Come on now, let's crack some more skulls."

While the words made Dave and Mike shiver, Jesse nodded his head in agreement. With the steel pipe in his hand, he chased them.

Ryder crouched down, undid the dog's leash, and whispered, "Go, Gazoo! Sic 'em!"

It required a high degree of self-discipline to suppress recurring pain without being at the mercy of a visible threat. Ben, whose gaze was fixed on the dark silhouette of the military hospital, found himself in such a precarious position. The rational knowledge that there were murderers at their backs could not lessen the pain, could not make it less acute. With every step, Ben felt a flash of pain. He could not have endured this agony, this road to self-destruction, if Nela had not been running behind him.

"Run!" she kept yelling from behind. "Run for your life!"

It didn't matter at all if they were heard now. The gang was breathing down their necks, they knew that. As the high grass flew past them, the hospital's outline got closer and closer. Hope energized Ben. He roared out his pain. It helped him ignore the agony. Like a whip, Nela drove him again and again.

"Come on, don't give up!"
"Uhhhhhhhh!" He spat and gasped.
"Just a few more feet! Don't you dare give up now!"

Ben felt sick. The pain was unbearable, rising from his leg to his stomach. He would have to throw up in an instant. An increasingly loud buzzing sound came to his ears. He could already read the first letters on the building in front of the actual hospital. Although he could not read the entire word, he knew that this had once been the emergency room.

Bushes and ivy had overgrown the entrance to the building. There had been no ambulance rides out here for a quarter of a century. The irony was even greater when he realized that he now was in dire need of assistance.

Ben felt his body refusing to support him. He wanted to run, but his legs slowed down with each step.

"Run!" Nela yelled at him, but it just didn't work.

The meadow ended, revealing an asphalt surface that appeared to be the access road leading to the building. Straight ahead, past the emergency room, concrete steps led to the main building.

Over the decades, grass and ivy had taken over the building as well. Lower floor windows were boarded up and plaster was peeling off the walls. Wind and rain had taken their toll on the facade. Feet-long cracks stretched across the outer walls. The old hospital was dilapidated, but not yet in danger of collapse.

Meanwhile, Ben had slowed down so much that he was only moving at a steady pace.

"Please, Ben! Run!"

Nela had not given up, forcing him to continue from behind. But the old man had reached his limits. The pain in his leg literally brought him to his knees. Finally, he just limped along in front of her.

"Listen," he urgently said to Nela, grabbing her shoulders with both hands. "The emergency generator is located in the basement. You will go so deep into the lowest vaults until you can go no deeper. Then you'll keep going south, in that direction." Ben pointed past the hospital. "There should be gasoline there. You'll start the generator, so the power in the house will work again for a short time."

"Fine," Nela curtly replied, "but we can do that together."

Yet, Ben did not allow himself to be irritated. "After that, go upstairs as fast as you can, up to the attic. That's where you'll find the radio equipment." He pointed upward. "See the antennas on the roof?"

Nela nodded. "Yes, I do. Come on now!"

She grabbed his hand and resolutely headed for the stairs, but Ben could not keep up with her pace. In severe pain, he ran after her, convulsing with each step.

"Go upstairs, open the door!"

Nela took two steps at a time, as fast as she could. The big glass doors looked at her like dark eyes. Verdigris had spread over the panes, blocking the view inside. What struck Nela, however, was the flashing metal lock and the thick steel chain that held the door handles together. Damn!

"Ben, the door is locked!"

"I never locked those!"

"There's a big old padlock on it."

Dog barking. The gang came running.

"Come on, let's get out of here!" Nela grabbed Ben's hand and pulled it. Powerless, Ben stumbled forward, buckled, and fell onto the stairs.

"Uhhhh!" Pain robbed him of all his strength.

"Get up!" She pulled at him with both hands. But Ben remained on his back, motionless.

"Get out while you still can, girl!"

"I'm not leaving you alone!" Tears rolled down her cheeks.

"We will both die then. Get help, this is our last chance."

Nela sobbed, covering her mouth with her hand. "No …"

The gang was getting closer.

"Run around the house, right now, as fast as you can, on this path." He pointed to a trail between the ambulance and the hospital. "A few yards around the corner, there's a window I didn't board up properly. Hear me? The top nails are missing. It is possible to climb in if you pull the board back."

Nela's tears were still running, but she focused on Ben's words.

"Did you hear me, young lady?"

Nela nodded hastily. She pressed her lips together, holding back tears. Nela took his face in both hands and gazed into his eyes.

"Hang in there, Ben Marshall. Please, hang in there."
"Don't worry about me, I will be fine." She gave him a kiss on the lips.
"I will come back and get you. I promise."

Gently, he pushed Nela away from him. "Here, take this with you." Ben handed her his heavy flashlight. "Hit it as hard as you can."

She nodded.
"Now get out of here."
Hesitantly, she started walking.
"Get out now!"
Nela ran.

As Ben turned to look at the field, the dog pounced on him.

HADES

The tears of grief had given way to those of anger. Yelka had gritted her teeth grimly, breathing through her nose. Her chest rose and fell evenly, her fists were clenched. Anger was an emotion Yelka had rarely felt. Her desire for harmony and balance was too great to give room for negative emotions. But deep inside her, the need to break through her barriers and let out her anger had lurked all along. The urge to retaliate sought a channel, drove her—indeed, kept her alive.

Determined, Yelka ran through the dark tunnel, fighting her way through the muddy ground. It smelled of lime and rot. Water dripped from the ceiling. Yelka's eyes had adjusted to the darkness. She could make out the old bricks of the tunnel walls, the muddy ground, and the insects and rodents fleeing from her. It was so cold in the tunnel that Yelka could see her own breath.

After a few steps, she recognized the end of the tunnel in front of her. The path ended at a massive wall, in which there was a rusty grate at eye level. With careful steps, Yelka approached the grating, breathed softly, and put a hand on the metal.

Carefully, she pressed against it, feeling only slight resistance. She could push it in, but Yelka hesitated. She sensed that she was not alone. Someone was on the other side. Yelka held her breath and peered through the bars.

She was unable to see much, though. The bottom edge of the grille seemed to line up with the floor of the room on the other side. So, whoever was there could only see her by leaning down. Vaguely, she heard footsteps and strained breathing. She tried to focus on the other room. Was there more than one person?

A shock ran through her bones when Yelka felt a tickle on her face. She tensed up, pressing her lips together to keep her breathing in check. The thin arms of a spider touched her nose and cheekbones. The critter ran from her forehead to her neck, reaching her chin. It was a dark spider as big as Yelka's face. She closed her eyes and pulled herself together, holding her breath. Finally, she resolutely grabbed a leg and pulled the spider away from her body. Gently, she set the animal down on the wall and continued gazing into the darkness of the opposite room.

But now, there was silence. Moreover, Yelka couldn't see any movements anymore. Whoever had been there seemed to have left the room. She waited a moment. Seconds passed like hours, but she had to be sure that she wouldn't attract any attention if she pushed in the grille.

What did she have to defend herself with? Yelka had nothing left on her. Her equipment had been lost during their escape. Her wallet and keys were the only things left in her pants. What was she supposed to do with them? Yelka carefully pulled out the keys and looked at them for a moment. She then clenched a fist and let the keys emerge from between her fingers. Now, they looked like little claws. With them, she couldn't kill anyone, but Yelka would sell her skin as dearly as possible.

"Come on, you scumbags! I'm gonna put some holes in you."

Determined, she pushed the grate forward and felt it slacken under her pressure. After a few moments, it had detached itself from the wall, laying loosely in her hands. Patiently, she lowered it until it lay on the floor. Yelka scanned the back of the wall and finally found a foothold at the top edge. It was time to get moving!

She jerked her body up, keeping her foot on the brickwork and holding on to it with her toes. Using all her strength, Yelka pulled herself up, as the edge of the entrance rubbed against her rib cage. She suppressed a painful groan, searching for support with her hands while her legs bobbed in the air.

Finally, inch by inch, she crawled forward. Small pieces of stone, splinters, and debris kept drilling into her hands and arms. But Yelka's determination drove her on, helping her to suppress the pain. When she finally made it, she rolled to the side and lay with her back against the wall.

After the effort, her lungs were screaming for air, but Yelka tried to breathe slowly and evenly. She glanced around the room, but she couldn't make out anything. It was pitch black, with only shadows to be glimpsed. Yelka could tell that the room was big. In front of her were wooden benches, the large windows were boarded up from the outside.

At the edges, cold moonlight fell through. Very slowly, Yelka pulled out her bunch of keys. She had to be ready for anything. Her heart was racing, her fist closed tightly around the steel claws. Yelka crouched down and let her gaze wander. In front of her were more wooden benches, lined up side-by-side. At the end of the room, she could glimpse a gallery. Jeez!

This was a chapel. Despite the darkness, she now saw the large cross hanging from the ceiling. Like any other medical facility, this military clinic offered a spiritual sanctuary for contemplation and solitude. For a moment, Yelka felt something like calm and relaxation. That urge for peace and harmony came back, settled on her mind like a false friend. Yelka shook her head, she had to be prepared for battle. She again tightened her fist and felt the cold metal between her fingers. She had to move on, find the exit and get help. As she turned to look for the door, she noticed a shadow behind her.

Yelka jumped back and raised her fist, ready to strike. In the darkness, someone was standing. Yelka tensed her body, about to strike. She yelled with fury and struck with full force, yet she hit nothing. Yelka whirled around, flailing wildly. However, the person in front of her skillfully avoided her blows. Finally, she heard a woman's voice ask, "Tess, is that you?"

Relieved, Yelka lowered her arms. Whoever stood in front of her wasn't an enemy.

"No, I'm not Tess, but I know her."
"Then, who are you?" The voice sounded soft, fearful.

Yelka realized that the woman in front of her was holding a heavy flashlight, ready to strike. "Hey, take it easy. I'm not going to hurt you. My name is Yelka. My friends and I were attacked by a gang of thugs. Fleeing from them, we ran into Tess."

"Where's Tess now?" The woman seemed to have calmed down, her tone becoming firmer.

"We lost each other. The gang murdered my sister."

Her counterpart lowered the flashlight. "Seems you're the hose girl, hu?"

"Right, that's how we were able to free my sis. Unfortunately, I wasn't able to save her." Yelka struggled with tears. She felt a lump in her throat.

"Hey, it's okay." Nela embraced her. "Let it all out, you're not alone anymore."

Yelka broke away from the embrace as tears made their way. "Appreciated, but it's not comfort I need right now."

"I got you," she replied, "Whatever you're looking for, I'll help you.

Yelka wiped the tears away and gave her new ally a grim smile. "You must be Nela."

"That's who I am."

"Tess has been talking about you. How did you get here?"

"The gang ambushed us before they chased you. I lost Tess in the process. Finally, I met a security man."

"So, there's security out here?"

"Yes," Nela replied with an icy stare. "The bravest guy in the world is out there." Tears ran down her cheeks.

"Oh my God … Is he …?"

"Yes," she nodded, sobbing. "He gave his life to help me escape."

Outside, a dog barked loudly.

"They are just about to beat him to death." Her voice sounded monotonous and ice-cold.

Loud voices mingled with the barking.

Their screams got louder.

Horror rose from their stomachs like an ice-cold fountain and paralyzed their limbs.

"They're about to come in through this window."

"What are we waiting for?" Determined, Yelka walked toward the bench under the boarded-up window. "Come on, give me a hand. We'll build a barricade."

While Nela held one end, Yelka lifted the bench and positioned it into the frame. Glass shattered, but that didn't stop her. With a deft twist, she wedged the wood into the frame, making it impossible to push open the heavy window from the outside.

"You guys are Urbexers, right?"

Yelka nodded in confirmation. "Yep. You too?"

"You bet."

"Then, I guess we just broke all the rules."

Nela and Yelka couldn't have imagined the shared laughter a few minutes ago. The threat made it even more liberating.

"It's nice to meet a friend."

She smiled. "It really is."

"Listen, Yelka. The security guy, Ben Marshall, told me about an emergency generator in the basement. If we find that and turn it on, we can use the transmitter on the roof to call for help."

That, at least, was a glimmer of hope. "Sounds like a plan."

"What tools do you have with you?"

Yelka laughed. "I have nothing left but my house key." Grinning, she presented her fist, ready to strike.

"Well, this is a good thing, as at least you won't have to worry about returning to a locked home."

They laughed. "Let's go then. Light our way!"

With Near flashlight, they left the chapel and went down the stairs into the basement. Compared to the escape tunnel that Yelka had just come out of, everything here seemed to be intact and clean. The floor was concrete, and the walls plastered. To the left and right, empty rooms kept appearing. Finally, they passed a large room at the end of the hallway.

"What is this?"

"That must be the utility room," Nela guessed. "See the fuse boxes?"

"Yeah, pretty impressive."

"I assume there is one for each part of the hospital."

"The emergency generator shouldn't be far away then."

"Probably not."

They left the basement through a massive steel door, behind which was a narrow corridor. Just like in the utility room, everything here was clean. There was no dust or dirt on the floor to indicate that there had been a long period of vacancy. At the end of the corridor was another steel door.

"Caution–to be operated by authorized personnel only. Danger! High voltage."

So, here they were in the right place. Behind this door was the hospital's power supply. But when Nela pressed the handle, the door was locked.

"Damn it!" she cursed.

"What are we going to do now?"

"I think I can open the door," Nela claimed. "But it's going to take some time."

"Let's do it. What are you waiting for?"

"We need to go back to the utility room."

"Why, what are we supposed to do there?"

"Do you trust me?"

"You're funny, Nela? If I didn't, you'd have holes in your chin by now."

"Come with me then!"

With a few quick steps, the two returned to the basement, where the large fuse cabinets were located. Nela rummaged through the pockets of her cargo pants and finally discovered a roll of wire.

"What are you going to do?" Yelka watched as Nela unwound the spool inch-by-inch.

Grimly, she gazed at her. "One by one, we will trap and hunt them down."

Yelka smiled. She liked the idea.

"Urbex style!"

288

Occasionally, a dog had to be put on its back to make it submit. Without that, he would become rebellious and would no longer accept his master. Dog breeds, such as Rottweilers, German Shepherds or Bulldogs, produced very dominant specimens.

Golden retrievers, on the other hand, were peaceful animals, usually integrating into their pack without any problems. As a puppy, however, Athos had been rebellious; Ben had to throw him on his back several times until he calmed down.

He was familiar with aggressive behavior in dogs and was not afraid to lend a hand himself. But Ryder's snarling, slavering mutt was a very different animal. It hadn't had any education and was as socially neglected as his master. With mad eyes, Gazoo had bitten Ben's forearm.

His head flew from left to right, his teeth ripped at Ben, trying to tear him apart. Ben felt a pulsating sensation of pain, similar to a flash of lightning. Already the dog must have bitten him to the bone. Blood splattered across his face.

"Off! Off! Off!" roared Ben, but the dog disobeyed. Drool mixed with blood as the beast kept tearing at him. "You wouldn't have it any other way," Ben hissed in pain. He rolled over the dog, pinning him down with both legs, then pushing Gazoo down with his bleeding arm.

The dog recognized his now inferior position and let go of Ben's arm. Wildly and uncontrollably, it snapped at him, biting his hand, his cheek and again into the open wound. Ben could no longer hold the animal. As soon as the dog broke free of his grasp, he would go for his neck. Panicked, he searched for help, his right hand groping on the ground and finally finding a big stone.

"Sorry, kid," he muttered and let the rock crash on Gazoo's head. The first time he barked in protest, after the second blow he whimpered, and the third silenced Gazoo. Exhausted, Ben dropped the stone and sank back to the ground. Blood spurted from his wound, running down his arm, onto his chest and neck. But it didn't matter anyway, no one would be able to help him now. He could already hear the gang coming closer.

Ben lay in the grass and felt the dry stalks tickling his face. In the night sky, the moon stood above him, shining brightly. Not far away, a cricket was chirping. Only when faced with death did he realize how peaceful this place actually was. Ironically, it was only now that Ben became aware of the uniqueness of the old barracks.

"Yo, there's the old hobo!" Footsteps arrived, destroying the peace. "Yep! Ryder, we got him."

Ben heard their heavy footsteps pounding on the dry asphalt. Branches cracked as the steps came to a halt beside him. His eyes were closed, he was breathing calmly.

"Look, it's old Marshall."
"I told you to fuck off!"
"Damn! So what?"

He didn't have to open his eyes to know who had built up around him. It was Jesse, Mike, and Dave's voices that echoed very close to him.

"Yo, old man!" Dave kicked his leg. "Wake up!"

"Grandpa, open your eyes!" He felt like someone hit him on the stomach with something.

"There he is." The voice spoke in another direction. More people joined in.

"That's a nice gift the cat brought."

Ben knew the raspy voice that had joined just now. He smiled. It was strange that Ben was smiling now, even though he had been in so much pain and suffering. He opened his eyes and said, "Hello, Henry!"

"Well, who do we have here? The man himself, Mr. Marshall, right?"

"It's nice to see you again."

"Got you pretty good, didn't it?"

"Don't you worry, I am doing fine."

"Ah, that's a shame, really." Henry turned to his gang. "You all know the old guy, right?" Hesitantly, they nodded their heads. "He's a man of high caliber, real old school. Isn't that right, Ben? Am I right?"

"That's right, Henry."

"You all know the story of why Ryder and I ended up in foster care, right?" Insecurely, they nodded again, since everyone was aware of the rumors about the death of Mr. and Mrs. Sherwin. "It's all right, don't worry about it. It was this man who found them both dead in their bed. Wanna know what he did after he called the cops? You remember that, Ben, don't ya?"

"Oh yes, I do, Henry. Like it was yesterday."

"He took Ryder and me to his house. Until Child Protective Services came. Isn't that right?"

"That's right."

Nodding silently, Henry glanced around. Dead silence reigned as Ryder shouted. "You killed my dog, bitch!" Alongside Henry, Ryder had fallen to his knees and held his lifeless pet in his arms. "That filthy coward killed my dog!"

A low humming sound reached Ben's ears, drowning out Ryder's wailing as it turned to pure hatred. Everything he perceived was through a calming filter, that blocked out all the horror that lay ahead.

"Ryder, listen, I'm sorry …"

But Henry wasn't done yet. "For one night only, he let my little brother and me stay with him. And then Child Protective Services took us away. For six long years, we went through hell."

Ryder had put Gazoo's carcass on the grass and was hatefully staring at Ben.

"Look at him, Ben. That's what that little fella has become. A stone-cold killer."

"You know that's not true, Henry."

Henry burst into demonic laughter. "I'm giving you one last chance, Ben Marshall. You tell me where that girl went, and we'll let you live."

Ben took a deep breath. He smiled. "Do you have another cigarette for me, Henry?"

Henry squatted down in front of Ben and shoved a filterless cigarette into the corner of his mouth. "Take a drag, dude."

Ben carefully inhaled the smoke. He had quit 20 years ago, but never really conquered his addiction. He had often imagined what it would be like to enjoy the aromatic smoke of a good roll-your-own again.

"Well, where did the bitch go?"

Ben pointed in the direction where Nela had disappeared. "You guys go around that house."

Henry's face was very close to Ben's. "Just down there?"

"Exactly. All along the facade."

"All the way?"

"Precisely. Until you get to a big fence."

"Guys, remember this. All the way down to the fence!" Henry looked at the gang with a weighty gaze. "And then what, buddy?"

"So, once you're over the fence, you keep walking, keep walking all around the entire house."

"We keep running along the facade."

"Until you finally get back here."

"What, right here?" Henry looked at Ben in irritation.

"Yeah, right here."

"No way!" He chuckled in disbelief.

"You bet. And you take a running start."

"I take a running start?"

"Yeah, you better be fast."

"All right."

"Then, headfirst, you run right into your brother's ass."

Henry laughed out loud.

"And that's where you take a look. Maybe she's somewhere in there."
Amused, Henry stood up. "I love that guy. Isn't he funny?"

Ben closed his eyes and smiled. He couldn't hear Henry telling the gang to finish him off. He didn't feel the kicks against his body and head. When darkness surrounded him, Ben Marshall was at peace with himself.

"Brother, what is so important in this hospital that we would kill for it?"
"Nothing of material value. Descend with me to Hades and I will show you. The rest of you fan out and find the girl."

Light-footed, Zander strolled through the forest, holding the knife in his right hand. He followed the path that led from the old settlement to the swimming pool, and then disappeared into the dense forest. If he wasn't completely mistaken, then somewhere there had to be the barracks. He would surely find them there–Yelka, Vivian and Damon.

And also Ryder and the rest of the gang. He was very eager to meet Henry. According to Tami, he would have to be Zander's equal. It would be a great rush to compete against him. He tingled when he thought about it.

After a few moments, the forest opened up. Zander's memory had been correct. Before him, there was the gate to the old military compound. What a sublime, challenging sight. The huge chain-link fence with barbed wire on top gave way to a place few had entered before him.

The gate squeaked in the night wind, the tall grasses on the old parade ground swayed back and forth. The barracks looked dark and frightening, testifying to military drill, punishment and a show of force. Fresh tracks indicated that the gate had been broken open. Zander knew, he was on the right path.

Upon reaching the center of the square, he saw two bodies lying in the dark.

A drama similar to the one Zander had experienced on the old open-air stage must have played out here not too long ago. With blood splatters everywhere, the first corpse lay in a red, dark puddle. It was a girl, horribly mauled. Judging by her clothes, these had to be the remains of Vivian.

She was wearing skimpy denim shorts, but Yelka's top. Or was that… ?

He pulled the arm off the corpse, turned it on its back, and looked into Vivian's face. At least, what was left of it. The left half of her face was intact, the eye closed. The right side, though, was barely more than a bloody, open wound. The skull was so messed up that an ear and some of the lower jaw were missing. Only blood, flesh, and gray matter were left of her head. Other than that, however, her body was unharmed except for scrapes and bruises.

Zander ran the tip of his knife over her skin, traveling from her neck down over her torso and legs. The remains of Yelka's younger sister looked pitiful and sad. Zander groaned. Whew. It seemed like someone had let out all his anger. Ryder had utterly lost it. But apparently, he hadn't even fucked her before.

This must have been about something else. The gang must have been pretty angry. At least, they hadn't caught Yelka. She had to have gotten away from the guys. Good thing. Zander straightened up and gazed into the darkness. He wondered where they had gone.

A soft rattle sounded behind him. Surprised, Zander turned around and glanced at the second body lying a few feet away. Was that Damon? With quick steps, Zander walked over to him. It was indeed Vivian's manager who was lying in front of him. They had definitely given him a good beating.

His face was bloodshot, his eyes swollen. Damon's nose was no longer visible. His mouth was bloody, his teeth broken. A thin trickle of blood oozed from his ear. Damon's body was broken, his fingers sticking out at unnatural angles. His right leg appeared to be broken in half.

"Help … help …" Damon gasped softly.

"What was that?" Zander put his ear close to Damon's mouth.

"Help … me… " He used up the last of his energy.

With feigned indignation, Zander said, "Well, I really can't understand what you are asking me to do. In fact, the rest of my program for this night is very tightly scheduled, so you better find the right words quick. A-S-A-P!"

"Get … help!"

"Hm …" Zander folded his arms in front of his chest. "Who did this to you?" He pointed at Vivian. "Was it Henry? Or Ryder?"

"Yes," Damon rasped softly.

"Yes is not an answer to a question with two options, Damon. You should be aware of this."

Without an answer, Damon groaned.

"Well, then I'll ask you something else, and I know you will do your best to answer me accurately. Where did they go? Huh? I would love to hunt them down immediately and at least free Yelka from their grip."

"I … don't … know …" In a gasp, his voice faded away.

"Damon, you're obviously not much use to me alive."

From a distance, Zander heard a dog barking. It had to be them! He saw the military hospital between the trees. That's where they were headed!

"Please … help me!" Damon reared up in pain, trying to reach out to Zander, but he could not. He slumped, losing all body tension. Tired, he pulled his arms and legs towards him, breathing shallowly.

Zander took one last look at Damon Duke. He had led a life of arrogance.

"I think we need to make a cut here, dear Grim Reaper. I think the whole thing is a misunderstanding. My name is Damon Duke, and I don't have time for you yet." Zander chuckled at his perfidious impersonation.

"My name is Damon Duke …" Suddenly, he liked the idea of incorporating Damon's behavior and expressions into his new self. Something in him had always envied the social media manager's style and bearing. He looked down at his lifeless body. Zander had always liked his red sneakers. They had to have the same shoe size.

"Duke, Duke, let me have a hand, will you?" Grinning, he pulled the right shoe off the corpse's foot and tried it on. It fitted like a glove. What next? Uh, that black designer shirt with its silver appliqué was a real stunner. Not so much the men's purse. As an Urbexer, he could only smile about it. But he liked the t-shirt, it fit just perfect. It had been affected by the unfortunate circumstances, but a little soap and water would fix it up. Wow, his new clothes suited Zander well.

But something was still missing. Something that would make him perfect.

"I think we need to make a cut here."

Zander drew his knife and bent over Damon's body.

Then, he did the unthinkable.

In her flashlight's glow, Yelka could see her own breath. Shivering, she glanced behind her. There was a tense silence, broken only by distant drops of water and the sound of her breathing. However, from the darkness, the faint voices of her pursuers seemed to reach Yelka. The tension rose even more as Yelka felt her entire skin crawl. Impatiently, she watched Nela, who was squatting in front of her, trying to unscrew the lock of the steel door that blocked their way to the power supply.

"Are you making progress?"

"The lock is fastened damn tight," Nela murmured softly. "I just have to …"

"Relax, take your time."

Nela gasped. "All the time in the world won't be enough to unscrew this lock."

"What happened?"

"Unfortunately, that screw needs to be drilled out."

In the pale light of the flashlight, Yelka saw that the head of the screw was worn out, no longer offering any grip. "Damn, what do we do now?"

"Well, screw the code," Nela shrugged.

"Excuse me?" Yelka was confused.

"I guess the only thing that helps is vandalism." She smiled. "Come on, give me that flashlight."

Nela grabbed the heavy lamp and hit the lock until it finally broke.

"Not too bad" Nela laughed. "Now, I guess I know why some kids fuck shit up."

"Girl's going bonkers" Yelka joined in her soft laughter.

"Hey, that would have been my part, actually."

"Well, there is always someone who is a little more reasonable."

"That better not be you."

"We'll see."

"Come on, let's go!"

The door opened silently, revealing a dark vault with a size, which could not be seen even in the light of the flashlight. The air was cold and smelled damp. Water ran down the gray concrete walls and formed greenish shimmering lime traces. A thin film of moisture lay on the floor. Nela shone the flashlight back and forth. On the wall to their left were blue barrels that appeared to be new and little used. To the right, someone had set up primitive steel shelves filled with various things.

"What the hell is this?"

"It looks like a stock."

"Look at this … bumpers, rims, tires."

"Here are radios, airbags, tools."

"See, there are cartons of gaming consoles here."

"Cameras!"

"This looks like a freaking thieves' warehouse."

"I bet this is where the gang hid their loot."

"They seem pretty kinky."

"Why is that?"

"There's underwear here."

"Oh, my goodness, here's a whole bag of women's clothes."

"I'm sure these perverts do some pretty bizarre things with them."

"Who knows what these weirdos are doing down here."

"What kind of sick fucks did we run into?"

"Maybe we don't want to know."

"It doesn't matter. We need to find that emergency generator."

Nela shone her light into the back of the room, looking for a way. She sensed Yelka close behind her, who had placed a hand on her shoulder. Very vaguely, she could spot a door at the end of the room that led her further into the depths of the building. When Nela took a step forward, she was held by Yelka.

"Wait, I want to know what's in there." Yelka pointed to the barrels on the opposite wall.

"Shouldn't we turn on the power first?"

"Sorry, I need to know what's in there."

"I thought you were so reasonable."

"You were wrong, obviously."

Determined, Yelka walked to one of the blue barrels, with Nela close behind. Carefully, she placed a hand on the container's rim. The plastic felt neither brittle nor fragile. It was, undoubtedly, new. The metal ring that held the lid in place was rust-free, reflecting the light of the flashlight. Silently, Yelka looked at Nela. She pulled at the barrel, trying to tilt it, but it was heavy.

"Give me a hand," she urged Nela.

With combined forces, they managed to rattle the blue plastic barrel. From the inside, they heard a soft splashing sound, like there was water inside.

"You better leave it locked as is."

Yelka, however, only shook her head. Vigorous, she loosened the hooks on the barrel's side. As she lifted the lid, air escaped with a soft hiss. A sweet scent, mixed with a hint of spirit, flowed towards them. Nela gagged, Yelka turned away, still holding the lid.

"Yelka, no. Don't look inside."

But Yelka pushed the lid away. The stench was almost too much for them. Finally, Nela shone a light into the container. Dark liquid reflected the beam.

"What is this mess?"

"It seems to be some kind of chemical."

"Wait a minute …"

Something moved under the black surface, floating beneath it.

"What the hell is that?"

"Oh my God …"

Very slowly, the thing broke through the surface. Something like an elongated black branch appeared.

At its end, five bright dots could be seen.

Toenails.

Yelka couldn't help but throw up.

A second foot floated to the surface. With a twist, Nela slid the lid back into position. Yelka spat out and wiped her mouth.

"I told you, they're sick fucks."

But Nela did not react. She gazed behind Yelka like she was frozen. "What is it?" Slowly she turned around.

Between the barrels, in a niche, there stood an old chair, like the one Nela and Yelka knew from their doctors. It was covered in scratches, rust and bloody residue, making it look like it had been dipped in blood.

"This ain't no fence's stock," Nela whispered tonelessly. "We're right in the middle of a torture nightmare."

The chair, apparently, had been brought here from one of the hospital's wards and had been anchored to the concrete floor with heavy-duty bolts. Someone had attached wide leather cuffs to the arm and leg rests. But the utensils' sanitary integrity was gone. Massive violence, blows, and hits had left dents and scratches. The chair's upholstery was slashed and torn apart. Everything was soaked in blood.

"Shitheads, you fucking shitheads …"
"They're going to pay for that."
"The cops will have to take care of that when we get out of here."
"We should move on now."

They tore themselves away from the torture chamber's horrible sight. Determined and without hesitation, they opened the door at the end of the room. There was a big hall in front of them with a huge technical device in the center. Pipes, valves and hoses ran together in what resembled an oversized engine block.

"I'm sure that's it!"

"We're just gotta get this little fucker going."

"Look for a large switch or lever, anything that could be used to turn it on."

"Maybe something like the one that says 'emergency power'?"

"Absolutely!"

When Nela pulled the red lever, a pumping sound rang out, as if a car had been started. At first, the machine was quiet, but it got louder by the second. Finally, a bright light illuminated the basement.

Yelka was dazzled by the radiant glow and had to cover her eyes for a moment. Nela hugged her.

"That's half the battle."

"Now, we only need to locate the transmitter."

"Come on, let's get moving."

When they left the utility, the overhead lights had turned on in the stockroom as well.

"Hi girls."

Like a pack of hungry wolves, Henry and Ryder's eyes were fixed on Nela and Yelka, spraying triumph and fury. The predators had their prey cornered.

"That cunt took my girl!" Ryder pointed his steel pipe at Yelka.

"That bitch over there? She is quite pretty, no doubt about that. Looks just like your little girl, before you beat her to a pulp."

Ryder gave his brother a serious stare.

"I bet they're sisters." With a malicious grin, Henry smirked at Yelka. "That's right, isn't it? My little brother digs you, really bad. With him, I bet, you will have just as much fun as your sister had."

The brothers approached slowly, circling Yelka and Nela.

"You filthy animals …" Yelka hissed angrily. Her grip on the heavy flashlight became so tight, her knuckles turned white. She lashed out, ready to strike at any moment.

Nela had flipped out her knife's blade. It didn't seem threatening, though, but properly wielded, it could cause significant damage.

"Not a step further!" she shouted in a firm voice.

Henry laughed in mock anger. "Ho, ho! You exotic little bitch." He grinned over at Ryder. "Looks like we both made a good catch, huh?"

"I mean it, boy!" Nela raised her blade, ready to stab.

"Or else?" Excitedly, Henry glared at her.

Slowly, the two men approached. Backs to the wall, Yelka and Nela moved together toward the exit. In front of them were those blue barrels with those gruesome contents. Henry and Ryder were standing nearby.

"Girl, you are here in my world, in Hades. Don't you ever dare threaten me." Henry's feigned smile was gone, his cold eyes flashing with hatred.

Nela, however, was not intimidated. With the knife raised, she stood her ground. "You guys are goddamn sickos, we've already figured that out." Nela pushed the lid off the barrel. "You into that, asshole?"

Rising from the barrel, the foul-smelling cloud took everyone's breath away. Henry, however, kept a straight face. Ryder, however, glanced back and forth between Nela and his older brother, confused.

"Yeah, come here, Ryder. Take a look." Henry kept his eyes on the two women as his brother hesitantly approached. Disgusted, he took a brief peek inside the barrel. When he realized what was floating within the chemicals, he averted his gaze and silently stared at Henry.

"Oh yes, accept reality, little brother. It is within you, too. You proved that perfectly well, earlier on."

Yelka trembled with fear and anger as Henry stared at her in disdain.

"There's blood on our hands," Henry smugly announced. "I don't know how many people I've killed, but it's been quite a few."

Ryder had his lips pinched together, his lower jaw muscles twitching.

"Little brother, I think it is time to make a confession to you." Henry's body had lost all tension. "You know why we grew up in foster care, don't you?"

Ryder silently nodded. After a brief silence, he finally said, "Because our parents died."

Henry put on his grim smile again. "I caught it early on. In fourth grade, I stabbed Mandy's dog. That was pretty awesome, but it didn't really satisfy me."

Ryder remembered the incident from his childhood and glanced at him in surprise.

"After that, I drowned René while he was playing by the creek. The little boy fought back like hell. But it didn't do him any good. They never found his body."

While Henry grinned with a smug, Ryder's eyes widened.

"Two years later, one night, I was at our parents' bedside. I had that big knife from the kitchen with me."

Henry's words were unbearable. Nela and Yelka were on the edge. Ryder was speechless. His big brother, however, seemed to feel something like relief as he described his terrible deed.

"They separated us after that, remember? They claimed I was in another place. But in reality, they put me in the loony bin until I turned eighteen.

Then, they let me out again." He turned to Nela and Yelka and laughed. "I'm officially cured."

Nela, however, was not watching Henry, but Ryder. He had lowered his steel pipe, and, with complete disbelief, was gazing at his brother. She blinked cautiously over at Yelka. Out of the corner of her eye, she realized that she was still high alert. Nela inhaled through her nose, making a noticeable sound.

For a brief moment, Yelka peered over at her. When their eyes met, she raised her eyebrows and pointed at Ryder. She also recognized his uncertainty.

"Yes, I am perfectly sane," Henry now claimed again in a serious voice. "And this is my torture cellar. Because killing is fun for me. There's nothing abnormal about it. Each of us harbors that certain passion. Even you, brother." He turned back to Ryder. "Earlier, you asked me why we kill. Now you know the answer. We kill for the sake of killing."

Yelka watched her sister's killer lift his chin as his gaze hardened. The seeds of madness that his brother had planted seemed to sprout.

"This, Hades, will become our common realm, my brother. This is where I bring all the ones that fall into my hands. Tramps, cable thieves and those jerks who call themselves newfangled Urbexers. All of them died by my hand down here."

With triumphant pride, Henry gazed around, determinedly eyeing

Nela and Yelka.

"These two," he pointed to the barrels, "were cable thieves who strayed here a few days ago. Their names were Billy and Scott. Oh yes, they were terrified, begging for their lives. See what's left of them now."

While Yelka and Nela waited for an opportunity to escape, Ryder silently peered at the barrels.

"What are you waiting for, brother? There are two more barrels left waiting to be filled."

Ryder swallowed. The parade ground events flashed before his eyes. Anger and hatred were gone. Emptiness and fear were back. Nela could see it working inside him. She had seen what he had done and how with each blow he had even killed himself. Now was the time!

"Hey, asshole!" She broke the tense silence. Henry's gaze turned to her. "You still wanna know what else?" For an instance, the ice-cold killer was caught off guard. "I'll tell you what else. I'm gonna cut that dick broom right out of your face, you sick freak!"

Dumbstruck, Henry stared at her; she had taken him by surprise.

"Uh, uh, being put on blast, Henry?" Now, Yelka attacked him as well. "So, do you know how we are going to do that?"
Together, they yelled, "Urbex style!" as Nela snapped the wire they had previously stretched.

When the lights went off, they knocked over the barrels. The floor was covered in a foul smell of chemicals as Nela and Yelka rushed towards the exit.

Out of the gloom, they heard their attackers curse, as they moved toward the door, step by step. That sudden darkness caught the brothers off guard, and Nela and Yelka ran to the exit safely, keeping the door's position in mind. Yet, when Nela pressed down the handle, it was locked.

"Them bitches really thought they would get off that easy."

Henry's voice approached with quiet certainty. The two murderers did not bother to hide their position. Nela and Yelka were trapped.

"We're coming!" shouted Ryder in a strange voice. With a scraping sound, his steel pipe slid across the floor, sending a chill down Yelka's spine.

Nela pressed the handle with all her might, bracing herself against the door, but it was useless. It did not move an inch.

Panicked, Yelka hammered the lock with the flashlight.

"We'll sell our skin for as much as we can," Nela hissed at her.

But Yelka did not give up. She had grasped the handle, shaking it obsessively. There was a last bit of hope in her left, feeling something on the other side.

"Well, we've got you now."

The voice was close, merciless.

Nela roared, slicing the darkness with her knife.

Yelka pushed down the handle one last time as the door opened. She grabbed Nela by the shoulder and dragged her along.

As they ran out, Yelka thought she felt someone next to her.

The last thing they heard was the door slamming back into the lock.

Darkness enveloped Ryder, hiding his confusion underneath. A buzzing reached his ears, becoming louder and louder. He was overwhelmed by his brother's confession, the excessive violence, the murders, the torture, and the chemicals' stench. Dizziness overcame Ryder, he threatened to collapse. He felt his strength fading, his arms sinking down. Weakly, he held the baton in his right hand as he heard his brother yelling from a distance.

"The two bitches thought they would get off that easy."

Suck it up, Ryder! He suppressed the nausea and took a wary step forward. A scraping sound cut the silence as his steel pipe dragged across the floor. Damn, they heard him that way! He lifted his arm just high enough to wield the weapon safely again.

"We're coming!" muttered Ryder, more as a motivation to himself than to scare the girls.

As he slowly staggered to the door, he heard a dull thump. They tried to escape, but they couldn't. Among the screams and curses, he heard Henry laughing maliciously. Ryder breathed heavily, hitting the floor with the pipe. Don't think, just do it. He struggled with his powerlessness.

Then, all of a sudden, the door slammed shut and there was silence. Ryder stopped, frozen. For a moment, he heard nothing but the pounding of his own heart. Then, the buzzing in his ears returned and increased to a steady whistle. Ryder raised his hands to keep his balance. Like a faint whisper in a storm, he heard his brother's voice. A hand brushed his face, shadows passed him by. Ryder closed his eyes.

"The bitches are still here!"

Henry's hissing voice snapped Ryder out of his swoon.

"What was that?"
"They were bluffing and speculating on us running after them. But they're still in here."
"Alright …"

Ryder took a deep breath, turning left and right. Slowly, his eyes became used to the darkness. Henry was standing next to him. Ryder noticed a dark shadow moving slowly across the room, not far from them.

Henry put one hand on his forearm, pointing in the direction of the shadow. With the other hand, he pointed to the left, indicating to Ryder that they should circle the girls. He nodded and was about to leave when a voice spoke to them.

"Ladies and gentlemen, it is my special pleasure and honor!"

Henry and Ryder froze. Who the hell was that?

"The infamous Sherwin brothers in an exquisite place like this."

The voice sounded familiar to Ryder.

"What I'm wondering, though, is there no light in an establishment as flamboyant as this one?"

That was how Damon Duke had talked, that snotty jerk. But that couldn't be, he was dead.

"Or is it, that you two cretins are so ugly that you're ashamed of me?"

"Who's that motherfucker?" whispered Henry.
"He kinda sounds like that Duke."
"Like who?"
"The guy you beat to a pulp."
"Nah, that one's done."

"I sincerely apologize, gentlemen. The practice of secrecy is not appropriate at this moment. I kindly ask you not to put any obstacles in the way of our mutual acquaintance so that we can finally turn on the light again. Furthermore, my time is limited."

"I don't know, man. I don't know …"

"Fuck it, let's finish him off for good now."

Henry tried to pull out his flashlight, but it seemed he had lost it during the recent events. Gruffly, he patted his jacket down. Henry growled angrily and grabbed Ryder by the neck. "You head left, I head right. We hit it on my command."

"All right," Ryder muttered absently.

Who was in the cellar with them? It could not be Duke, never. Henry had beaten him to death. Even if he was still alive, he would not ambush them down here anymore. But there was no other way. Nobody else had that arrogant, smug tone.

Duke had come back to take revenge on them. That buzzing sound grew louder again. A stinging tingle spread through his stomach. He felt sick. Duke, Duke, death. Duke of the Dead. Duke of hell.

Ryder's eyes searched the gloom for the dead man. His legs trembled. Next to him, Henry disappeared into the darkness. Cautiously, Ryder raised the steel pipe, pointing it forward like a skewer. The baton swung back and forth, but Ryder wouldn't hit anything.

With a trembling voice, he finally called out, "Duke, is that you?"

"That's right" sounded not far from him. "My name is Duke, Damon Duke from Duke Executives!"

An angry yell immediately followed the triumphant voice. "There he is!"

Panicked, driven by fear, Ryder stumbled forward, letting the steel rod cut the air.

Desperate cries of pain rang through the darkness. In the midst of this, he felt the impact as his blow hit its target. The air seemed to hold its breath for a moment, followed by a faint, rasping gasp that pierced the chaos.

"Henry?" But no one answered.

"That oh-so-notorious Ryder lashes out in fear and hits his very own brother. What a cynical twist of fate."

The emotional chaos inside Ryder calmed as a familiar companion re-emerged in his heart. Damon's words gave new life to his old friend, anger.

"If only your little girlfriend Tami could see this. For heaven's sake, what an embarrassment that would be for you."

With the old anger in his voice, Ryder hissed "Shut the fuck up," and took off running.

His steel pipe cut through the air; a shriek of rage came from Ryder's throat. Hateful, he ran into the darkness, straight toward the voice.

Fear and panic had given way to the only feeling that made Ryder feel safe: dead hatred. Frenzied, he lashed out, with only destruction in mind.

He didn't notice his fist hitting concrete and his knuckles cracking. Adrenaline numbed the pain, drove his frenzy.

"I finally got you," whispered a voice beside him.

Ryder turned and struck with his baton. It didn't hit anything.

"It's either you or me now."

Muffled thuds. Gasps. Silence.

"Ryder?" Henry had regained consciousness. He lay on the cold floor, his head pounding with pain. Someone had knocked him down. Probably his own brother. If only he could get his hands on him! "Ryder?" he called out again, but no one answered.

He was surrounded by a strange silence. What the hell was going on? He got back on his feet and tried to find his way in the darkness of the cellar. Henry squinted his eyes, wrenched them open again, and searched for a clue. To his left would be the door and to his right the emergency generator. With arms stretched out, he inched his way to where he suspected Ryder was.

A creaking noise made Henry wince. Metal squeaked. What was that?

"Ryder?"

Again, the darkness sucked in his voice. What was going on? Where did the noises come from? Henry's gaze wandered, but he couldn't see anything at all. He knew that sound, had heard it many times before, had even caused it himself. Of course, it was his chair that squeaked so hard when he strapped his victims in. His heart was beating faster.

Someone was in his sacred place, had entered his Hades! With cautious steps, Henry crept through the cellar, approaching his sanctuary. Nervously, he listened into the darkness, but it remained dead silent. Then, Henry heard soft but frantic breathing as he got closer. It had to be his brother.

"Ryder?" he now called out in a firm voice.

He heard him trying to answer, noticed the vibrations of his voice–but it became an uncontrolled gurgle. Like he was going to throw up. Then, a rattle. Henry's stomach clenched. He wanted to go on, to rush to Ryder's side, but he just stood there, trembling. Paralyzed with fright.

Liquid dripped onto the cold floor.

"Ryder?"

A demonic laugh made his blood run cold.

Then, the devil stood before Henry.

The haunting images were etched into Mike's memories. Ryder's big brother is standing over this guy, mercilessly pummeling him, kicking him with precise accuracy. At first, the boy had tried to protect himself, but eventually tension had drained from his body. His hands dropped to the floor, his head rolled to the side, powerlessly.

Mike just couldn't forget the image of Henry kicking the head–it rolled to the side and then tipped back to its original position, just like that. A thin trail of blood ran from his nose, irritated with each kick, finally forming the grotesque image of a cardiogram.

Mike realized it was better not to get in Henry's way, as he would punch him in the face as well. And you certainly should not disappoint him.

That was the reason he had given old Marshall a good beating. He should be aware that he could count on him. Better to live by his side than to die by his kicks. Now, if he could only find the girls, Henry would respect him and forget the smack he gave him earlier.

Mike nodded his head, as if reassuring himself that he was doing everything correctly. And when he would finally catch them, he'd claim his right and crush one of them with his own hands. Then he would be a made guy. Even ahead of Dave. But for that, he had to grab them first, even in this darkness.

With a loud bang, the lights suddenly came on, sending a thrill down his spine. The dim yellow lamps on the ceiling began to flicker unsteadily, and some of them went out after a short time. They had been out of service for much too long. The yellow, flickering light combined with the hum of the electric wires created a distressing atmosphere.

Mike clung to his steel pipe and took in his surroundings. This was not a medical area. There were no treatment rooms or operating theaters to be found here. Rather, this had to be a storage complex. Behind a rusted trolley, there was a heavy metal door. Carefully, Mike pushed down the tall latch and slid the door forward an inch. Glancing through the gap, he found a large, tiled room, its walls lined with metal shelves and sideboards.

The shine of the furniture was long gone, the chrome had become dull, the tiles were dirty and cracked. Still, one could guess that this must once have been the hospital's kitchen. Quietly, and with hesitant steps, Mike entered the huge cooking room. Behind him, the door creaked shut. Damn, he had not been careful enough! Startled, he gazed around and made sure that no one had heard him. After a moment of silence, he continued to sneak through the kitchen, searching for possible hiding places. Those two sluts had to be somewhere, after all.

For a moment he stopped and listened, then Mike crouched down and peered under the shelves. In the dust on the tiles, he could find visible traces. Someone had been here recently. But they hadn't expected Henry and Ryder to turn on the lights and for him to spot their tracks. Triumphantly, Mike stretched up and grinned. They were here!

Clutching the steel pipe tightly, he inched on, imagining what it would be like when he got a hold of the girls. He'd be having a blast with them, right? He'd really take it on both of them. Mike remembered the dark-haired one who had been out with Marshall. A stunning beauty! With her dark skin and black straight hair, she looked really exotic.

The other must have been the bitch who almost slapped Ryder that night when they pretended to be security. Not bad, either, but Mike wanted the dark princess. Anyway, what would he do with them after the party? Should he hand them over to Henry and Ryder? Or should he waste them right here and bring them back to the gang as trophies?

Today, Mike had already learned how to end a life.

Lost in his fantasies of omnipotence, he was wandering the kitchen hallways when he tripped over something lying at head height on the sideboard in front of him. At first, Mike was confused, unable to connect the canister to the kitchen. But then he opened the container and smelled it. Sure enough, it was gasoline. The canister seemed to have been here for a long time, a thick layer of dust had covered both the sideboard and the canister itself.

But why was there a canister of gasoline in the kitchen? Monstrous thoughts were already forming in his mind when he heard a noise behind him. Mike cast a hasty glance over his shoulder, frantically looking around, but he found himself alone in the large chamber. He lowered his breath and tried not to move. He sensed that something was shifting. Or did his mind just fool him? He slowly turned his head and took a look around the kitchen. But there was no one there.

Didn't he hear soft voices, though? He took a deep breath, closed his eyes and focused on his hearing only. A nervous tremor came over him, his hand tightened around the steel pipe. The tension had made Mike's violent fantasies disappear. Doubts now gnawed at him; fear sprouted.

Yes, there were voices there, for sure! Mike opened his eyes and stared ahead. He could hear them, and they were whispering to each other!

While his emotions swung back and forth between anger, excitement and fear, he carefully felt his way forward. Now, just don't make any noise, pay attention to every step. Every grain of dirt could cause a noisy crunch. Anyway, he was on the right track. In the twilight, he noticed a massive steel door, behind which those voices seemed to emanate.

It was broad and heavy and stood open just a slit. This was how he had always imagined the door of a bank vault. Mike paid attention one last time and could now distinctly hear the suppressed muttering behind the door. Firmly, he raised the baton and yanked on the latch. The massive door, however, was slow to open, heavy as it was. Finally, Mike pushed his body through the opening gap and hollered, "I've got you now!"

But there was no one there. Mike found himself in a cooling chamber with empty shelves on the walls. From the ceiling, hooks flashed where meat used to hang. Freezers stood open, locked cabinets concealed the last remains of the military kitchen. Astonished, Mike lowered his baton. Had the girls been hiding in those closets? They had to be here, as he could still hear the voices. Indeed, they were louder, but they sounded muffled. They had to be here! Mike decisively walked up to one of the closets and yanked it open.

"Come out, it won't do you any good. I will find you anyway!" he shouted angrily.

Door after door flew open, Mike didn't pass up a single closet. For he still heard the faint voices. What the hell was going on? When he opened the last locker's door, it hit him–it was just a cell phone playing a video. Puzzled, he picked up the mobile and took a look at it. The video showed those sluts he was looking for. They were in the kitchen, whispering to each other. It was precisely where he had just been standing!

"Think the fool has found us yet?"
"I don't believe so, we've only been talking for five minutes."
"Couldn't we just turn on the loop feature?"

In disbelief, Mike stared at the display. He got run around by a video. But what …

With a loud crash, the heavy security door slammed shut behind him. A soft giggle was the last thing Mike heard.

When the bolt crashed into the lock, the cold storage door was firmly closed. Yelka and Nela embraced each other. Their plan had worked, the first assailant had been overpowered. Only now did they realize how strained they had been until just now. Hugging each other tightly, they felt their hearts pounding fiercely. Angrily knocking signs from the other side proved to them that their opponent was trapped. A burst of euphoria came over them.

"Bitches!" Mike shouted from inside. "Wait and see what I'll do to you when I open the door!"

However, the threat was idle. "Yes, well, we're waiting," Nela exclaimed with a mischievous smile.

"I'm gonna to bash your heads!"

"I rather think you're going to bash your own head in, if you go on like this!" was Yelka's answer to Mike's impetuous blows.

"Have fun in there!" Nela laughed and was about to leave.

Yet, the knocking on the other side faded, and anger vanished from Mike's voice, as he called out, "Come on, let me out. I won't hurt you either, I promise."

"Surprise, surprise …" Nela raised her eyebrows.

"For real. Please, give it a rest." His voice sounded shaky.

"We didn't start out killing people!"

"I'm sorry, I didn't want this to happen. Henry pushed Ryder to do it. This is all his fault."

"We don't give a shit. Cling together, swing together!"

"I'm going to starve in here! Please!" Mike's voice sounded tearful.

"Hey," Yelka said quietly, "wait a minute. We can't let him die."

Astonished, Nela gazed at her. "What do you mean by that? Are you willing to let him out?"

"I don't know …" murmured Yelka.

"But I know. He was about to attack us. We can't let him go."

"We could tie him up and leave him here. At least then he'd have a fair chance."

"A fair chance?" Nela was stunned. "You want to give that scumbag a fair shot?"

Embarrassed, Yelka shrugged her shoulders.

"What chance did Ben have? And what chance did your sister have?"

Defiantly, she squinted her eyes. The memory of Vivian's fate shook Yelka deeply. For a moment, the two women silently eyed each other.

"Hey, please! Come on, I can help you!"

"Shut up!" Still challenging, Nela looked at Yelka.

"Now, we can't put ourselves on the same level with them by simply starving him to death," Yelka finally replied.

"Yeah, we might want to consider that" Nela hissed back.

"But we can also be better than them and give him a chance."

Yelka had raised her chin in anticipation of an answer from Nela.

"Please! I'm going to starve to death in here!"

Nela threw an annoyed glance at the door. "So, what would this chance look like then?"

"We'll let him out, tie him up, gag him, and take him with us. Remember, we'll need a witness when we talk to the police." Thoughtfully, Nela chewed on her lower lip. "I demand a major investigation, and I want every single one of them held accountable."

"Great plan," she finally countered. "What if it doesn't work and the guy attacks us?"

"I really won't hurt you!"

"I'll leave that up to you," Yelka replied. "You call the shots."

"Agreed." Nela joined in with a grim look. "How shall we do it?"

"Tell him to lie down flat, and we'll open the door."

"I will hold him …"

"… and I'll tie him up."

"That sounds like a good plan. Got a rope, though?"

"Let's use the wire that we took for the trap."

"This is going to hurt him big time."

"Nobody said it was going to be easy for him."

"Hey, please, let me out of here now!"

With a scowl, Nela and Yelka looked at each other."What's your name, dude?"

After a few moments of silence, the voice answered, "My name is Stanley. Who are you?"

"You can take your pick, Stanley!"

"Our names don't matter!"

"We'll tell you how this is gonna go down. You're going to lie down on the floor. Hands behind your back, feet to the door. All right?"

Silence.

"Alrighty, Stan?"

"Umm, yeah, okay. All right."

"Then we'll come in, and you'll be a good boy and stay down."

"Now, lie down, Stanley!"

"All right!"

"Are you lying down flat?"

"Flat as a board!"

"What do you see?"

"Nothing, it's dark."

"Do you see the wall in front of you or the door?"

"Um ... I believe it is the wall."

Nela rolled her eyes.

"On the count of three, we tear open the door and jump in," Yelka whispered.

"Okay, then I'll sit on him, and you tie him up."

"Deal!"

"One ..."

"... two ..."

"...three!"

With combined forces, the two tore open the door and rushed into the dark. Nela was about to pounce on her victim, but Mike was not on the ground.

"Where are you?" she yelled into the dark, cold room.

Yet instead of an answer, she was punched in the stomach. Mike pushed her to the ground hard. Yelka jumped back as the bulky shadow came charging toward her.

"To me, you're just 'slut' and 'cunt'!" he triumphantly shouted.

Yelka kept backing away until she felt cold tiles against her spine. Wielding his steel club, Mike murderously grinned.

"How do you want me before I fuck you up, bitch?"

With her eyes closed, Yelka felt her legs give way as she slowly sank down the wall. Either way, hopefully it will be over fast. She regretted her naivety. If only she had listened to Nela. This gang was not worthy of their favor. Yelka felt the baton rise above her. She tensed up. Any moment, the pain would set in.

Yet nothing happened.

"Hey, you can open your eyes again, it's over."

Before her, Nela smiled, holding that heavy flashlight in her hand. Mike was lying on the ground, bleeding from a gash on his head. Relieved, she hugged Nela.

"Oh my God, I'm so glad …"

"Yeah, come on, we don't have any time to waste." Nela gently pushed her away. "Help me."

"What do we do?"

"We follow through with your plan," Nela replied.

Together, they pulled Mike to one of the steel worktables and wrapped his hands around its leg. Quickly, Nela wrapped the wire around Mike's hands, so he couldn't loosen them.

"This is where we'll pick him up later. If something happens, he'll be able to free himself."

"Okay, that's how we'll do it. Now let's find the transmitter."

"Wait a minute," Nela interrupted her. "You need a weapon as well." She pointed to the steel pipe Mike had dropped.

Silently, Yelka gazed at the baton. "Uh, uh …" she moaned, shaking her head.

Uncomprehendingly, Nela looked at her. Then, she understood. Carefully, she lifted the pipe and held it up. It was blank, no blood could be found on it. "This thing has never hit anything but the hay," Nela guessed. "Take it."

Hesitantly, Yelka reached for the striking weapon, slowly clasping it in her hand.

"You're going to need something to defend yourself."

"You're right," she replied softly.

"And we will have to rethink our strategy," Nela added. "No more mercy."

Yelka rubbed her eyes and gazed at the ground.

"Hey, that almost went wrong."

"Yes, that's right," Yelka replied. "But …" Nela put her index finger to her lips.

"No buts, ifs or ands. You will support me and put responsibility in my hands. I will take any consequence on myself, but for that, I need your help."

Mutely, Yelka nodded.

"I understand your moral concerns and your fears. But this is a matter of bare survival. Do you understand that?"

"Yes, I understand you," Yelka said. "And I will promise you that if we survive this, I will bring you back from this darkness."

As they walked together up the stairs to the tower, Nela thought about Yelka's words.

Henry had armed himself with a thick cable. For the first time in his life, he felt something like fear. Rather, it was a nervous feeling in his stomach that made him hesitate, his legs feeling heavy. Every step forward cost him enormous energy. It was like a throwback to his childhood when Henry heard his father yelling. Even as a little boy, he knew how hard the old man's belt would hit him if he called for him like that. Each time, he had walked up the stairs with slow, heavy steps to where he was to pick up his punishment. Damn, what had happened that this fear had come back?

"So, Mr. Sherwin. Now for you. The sooner you face reality, the more painless it will be."

That arrogant voice was back. Henry swallowed. He felt dizzy. His old man had been the only one who had known about his dark side. He had caught him with Mandy's dead puppy. As punishment, he had beaten him black and blue. Henry also got a painful punishment from his father for the René incident, although he couldn't prove it to him at all. That rotten, unjust bastard!

Henry tensed his muscles, squeezing the massive cable in his fist. He would pack quite a punch. Just as he had gotten even with the old man, he would now take on this bumbling son of a bitch.

"Show yourself, fucker. Let's see what kind of man you are in daylight."

To back up his words, Henry let the cable whiz onto the sideboard. A dull bang sounded. He took a step toward the voice.

"Come out, you dirty motherfucker, and get your ass kicked!"

Henry had worked himself into a frenzy, his pulse racing. It was the same feeling he had back then when he had taken the kitchen knife and …

"Well, well, well, I don't like the tone of this at all, Henry. I had hoped for a debate at eye level, but I guess I'll have to lower the bar for that."

Henry paused. He didn't like the way this guy was talking to him. Who did he think he was? With a powerful blow, he hurled the cable through the air, accompanied by a hissing sound.

"Come on out, you …"
"Shut the fuck up, you bastard!" A rough voice harshly cut Henry off.

It was loud and aggressive. "Who do you think you are, lil' hooker whore?" Henry froze. If he hadn't known better, he would have thought it was Ryder. "To me, you're nothing more than a cheap fuck!"

Henry was confused beyond belief. Now, were two enemies invading his Hades? What was going on, anyway? He spun around, flailing wildly. His eyes searched the darkness for a silhouette, a shadow, or a movement while he spread his hands wide from his body. But he could see nothing, only hear his very own breathing.

Silence. Where were they?

Henry needed to find Ryder, there was no other choice. Furthermore, the light would have to be turned back on, then momentum would be back on his side. But to accomplish that, he would require strategic thinking and the ability to control his emotions. He breathed in and out calmly, fighting his racing pulse. Where was the front door located? The light switch would have to be found there. If he could get there safely, he could turn on the light and start a surprise attack.

Henry, contrary to his habit, crept silently in the direction where he thought the door was. In his mind, he went through each step, one by one. With his back against the wall, he would turn on the light, spot the opponents and immediately charge at them, yelling. Like this, he had successfully intimidated and overwhelmed several opponents, more than once. Hit them and break them.

A gasp made Henry wince. He heard soft whispering. Listening into the darkness, he paused. The rattling grew louder. Someone was giggling. Noise and bluster.

Silence.

"Ryder?" whispered Henry, not expecting an answer at all.

Liquid dripped onto the floor.

Splat.
Splat.
Splat.

The rattling stopped.

Henry pulled himself together, kept searching the wall for the light switch. It had to be somewhere! His fingers touched cold concrete. Blindly, he continued to pound until he finally hit plastic.

With an increasingly loud buzz, the light began to blink, then slowly spread, illuminating the basement in a flickering yellow. Henry's eyes were dazzled by the sudden light. The cellar, which he had entered so many times before, seemed strange—like someone had soiled it. Henry's gaze wandered over the barrels and shelves, but he could not spot anyone. Where were the intruders hiding? Walking on, he thought he heard voices coming from his torture chamber.

Glancing around the corner, he recognized his chair where he had already strapped numerous victims. But the person who was now fixed on it was not one of those. His limbs were extending from his body at unnatural angles. His right forearm bent in the middle, his hand touching his elbow. The left leg was taped with the knee pointing outward.

The wire holding his head to the back of the chair was tightened so much that it had cut bloody furrows across his flesh. His eyes were open, staring at the ceiling motionlessly. From a gaping wound on his neck, blood spilled onto the floor.

Henry staggered, strength leaving him as he dropped the cable. Fainting, he sank to his knees.

"No …" Henry stammered softly. "No …"

He could yet see someone coming out from behind the chair. A gangly, bloodstained figure wearing golden sunglasses, a black designer shirt with silvery appliqués and red sneakers. The guy looked like that Duke dude he had just bludgeoned to death. How could that be?

"Henry, at last we meet face to face. It's a pleasure."

It was one of the voices that had spoken to him from the dark.

"Oops, not exactly," the person morbidly chuckled.

When he took off his sunglasses, his blood smeared face looked dead, like a mask.

"It's not my true face, though. Wait a minute."

With a firm gesture, he grabbed his cheek.

Henry was paralyzed by fear.

Duke's facial skin dangled between the guy's fingers.

That bump on his lower jaw was thick and swollen. Grinding pain spread where Henry's fist hit him. The fear of Ryder's big brother made Jesse do things he had never imagined before. Jesse had joined the hunt for the girls to impress Ryder, but he wasn't going to do to them what he had done to old Marshall.

That was because he dreaded Henry too much. Fear and panic had morphed into blind rage as they had stomped on the elderly man. As he lay lifeless before them, Jesse knew how Ryder must have felt when he had beaten the bitch to death.

Yes, they were on the same level now, no one would ever mess with them again. Dave and Mike should shut the fuck up. From now on, the gang's killers were calling the shots! If he found those girls now, he would share them with Ryder. Whatever they did to them would become legendary. Jesse felt omnipotent. Nothing was unthinkable anymore; nothing would stop him.

Their outrages would be beyond imagination.

Yet, how could he smoke the rats out of the hole? Cautiously, he crept through the dark corridor, lying in wait like a prowling wolf. Then again, wasn't it easier to find the little ones and bring them into the light? He felt their proximity, could smell the fear wafting through the darkness. Oh yes, they were not far away.

"I can smell you …" Jesse hissed, lurking. "Come out, rats. Pest control is here!"

At the end of the hallway, he groped on the wall for a switch. With a soft whirring sound, one lamp after another went on until all the lights in the hallway were lit.

"Come out of your holes!"

Jesse let his steel pipe screech across the floor. Smug, drunk with power and filled with a lust for murder, Jesse strolled down the deserted infirmary hallway. Casting a glance into each of the empty surgery rooms, Jesse planned new, horrible operations and treatments. In his fantasies, he detached himself more and more from the excesses of the last evening, further and further away from his fears. He now was the one they should be afraid of! He would tie them to the beds, dehumanize them and abuse them to death.

Jesse's gait swayed as he stood in the stairwell, drunk on his own violent fantasies. His gaze roamed restlessly, wandering up the stairs. He wondered if they were hiding up there. But why hurry, when he had all the time in the world? Jesse strolled on, carrying his baton loosely across his shoulder. The end of the corridor was not far away. Most definitely, his prey was waiting for him, trembling.

Oh yes, it would be a bloody feast.

Opposite the toilets, the elevator shafts gaped, their doors carelessly left open. Jesse hesitated. Now, first he should probably check the toilets. With a diabolical grin, he lifted the steel pipe and knocked on the men's room first.

"Anybody in there? I have to poop!"

Jesse laughed and was about to kick the door in when he heard a cough. It was soft, suppressed. And it wasn't coming from the toilet. He wheeled around, but there was no one behind him. Very slowly, he crept back across the hall to the elevators. Tensely, he raised his pipe and sneaked towards the open shaft.

There it was again!

Obviously, he heard someone.

He got them!

Cautiously, Jesse approached and peered over the edge of the shaft. It was dark below him. From above, some light fell into the opening. There was that sound again. But it was not coming from below, but from above. Jesse shifted his weight to his front foot, pivoted his body, and looked up, into the light. There was someone there. Damn, it was one of the girls!

"Hello!"

She was standing right above him, waving at him. What the heck?

Just then, the toilet door behind him was ripped open, and a black-haired fury pounced on him. A large, black flashlight was pointed at him like a skewer. She shrieked like hell. Jesse tried to strike back, but it was too late. He lost his balance and fell into the dark shaft, screaming.

Pain shot through his spine as just a moment later he crashed onto the concrete floor. Jesse cussed and screamed in pain, but he was alive. He rolled to his side and held his back. Panting, he got back to his feet and surveyed the site. Sure enough, he had been on the second floor and fell just one floor below. He saw the locked elevator door in front of him. When he looked up, the women were staring down at him. Above him, a flashlight was turned on. Jesse was blinded.

"How's pest control going down there?"
"Did you find any rats?"

Jesse turned away and raised his arm to cover his eyes. The bitch was not far above him. Just a few feet. If he leapt, he might have been able to grab the edge and hoist himself up. He picked up his baton and glared past the blinding light.

"You stupid little cunts! Wait till I get back up there!"

On the walls, he could make out the fixings of the elevator. Steel cables led upwards to the left and right. Testing, he reached for them and, with only one arm, tried to pull himself up. Yet, he wasn't strong enough. Damn it, he would have to use both hands and leave his steel pipe. Anyway, he would beat them up with his bare hands, those lousy bitches!

"Hey Yelka, he really tries it!" the one above him shouted.
"Shut up, I'll be right there!"
"Have you ever thought about why the ropes are still so tight?"
"Fuck you!"
"Little advice, asshole," the other one shouted, "just because the light is turned on does not mean that the security system is activated as well."

But Jesse did not listen, he would rather try to climb.

"He doesn't understand."
"Fair enough!"
"Yelka, send down the elevator."

Their revenge was to be cruel.

When Jesse's screams had died down, Yelka took her hands off her ears and gently touched Nela's shoulder. Her friend was gazing into the dark abyss that ended just inches below her. The elevator's roof hid the horror that lay beneath. She hugged Nela, but she seemed frozen.

"Thank you very much," she said softly.

Finally, Nela turned her head and asked, "What for?"

"It was a matter of bare survival, you were right."

Nela glanced at her and nodded grimly.

"But now it's time to move on. We have to look forward."

Finally, Nela smiled. She was right. Now the words Yelka had said in the kitchen dawned on her. Nela shook her head, blocking out the screams. If they were to survive this nightmare, she would definitely need more sunshine and fewer dark buildings in her life.

Yelka had grabbed her hand and pulled her up the stairs. With soft but determined steps, they moved up one floor after the other. The higher they got, the mustier it smelled. Rain and humidity had caused the walls to become dark and brittle.

As they left the stairwell, Yelka and Nela entered one of the top floors of the hospital. This was the old part of the building, built at the turn of the century. The wallpaper was hanging loosely and the wooden floor creaked. Puddles of water had pooled in front of some open windows. It smelled of mold and mildew.

"Where should we go?"

"Let's turn to the right. Over there, we should be able to access the garret."

"The floor doesn't look safe at all."

"Alternatively, we could try to find a way around to the left, however ..."

"It's okay, I'll shut up. You lead the way."

Nela smiled.

As close to the wall as possible, the two women felt their way down the hallway. Yelka felt the damp concrete against her back as she watched Nela disappear into a room. Cautiously, she poked her head around the corner. The odor of mold and mildew hit her. Instinctively, Yelka turned away, squinted her eyes and exhaled.

"For heaven's sake, what is that?"

"Don't be like that," Nela whispered. "Never seen an abandoned laundry room before?"

Only now could Yelka cast her gaze back into the room. The once white-painted room was infested with black mold, and the windows were tarnished. There was only sparse light falling into it. Holes opened up in the ceiling. Through rotten beams, the room above could be guessed. The remains of bedding, clothing, and towels were scattered on the floor, situated above shattered shelves, debris, and fragments. Clearly, time had left its mark. Nevertheless, the floor in this room did not seem to be rotten.

"Breathing masks? Anyone?"

"Come on, if we survive this, mold is the least of our problems."

"At least cover your face with your sweater."

"Good point." With her mouth and nose covered, Nela squatted down. "Here is where we can prepare for what, we hope, will be the final trap."

"Fab. How do we do that?"

Yet, Nela did not reply. She eagerly rummaged through the pile of wet fabrics. Finally, she pulled out a large pillowcase that had not yet been eaten away by mold and wetness. Triumphantly, she held it up in the air.

"Let's go."
"Say what?"

But again, Yelka got no answer. This time Nela handed her the bag and filled it with broken pieces, glass wool, screws, and nails. Yelka observed her with a curious gaze.

"Don't look like that, it makes everything …"

Steps.

They froze. Nela put her index finger to her lips. There was someone in the stairwell.

"We have to go on," she whispered just audibly.
"Go ahead, I'll take the bag."

Again, they heard noises from the lower floors. But this time they had come closer.

"Quick, this way." Nela pointed in the direction from which they had come.
"Back to the stairwell? Then, we'll run into them."

"Trust me," Nela insisted, "but we have to hurry."

They softly opened the door and crept up the stairs. Quiet footsteps approached below them. Arriving at the top floor, they entered a rotten hallway littered with holes.

At the end was the attic. In front of them, one got to the roof truss and finally to the transmitter. Yet, behind them, death was lurking.

Under the human skin mask, the bloody face looked boyish, almost innocent. Only by the blood and the obscene grin could Henry tell which demon he really was. With slow, short steps, the boy paced around the surgical chair. His left hand slid gently, almost tenderly over Ryder's corpse. His fingers brushed his face as he pinned Henry with flashing eyes.

"You didn't expect that, did you?" he finally asked in a calm voice. "Are you surprised?"

Henry fought the faintness that threatened to overwhelm him. "Who are you?" he stammered, barely audible.

The boy chuckled softly. He playfully held a hand over his mouth like he had to suppress laughter. His eyes wandered searchingly as he said in a childish voice, "Maybe I'm Lil' Mousey?"

Henry's mouth was open, his eyes wide. What was happening?

"Or perhaps, I am that little slut, Tami," he purred in a high, quivering voice. He bit his lower lip lasciviously while slowly stimulating his breast with a single finger. "Hmm, Henry, did you like your brother's little girl-friend? Would you have liked to fuck her?"

Stunned, Henry swallowed. The boy bowed and remained standing in front of Henry like a lifeless puppet. Seconds passed, there was dead silence as he rose again. His expression was triumphant, mocking, challenging. Henry was almost losing his mind when he heard him speaking in Ryder's voice. "I can tell you that I enjoyed every moment before I slit that cunt's throat."

The boy was not only imitating his dead brother's voice, but also mimicking his posture and gestures. White dots danced in front of his eyes. Henry tipped forward, managed to brace himself at the last moment.

"Who are you?" he stammered tonelessly.

"Don't act like a pussy," he heard Ryder's voice from above. "Bad rep for me when my big bro' is acting like a wimp."

"Who … are … you?"

The guy laughed roaring, just like his brother did. "I'm Damon Duke, from Duke Executives. I'm Mousey Gilman, an innocent little boy. I'm Tami Butcher, that schoolyard skunk. And I'm Ryder Sherwin, calling the shots!"

"You're freaked out of your mind!"

Henry heard the guy's voice close above him.

"No, I am not insane. I'm all those whose lives I've taken. So, the question is rather, 'Who was I once?'"

Henry raised his head and tried to look at him, but he could not. "So," he hesitantly asked, "who were you?"

"I was a diminutive and insecure individual. I didn't know what to do with myself and the emptiness inside me. I felt misunderstood. I thought I wanted love, but I couldn't find it. I longed to be a man but didn't know how. I wanted to be respected, but had no self-confidence. I also experienced those ominous urges, akin to yours."

Henry wanted to get up, but failed. Again, white dots were dancing before his eyes.

"But that doesn't matter anymore," he continued. "No longer am I afraid of anything or anyone. Today, I am everything I was looking for yesterday."

A roaring, demonic laugh bellowed from Zander's throat. Seconds later, the echo of his voice was still reverberating off the basement walls. Henry perceived the red sneakers in front of him, could smell the blood and filth on them. Behind it, he saw the chair upon which his brother's violated corpse lay.

Henry felt dizzy like he had never felt before. His sanctuary, his Hades, had been desecrated and raped. The place where he could live out his omnipotence and cruelty had been taken away from him—by a boy he had beaten to death.

An unbearable, paralyzing weakness came over Henry. Last night's events unfolded before his eyes like a maelstrom, dragging him down. Starting with the intruders on the compound, the out-of-control gang, his effeminate brother, the discovery of his hiding place, and ending with his fainting.

"Now you know who I am, Henry Sherwin. And who have you become?"

"I …" Henry tried to sit up, but dizziness overcame him immediately again. He lay at Zander's feet, gasping.

"That's what I thought. You are nothing. I feel so disappointed, so let down."

"Kill … me …" Henry rasped, barely audibly.

"Excuse me? That's outrageous. Did you really ask me to kill the infamous Henry Sherwin? Unbelievable!" Zander had returned to the arrogant tone of a Damon Duke. "Look, dear Henry," he continued in a chatty tone, "you and me, we kill for different reasons. For you, I suppose, the torture-murder of two cable thieves is like getting your libido back. Isn't it?"

Henry tried to counter something, but he could not.

"What was that? I can't hear you!" Without transition, Zander had shifted into an aggressive tone. Henry almost felt as if he could hear his very own voice. "You're just too quiet, wimp!" Zander snapped at him, only to lapse back into Damon's tone. "Composure, monsieur. Let's not stoop down to the level of a redneck." Zander smiled as if in agreement with his own words. "Well," he continued, "I, on the other hand, kill in order to grow on the spirit of my victim."

With empty eyes, Henry looked at him. He was defeated. "Please do it, kill me."

Zander crouched down, blinking at him with wide eyes. Tenderly, he stroked his hair. "Honey, I'd love to, I really do," he whispered in a soft voice. "But alas, you have nothing left in you for me to grow on."

Taking Henry's head between both hands, Zander kissed him on the lips.

"You're not desirable anymore, honey. Adieu."

Through the ceiling above him, water dripped onto the floor. The heavy smell of mold and mildew was in the air. The old hallway had moss and ferns growing on the wooden floor. Every step had to be taken carefully. Where there was no water on the floor, holes opened up through which one could see down to the lower floor.

He was glad that he had reached the new wing, where the stairs were made of concrete.

Dave had heard the kittens scurrying down the hall. Flitting on quiet paws, like they could escape him. But the dog had caught their scent. He crept up the stairwell in a crouched position, holding the steel club firmly in his left hand. With his back resting on the wall, he could strike at any time. He would take what he could get. Fuck Ryder. Dave had seen what kind of man he really was. Without his big brother, Ryder was a just coward. It was time for him to call the shots.

When he reached the top floor, Dave found himself in a hallway with sizable holes in the roof. In the dark of night, he could see the starry sky above him. Lamps and wiring had long since rotted away and no longer existed. Up here, nature had prevailed against man. Any step could cause the rotten floor to collapse. Still, Dave recognized footprints on the damp surface of the floor.

They had walked here, those little kittens. He would only have to follow their footprints to catch them easily. With his back to the wall, he crept down the hallway, following the prints in front of him. They couldn't be far away, as the only way out was to make a jump out the window. Listening into the night, Dave believed he heard voices. They were very close, in one of the surrounding rooms. He paused, clutched his baton tighter, and inspected the corridor ahead.

There were two more rooms to the left and right on either side, with a large hole in the floor between them. Ahead was a final door where the hallway ended. Dave grinned. There was no more running away, a dead end lay before him. Even if they tried to get away from him, they would not survive the escape down the potholed hallway. He grinned, triumphantly slammed his steel pipe against the wall. A dull clang sounded. Damp plaster peeled away. Dave relaxed. There was no need to be careful anymore.

"Awooo!" Dave howled into the night. "Ah-Ah-wooo!"

Leisurely walking around the holes in the floor, Dave headed for the last door at the end of the hallway.

"Pussy, pussy, pussy! Come out, I got treats for you!"

Dave laughed off his own nonsense. He hit the rotten floor as if to prove his words. Wood shattered; splinters flew. Focused, he approached the door. In the darkness, he could make out movement. That's where they were, in the final room. The door at the end of the hallway.

Dave's heart was pounding hard. He had them. Now, it was the hour of triumph. Since he could not have Vivian, he would now take the other bitch. She looked equally good, if not better. And who knew how the other skank looked like. Up here, he would have all the time in the world to enjoy with those two pussies. After all, he wouldn't have to let them go. Heck, Dave could probably lock them up in here and keep them as sex slaves. The idea aroused him.

Suddenly, he could see them! The door at the end of the corridor gave a glimpse of an empty room, at the end of which two figures were moving.

"There you are my little pussies! Do you feel like playing?" Again, Dave laughed maniacally.

With swaying steps, he approached the room, letting the bat whiz through the air. Dave could scent his prey's fear. He pursed his lips and grabbed his crotch.

"Come on, you little scamps, Daddy's got food!"

Dave entered the room. Moonlight streamed through the windows, creating an eerie atmosphere in the empty room. At the very end, the two girls were standing close together. They had raised their sticks hesitantly, as if they really believed they would be able to defend themselves against him. He saw the fear in their eyes, felt their broken will. He just had to tear, to take down the prey.

"Hello there, little ones," Dave whispered lustfully. "If you'll lower your weapons, I'll make sure we'll have all the fun in the world together."

"Piss off!" The dark-haired beauty fought back with the last of her strength.

"Oh, how cute you chicks are. I love it when the prey fights back."

"Go home before it's too late!"

Dave laughed hoarsely, spreading his arms. Smiling, he gazed up at the sky through the hole in the roof. The moon was shining brightly, signaling its approval. Whether they liked it or not, they would have to comply!

"Three, two, one, here I come!" Dave pointed the baton at the women and kept going. Now, there was no escape anymore.

A crackling sound appeared under his steps.

Irritated, he stopped and looked down. The floor looked rotten; water had accumulated. It was only where the women were standing that the ground seemed stable. But how had they gotten there?

It was too late.

Dave fell.

The collapse knocked Dave off his feet, he staggered and fell backwards. But the fall didn't last long–he hit the ground, even before he realized it. Although harsh lightning flashed through his body, he landed softly. Astonished, he averted his eyes from the hole in the ceiling and considered his position.

Dave found himself in a cushion of glass wool, the kind they used to insulate walls and roofs. He got lucky! It could have been much worse. If the floor down here had been rotten, too, maybe he would have fallen down another one. A smile spread across his face, but then he noticed a strange taste in his mouth.

Iron, warmth ... Dave tried to get up, but he couldn't. Neither his arms nor his upper body were under his control. With great effort, he lifted his head and looked down at himself. What the hell was that? A large shard protruded from his chest, another one from his abdomen. Breathing was difficult as blood ran from his mouth. The wool beneath him was peppered with shards, screws, and splinters that had drilled deep into his body.

"Help …" he rasped hoarsely. "Help …"

Something moved above him, someone was there. Those girls …

With their backs to the wall, Nela and Yelka tipped a long plank onto the floor and now walked safely across the rotten hallway. Glancing down, they were relieved to find that their plan had worked. Dave was lying on his back, impaled by lengthy shards, threaded screws and nails. Blood poured from his mouth and nose. His gaze widened upwards.

"You must …," he whispered with the last of his strength, "call a doctor …. call."

"Yeah, maybe we should," Nela replied matter-of-factly.

"And you should have called the police," added Yelka. "But now it's too late."

"Help … me …" He tried to breathe. "Please." His body buckled, blood oozing from his wounds. The yellow glass wool turned red.

"The girl you murdered was called Vivian. She was my sister."

"You could have helped her when you had the chance."

"It's too late now," Yelka said. "Each one of you will meet your maker."

"You will die here, alone."

Dave coughed. A gush of blood shot from his mouth, ran down his chin and cheeks. His lungs gasped for air, but he choked on his own blood.

When life was gone from his gaze, Nela and Yelka hugged. Bloodlust and arrogance had literally plunged the gang member to his death.

"He chose his own fate." Nela clutched Yelka's shoulders as she gave her a determined glance.

"He did," she replied firmly. "They all have."

"There shouldn't be many of them left."

"If I understand correctly, only the two sickos from the basement are still after us."

"You don't," Nela asserted. "They're not after us, they're the prey."

Yelka smirked. "That's right."

Cautiously, they left the ramshackle chamber and stopped in the hallway in front of a still intact window. The night air was fresh, the sky starry. From up here they had a clear view of the whole building. Eerily, the old military hospital was beneath them, like a relic from the past, now surrounded by spruce forest. One day, it would collapse and be devoured by nature.

Yelka turned her gaze to the sky. Even when the hospital was long gone, the stars would still be there. She took a deep breath and closed her eyes. Now she could feel her friends who she had gone out with that morning. Her sister Vivian, and Damon, as arrogant but lovable as he was. She wondered if he and Tess had escaped. And finally, her old friend Zander. She wondered where he was.

"Come on, let's keep moving. We're almost there!"

Yelka opened her eyes and saw Nela smiling. "Let's go!"

They carefully pressed against the wall and walked down the hallway. Gaping holes decorated the middle of the corridor, water dripped from the ceiling. At the end was a tower with a concrete staircase. The transmitter had to be up there, in the attic. They could see the antenna sticking up on the roof. When they opened the heavy glass door, a dark room lay before them. The tower's staircase ended on a barren last floor, where a wooden staircase led up to the roof truss. It had to be up there!

"Go ahead," Yelka pointed in the direction of the stairs.

Nodding, Nela immediately grabbed the railing. With firm steps, she went up and pushed against the attic hatch. "Closed," she said somberly. "It's locked."

"Damn."

"So close!"

"No way," Yelka cursed. She let her gaze wander and finally opened one of the two small windows, where sparse moonlight shone through.

Yelka leaned out and turned upward to catch a glimpse of the roof.

"Nela, come here!" she hollered euphorically.

"What did you find?"

"Look, here's a kind of outside wall fire escape."

Nela's gaze wandered from the window where the ladder ended, down into the darkness. It went down a good twenty yards. The ladder was old and rusty, the screws had surely loosened. Determined, they looked at each other.

"There is no alternative."

Nela grabbed the rung, shook the ladder as a test, and looked down one last time. Fortunately, the deadly height could not be estimated at night's darkness. Even though she knew the ladder had rust and wear, Nela pulled herself up. The cold night wind made her shiver, her heart beat faster. Determined, she worked her way up. Under every step, bits of mortar crumbled off the wall; time had made the ladder wobbly. For the first time, Nela felt a fear of heights rising inside her. Her heart raced as she felt a slight movement. Like frozen, she held on to the rusty rungs.

"What's going on?" Yelka shouted from below.

But Nela did not answer.

"Nela?"

"I can't," she finally replied tonelessly.

Yelka leaned out of the window, reaching out to her. "I'm with you," she soothingly whispered, placing her hand on her lower leg. "Take a deep breath and focus on a point in front of you."

Nela's gaze fell on a clump of moss growing on the wall.

"Focus on your breathing, Nela." She squeezed Nela gently. "In and out. In and out."

Nela followed her voice. The dark green calmed her. In and out.

"You can do this. Everything will be fine."

"Everything will be fine," Nela finally replied softly.

She climbed up slowly, but with a firm hold, until she reached the entrance on the top floor. Yelka saw her legs disappear into a hatch. It took a brief moment, then Nela looked down at her with a smile.

"You go!" she encouraged Yelka.
"That's right ... Now me..."

Yelka thought of her own words as she climbed out of the window and pulled herself up the rusty ladder. Wind crept under her T-shirt, made her hair fly. A shiver ran down her spine. With a jerk, she finally grabbed hold of the next rung and climbed determinedly upward. Just don't think, focus on your breathing. One movement mechanically followed the next until she eventually reached the top. She felt Nela's hand around her arm and was finally pulled into the roof hatch of the tower.

"We did it!"

They embraced each other and took one last look down. Treetops were swaying in the night wind; it was getting stormy. Above them, the transmitter's antenna bent to the left and right. It was time to get out of here.

The roof truss was narrow, old wooden beams held the rotten roof structure. It was only the cables leading down towards the transmitter underneath, that had been renewed not too long ago. To their left, a narrow spiral staircase led into the room, which had been closed off from below.

Cautiously, Nela put a foot on the first step and tested its condition. A soft squeak sounded as she slowly descended further. Yelka was about to follow her, but Nela abruptly stopped, raising a hand. Silently, she pointed down into the room below them. Light flickered, a soft murmur could be heard.

"There's someone there," Nela whispered tensely.

"One or more?"

"I can't tell, the voices are too quiet."

"What do we do?"

"We will stalk slowly and strike once we know who we are dealing with."

"Fine, I'll stay close behind you. Once you start hitting, I will join in."

"That's how we do it."

They remained on the stairs for a moment, listening. The light moved back and forth; voices seemed to be talking.

"It's more than one, I guess."

"Yeah, I think so, too."

"Hit it as hard as you can."

"I will not stop until they are done."

Yelka pulled the steel pipe out of her waistband. It was cold and felt brutal. One of her sister's murderers had carried it with him. Yelka was disgusted by the baton, and had actually hoped not to have to use it. However, now she took the rod in her hand tightly, clenching her fingers together. She put her other hand on Nela's shoulder and stayed close behind her. Yelka had seen this on TV once, when police officers had gone out on a call. Whatever they were doing it for, it made sense.

Slowly, avoiding any sound, the two crept down the stairs. The room they now entered was dark and winding. The light moved at some distance in front of them. It was obviously a cell phone that had been converted into a flashlight. The person holding it was alone, standing with his back to them.

Nela turned her head to Yelka and nodded silently. Attack! They ran at the same time, weapons raised to strike, but without uttering a cry. Their opponent had to be defeated silently.

It wasn't until the very last moment that the person seemed to suspect what was coming. Startled, he whirled around and directed the light at Yelka and Nela.

Nela was about to strike when Yelka grabbed her arm and held her back.

In the vague glow of the phone, she recognized who was standing in front of them.

"Zander," she cried with relief.

Instantly, Yelka pushed Nela to the side and hugged her lost friend. Tears welled up in her eyes, running erratically down her cheeks, soaking into his t-shirt's fabric. Sobbing uncontrollably, she held her last remaining friend. Just a few hours ago, they had climbed over the wall by the dirt road, looking forward to a weekend of adventures. They were going to explore an old world, of which only ruins remained. A world from which something new had emerged.

But now, at the moment of their reunion, Yelka realized that this world no longer existed. Her life lay in ruins, just like the ones they stood in. But in Yelka's new world, there were no aesthetics, no beauty of decay. She had woken up in a dystopia filled with abuse and murder that stared back at her with harsh and brutal hatred. All the more, Yelka clung to Zander, her last bridge back to the old, perfect world.

When he finally put his arms around Yelka, her tears dried up and the trembling inside her subsided. Relieved, she inhaled deeply, taking in Zander's scent and feeling his warmth. She didn't care that he smelled bad or was sweating. The only thing that mattered was that they had again found each other.

"Zander, I missed you so much. Where have you been? How are you? How did you get here?" she blurted.

Nela had lowered the steel pipe and sheepishly glanced around. She felt uncomfortable watching the two friends' intimate moments. Unsure, her eyes wandered around, perusing the dim room. She would let them have their moment of togetherness, there would be plenty of time later to get to know each other.

However, Nela had to pull herself together, because she also missed her friend Tess. Where was she? Had she been able to escape? Was she all right?

She had to get rid of those thoughts. She would take care of Tess if they made it out of this nightmare alive.

Quietly, she crept around the hugging friends, turned on her flashlight, and examined the room. Somewhere here, the transmitter had to be found. In the light of the lamp, a clear path could be seen on the wooden beams of the floor. Dark spots described the path that technicians had walked many times before. After a few steps, Nela turned a corner and found herself in front of a large metal cabinet. Buttons, displays, and switches were waiting to be operated. Finally! This had to be the transmitting equipment.

But as the flashlight's beam passed over the instruments, she spotted broken screens, torn cables, and malfunctioning buttons. The transmitter had been destroyed. So close to the finish line! Nela lowered the flashlight and was about to close her eyes in resignation when she noticed something. Thick layers of dust stuck to the equipment everywhere, only on the destroyed parts had it been wiped away. So, the transmitter had been demolished only a few minutes ago!

Nela turned and looked at Yelka and her friend.

"Yelka?" she called out with emphasis in her voice. "Yelka, would you please come here?"

Yelka slowly distanced herself from Zander, who still had not responded. He quietly lowered his arms and stared past Yelka into the darkness. Zander appeared to be apathetic and empty. Fear struck Yelka as she hesitantly took a step backward.

"What is it?" she called in Nela's direction without taking her eyes off Zander.

"Come to me, I have something to show you right away."

Life returned to Zander's gaze. He emerged from the darkness, staring straight at Yelka. Something lurking lay hidden in his eyes. He seemed to smile, but there was something treacherous in it. It was a stare that was unknown to Yelka. Only now did she notice that Zander was wearing Damon's T-shirt and shoes. Among the dirt on them, she could also spot blood. Her heart pounded faster.

What had happened? Slowly, with careful steps, she sneaked around Zander and approached Nela. He held his position; his body did not shift. Only his head turned in Yelka's way.

"What is it?" she again asked as she stood next to Nela. Her new friend's closeness provided her with a sense of security.

Nela quietly pointed to the destroyed transmitter. Then, her eyes shifted to Zander, who watched them like a mute insect.

In disbelief, Yelka shook her head. It could not be. Not him, not Zander. Why should he?

But Nela nodded resolutely, pressing her lips together. Her fist clutched the flashlight.

Yelka's mind was swirling. What was going on? That wasn't Zander at all. And yet, he was. Like a paralyzing fog, confusion overcame her. She had to have clarity.

"Zander, was that you?"

He remained in his position, standing sideways from them. Just his head was turned toward them. A smug smile spread across his face.

"Did you do that, Zander? Did you destroy the transmitter?"

Zander's tone of voice and his words made Yelka's blood run cold.

"Oh, Starlet, please don't make it a big drama."

Yelka felt horror run down her spine. It had been Damon's voice that Zander had spoken with–it had been his words. To make matters worse, he was wearing his clothes! They slid from one disaster to the next. This couldn't be real! Yelka's knees trembled. White dots danced in front of her eye. Dizziness overcame her. Her gaze flickered as Zander turned to them and spread his arms.

"Girls, please do not be concerned about your safety. I've got everything under control."

"Fuck off, you sick bastard!"

Nela's words snapped Yelka back to reality.

"Now now … Who's going to get vulgar?" chattered Zander in Damon's tone. "I am confident that we will locate a suitable space where we can fulfill all our immoral needs with each other. Until then, however, let's maintain decorum, my dears."

Nela grasped Yelka by the upper arm and dragged her behind her. The closed hatch that would take them back down the stairs was just a few inches away.

"Distract him," Nela whispered as she crouched down and unscrewed the lock.

"Zander, what happened to you?" asked Yelka.

"I'm glad you noticed my change, dearest friend!" With a rapturous smile, he stopped and spread his arms. "Do you like me? Believe me, I've done everything I can, now we can finally be together."

Yelka gazed at him in amazement. "Do you want to be my boyfriend?"

"Of course," he interrupted her, "don't act as if you have missed my affection." Indignantly, he thrust his arms into his hips. "It's okay, I think we were never in the same league, I realize that now." He gave a placating nod. "Last night, though, I caught up on all the things I've missed since I was a teenager." He squinted at her.

"Zander, I had no idea …"

"Yeah, I'm not a virgin anymore" he laughed part coquettishly, part mischievously. "My first time was a …" Zander raised an eyebrow, "… drastic experience."

Yelka looked at him in horror.

"Wow, you don't begrudge me?" His mask fell, revealing a hideous grimace that she had never before seen on Zander. "I get it," he continued. "To you, I'm just a little jerk following your ass around, huh?"

Zander's words hurt Yelka. However, they also brought her back to the threatening position she was in. The guy facing her was not her friend, but just another enemy. She sucked it up.

His voice pitch had changed, it was no longer Damon he was imitating. Yelka had already heard this voice the previous night.

"You never perceived me as a man, but always as your little puppy, you fucking cunt!"

"Yes, that's precisely how it is," Yelka now replied in a firm voice. "You were never more than a friend to me." She paused for a moment. "My best friend. And you never understood that that mattered more to me than anything else in the world."

For a brief moment, Yelka was under the impression she had reached Zander. His gaze loosened, wandered from left to right. His hand trembled until he clenched it into a fist. Then he shook his head and roared in a deep, thunderous voice, "Who do you think you are, you little whore? Have you ever listened to yourself? Who do you think you are?"

"It doesn't even matter anymore, Zander," she replied with a glance over her shoulder. Nela was almost finished. "The only question now is, what I think you are."

"Shut up! You're nothing more than a cheap fuck!" he roared in Ryder's voice.

"And I'm afraid that you've become a pitiful freak."

With a loud crash, the hatch flew open. In a split second, Nela and

Yelka jumped through the hole and ran for their lives, the raging psychopath breathing down their necks.

"I'm going to slice you up, bitch!" Zander pulled out his knife. "I'm gonna slaughter you like the chicken you are!"

Nela and Yelka fled in a panic. Their steps flew over the rotten floor, dodged holes and finally escaped into the stairwell.

"Turn off the lights."

"Take my hand."

"Go on, go."

"If we're lucky, he'll fall through one of those holes, just like that other idiot."

"Not Zander, he's an Urbexer. We have to be alert."

"What's wrong with this guy?"

"I have no idea. Something must have burst his mind last night."

"Yes, we are all struggling to keep our sanity, that's true."

Behind them, they heard Zander's shouting. He didn't even bother to hide his location anymore. Hatred and madness drove him.

"We can't have him at our backs all the way to the city."

"Let's shake him off."

"And how are we going to do that? We can't get rid of him."

"A trap. We have to set a trap for him."

"It better be a good one, or God help us."

"We need to end it here, in the house. In the open field, he will catch us."

"Any ideas?"

"Yeah, follow me."

Silently, they hurried down the last steps. Yelka and Nela were back in the basement.

"Remember how we saved ourselves here?"
"Yes."
"Let's go then, we got nothing to lose."

Zander might have become a schizophrenic killer whose fears had turned into driven murderousness, but within him there still slumbered that planful Urbexer who had survived until now. The ruins of his own self stood on a firm foundation.

They were back in the basement, where it had all begun. Oh yes, back into the Hades of his soul. Down here, there was no way out, this was where their fate would be decided.

Long I've yearned for your arrival,
Alone, in patience, I've made survival.
Now that you're here, stay a little more,
I won't hold you captive, that's for sure.
Yet, forever in my heart, our bond, a revival.

He warbled his favorite song. With a hoarse laugh, Zander thought about the new meaning of the lines.

"Glide with prey in shadows stark," Damon urged him.

"Echoes haunt, their voices hark," mumbled little Mousey.

"Yield your soul to the silent dead," moaned Tami, "Temptation's grip, all reason shed."

"Within a fractured, twisted mind," Ryder grinned, "Fantasy and reality are entwined."

His instinct led Zander to the kitchen. Here's where they were hiding. He would find them here. Playing casually with the knife in his hand, he strolled through the deserted kitchen. Light-footed, he kicked the cabinets, ramming the blade haphazardly through doors.

"You won't escape me" he purred in Tami's voice. "We're going to have a lot of fun together."

He had heard them. They hid next door in one of the many pantries, whispering to each other. It's a shame they were hiding out of fear. He had longed for a hard fight to conquer his women.

Zander paused. He thought of the dark-haired woman, and how snappish she had seemed to be. He was also struck by Yelka, who had approached him with tremendous sass. Something didn't add up. They were vivacious women who would not hide from him whimpering.

"I heard you," he shouted again. "One, two, three, four! Ready or not, here I come!" Mousey chuckled in amusement.

However, Zander ran straight towards the voices. They were hiding behind a steel door. He heard them whispering repeatedly. Zander grabbed the heavy door handle, held on to the knife, and pushed the door open. Darkness lay before him. Still the girls whispered. Ahead of him, he could make out a shackled person on the floor. It was Mike, the last member of the gang. But it wasn't the girls.

"I'm coming in now," he shouted maliciously, pretending to proceed.

At the last moment, however, Zander spun around and swung the knife at them. Yelka just managed to dodge him. They had snuck up behind Zander, trying to lock him in the cooler.

"Who do you think I am?" It was Zander's genuine voice, with a hint of disappointment in it. "Did you think you could lure me with a cheap trick?" Again, Zander stabbed at Yelka.

"Maybe we couldn't fool you," replied Yelka "but, for sure, we could fool the freak you became!"

They ran away, sprinting towards the exit.

"Don't you ever call me that again! You just don't!" Zander raged. "Freak, freak, freak! You fucking freak!"

In blind rage, Zander ran after the girls, ignoring every red flag. He didn't see the wire coming they had strung across the floor. Zander didn't feel it until it cut his ankle and knocked him off his feet.

He fell to the floor, hitting his chin on the cold tiles. Blood spurted from a cut. A tooth dropped out of his mouth. Zander spat and jumped back up. Ryder spurred him on. "Don't fuck with me, cunts!"

Yelka cast a horrified glance over her shoulder. This couldn't be true! Their trap had failed, Zander wouldn't let them get away! Bleeding and cursing, he stayed close behind, knife raised for a final stab. They were done.

"This far and no further!" Nela had stopped, arms raised above her head. She held up a canister. Yelka smelled gasoline as Nela spilled the liquid in front of her. "We'll light you up like a candle," she yelled with conviction.

Zander slowed his pace, strolling toward the two of them. "Kids, don't do things like that," he demanded in a matter-of-fact tone. "You can't start a fire down here."

Zander knew they were betting big. Just like their role model Damon Duke had. But Damon was dead, the time for games was over.

"What happened to the cherished Urbex code, girls? Take nothing but pictures …" Zander grinned victoriously as he kept walking toward Yelka and Nela.

Yelka, however, shook her head. "I've had enough of you," she replied, "… leave nothing but ashes!"

Horrified, Zander realized that a sea of flames erupted around him.

The blazing fire took their breath away. For a split second, the flames embraced Yelka. Unbridled heat burned on her skin, on her face. Screaming, she stumbled back, struggling to keep her balance. She was blinded by the fire's intense light. Like an easy victim for the flames, she almost fell, but Nela held her up from behind. From a safe distance, they took one last look back. The sea of flames now burned between them and Zander. His screams echoed through the underground. It was uncertain whether it was anger or pain.

"Come on, we need to get out of here!"

As the flames spread, Nela and Yelka ran back into the stairwell. Heat and fumes took their breath away. White smoke spread up their backs. Only when they had climbed the first steps did they dare to look down. Thick fog was rising from the cellar. Unceasingly, the fire's yellow glow approached.

"Where is the exit?" Arriving at the first floor, Yelka tried to get her bearings.

"This way, down the hall!" Exhausted, Nela pointed ahead.

"Did you go in through the main entrance?"

"I had to pass through a side window." Nela replied. "However, if my sense of direction is not deceiving, the main entrance is right there."

Nela thought about how she had left Ben Marshall alone. She was trembling, had to hold back the tears. Yelka held her back.

"No matter what we will find out there, I'm with you."

Nela nodded. "Thank you."

"Now let's move on before the fire reaches us."

With determination, Nela took a step forward. From the basement, they heard explosions as the lights went out. The fire must have reached the power supply.

Outside, the sun was slowly rising. The first rays of daylight fell through the ajar entrance door. Nela pursed her lips as she looked at Yelka. She took her hand. With a firm grip, Yelka opened the door.

In front of them lay the hospital forecourt, overgrown with grasses and bushes. The rising sun engulfed the meadow in a hue of red light, and birds chirped. A new day dawned, displacing last night's horrors. They took a deep breath and paused on the top step. Nela's gaze shifted to the spot where she had left Ben. She was trembling, would rather not see his body, but she owed it to him.

"Nela!" they heard a voice call out.

There, where the gang had attacked Ben Marshall, stood a girl.

"Tess!" Both immediately rushed toward her. "You're alive!"

They embraced each other, holding tightly and didn't want to let go.

"Oh my God, I was so worried."

"Me too. I'm so glad you're alive."

"She's not the only one still alive," said a rough, firm voice from below.

It was Ben. Tess had treated his wounds and put him in a position to recover. Nela slumped in front of him and could barely hold herself up. Tears ran down her cheeks without restraint. Her whole body was shaking.

"You're alive, Ben, you're alive ..."

"Do you believe a bunch of hooligans could kill me just like that? Better think again, young lady."

Sunk to her knees, Nela put her hands on Ben's face. "You're alive ..." That was all she could say.

"Obviously. And I owe that to this other young lady, who took excellent care of me." Ben looked terrible. His right eye was swollen, his nose bent, and his lips cut. Blood was all over his body. Still, he managed to wring a smile from himself.

"Oh my God, what have they done to you?"

"Most of it wasn't too wild," Ben claimed. "I'm a tough dog, after all."

Yelka smiled, touched, tears coming to her eyes as well. "Tess, so good to see you again," she said and hugged Nela's friend.

"I'm excited, too!"

The two of them held each other tightly.

"Your sister is she ...?"

Yelka burst into tears. Nela looked at Tess and quietly shook her head.

Silently, they held each other for a while. When Yelka's tears had dried up, she let go of Tess and looked at her with a steady gaze.

"After we rescued her, we were able to escape at first. But Vivian was too weak. I could only save myself at the very last moment."

Tess's cheeks were covered in tears.

"After the rescue, were you and Damon able to save yourselves?"

"At first, yes," Tess replied, "but then we were attacked by a security guard. He knocked Damon out and came after me."

"A security man?" Ben was irritated. "I'm the only one here."

"A little older guy with a mustache."

Nela and Yelka exchanged glances. "That was Ryder's brother."

"Henry Sherwin," Ben confirmed them.

"Was Damon able to escape?" asked Yelka.

Tess shook her head silently.

Yelka sank into herself. Vivian, Zander and Damon were dead. She was the only survivor of that night. Yelka could no longer hold it, and she sank to her knees. She had no more strength left to cry. Silently, she sobbed, supporting herself with hands on the floor. Like in a movie, the events flashed by. Together, they climbed over the wall, took amazing pictures, met the gang, and then it got grim. Rushed scenes lined up, blood and death everywhere. Yelka felt dizzy.

Ben took Nela's hand and pulled himself up. With her help, he got back on his feet, and made careful steps forward. He felt pain running down his entire body as he approached Yelka. Nela held his arm, supporting him. He lay his heavy hand on Yelka's shoulder.

"You are not alone, girl. We're all with you. You survived."

Yelka took a deep breath, feeling the warmth of his touch. His rough, fatherly voice soothed her.

"My name is Ben Marshall, and I would like to thank you."

"What for?" Yelka's answer was quiet and feeble.

"For saving this young lady here." Ben pointed to Nela. "She never would have made it without you, after all." Nela gazed at him in irritation. "She's far too hotheaded for that."

Nela and Tess laughed. When Ben joined in, Yelka smiled again. Obviously, the old man knew Nela well.

He reached out his hand to Yelka. "I am deeply grateful to you."

"That's okay, my pleasure." Yelka took his hand and pulled herself up. "Without her, we wouldn't have survived the night anyway," Yelka claimed, pointing at Nela.

"Where are Ryder and his gang all at?"

At that moment, a window shattered. Flames blazed out of the building. The fire had reached the first floor.

"We took bloody revenge."

"They're all dead."

Grimly, they looked at Ben when the door behind them burst open.

"Not all of us. You can't kill me!"

His mad gaze wandered over Nela, Tess and Yelka and eventually lingered on Ben. Behind him, flames blazed from the windows, smoke rose into the air. The hospital was on fire, Henry had barely escaped death.

"No one can kill me!" Henry was out of his mind. He raised the steel pipe that had once belonged to his brother Ryder and lashed out. "No one!"

With staggering steps, Henry walked down the stairs, a delusional grin appearing on his face. "But I can kill you! One by one!"

Ben bent forward. "Get behind me, young ladies. This is my job." When he got back to his feet, he was holding a large, blood-stained stone. "Come on, Henry. It's you against me. Right here, right now. Let's finish this."

Henry laughed like a lunatic. He thrust the steel pipe into the air and ran towards Ben. "Deeeath!"
Ben dodged the baton that came at him, stepped aside, and slammed the rock right into Henry's face. Like struck by lightning, the murderer Henry Sherwin fell to the ground, motionless.

"Do you know what I did with this rock?" Ben asked lifeless Henry. "I finished your brother's dog with it. Seems like today is not a good day for rabid mutts."

Sirens sounded; blue lights illuminated the meadow.

As they watched, two fire trucks pulled into the area, followed closely by ambulance and police. Loud voices rang out, ladders were extended, doors slammed.

Yelka, Nela, Tess, and Ben looked at each other in amazement. It felt like reality had caught up with them. The silence, the hush, and the whispers of the last hours were harshly broken, those rescue workers and policemen seemed like aliens from another world. Ben dropped the stone and protectively positioned himself in front of the group.

"Please leave the premises immediately," a firefighter instructed them. "You are endangering our operation!"

"I … we …" Even hardened Ben Marshall was at a loss for words.

"Ben, is that you?" The incident commander grabbed him by the shoulders and looked at Ben in horror. "What happened to you?"

"It's nothing," he finally replied. "Just a pack of dogs gone wild."

"You need to go to the hospital now!"

"We'll take care of him," Nela interjected.

Together with Yelka, they walked Ben toward the ambulance.

"We saw the fire from a distance," the commander continued. "It appears that we arrived just in time."

"No," said Nela, Tess and Yelka at the same time. "It's over already. You guys are much too late." Puzzled, the commander glanced at them.

While the firefighters played the hose on the flames, the women took Ben to the ambulance, where he received medical care.

"Good morning" they were addressed from behind. "May I ask you what you were doing out here?" They were surrounded by five policemen, who had their hands on their hips, expectantly eyeing them.

"Oh, it's quite a long story," Ben replied. "Best we discuss it tomorrow at the station."

"There's a lifeless person up ahead," the officer replied. "By all appearances, he was beaten to death. I strongly suspect that you are involved in the person's death."

"Matthew, it's okay," the firefighter intervened. "Don't you recognize him? That's Ben Marshall, security guard in charge."

In amazement, he looked at Ben and finally nodded. "Apologize. I didn't recognize you."

"That's all right," Ben replied. "Those young ladies saved my life from that guy."

"Excuse me, could you please tell me what happened?" A young woman in a red pantsuit held her microphone out to the group. "Did you start the fire? How did this man die?"

"Tell me, who allowed you to be on the compound?" The policeman gruffly drove at her. "This is a no trespassing area!"

"This does not apply, though, if the access is unsecured and no signs visible!" replied the reporter pointedly. "I am Christine Harlow from Channel 6. Are you the officer in charge?"

"You get the hell out of here, right now!"

While the press set up their cameras all over the site, the paramedics took care of Ben, Tess, Nela and Yelka. However, the sudden commotion overwhelmed the group. Yelka became dizzy. This was too much for her. She dropped to the grass and bent her legs, resting her arms on her knees.

While one of the rescue workers cleaned up her abrasions, Yelka realized that she had survived.

The last night's stress fell away from her, leaving her body feeling heavy. With her adrenaline level dropping, Yelka was getting tired. The fight for survival finally was over.

Silently, she let the paramedics do their work, watching the police officers and firefighters. By now, the flames had reached the third floor. Two firefighters played the hose on the main entrance, spraying a powerful jet of water at the building. The flames that had been extinguished on the lower floor, however, continued to rage above.

Flames blazed from a window. Someone was standing there. It was Zander. His and Yelka's gazes met. There was no emotion in his blank face. Whatever had happened to him, made her friend only a shell of his former self. Zander lifted his chin and looked at Yelka for one last time, then vanished into the burning building. A last tear ran down Yelka's motionless face.

When the paramedic had treated her wounds, Yelka got up and glanced over at the ambulance, where a cluster of journalists had formed around Ben.

"… This brave young lady saved me from a certain death," Ben told the astonished reporters.

Cameras flashed, microphones were shoved in their faces. Everyone wanted their part of the story.

Nela added, "And you'll soon be able to read all about it on my adorable friend's Insta. What's the name of your account again, my dear?"

But Tess waved it off. "Oh, stop it. I've had enough of that," Tess announced with a smile. "From now on, no more influencer b-s on my end. Just plain and honest bando photography!" Nela and Tess laughed along loudly.

Yet, Yelka sighed. Life would go on for them, but she had lost everything–her friends, her sister, her life. Now, Yelka was alone.

"Hey!" hollered Nela. "Yelka, come join us."

Tess and Nela wrapped their arms around her.

"You know," Nela said, "my friend Tess has this crazy idea to grow up now and leave all the social media nonsense behind."

"Exactly," Tess added. "Even if it means the world will miss out on something." A coquettish smile played around her face.

"So, we wanted to ask you …"

"… Our team still needs an experienced Urbexer."

"You up for it?"

"Of course, I'm in!" This time, Yelka cried with happiness.

From his stretcher, Ben watched the three women embrace. He smiled with satisfaction.

He, finally, could call it a day.

Fire at abandoned barracks under investigation

The old barracks near Highway 591 is known as "Bando," which means "abandoned place," and has gained a certain notoriety among photographers. Nevertheless, "Bandos" are frequently set on fire. It was only a few weeks ago that an abandoned children's hospital burned down, and now it has struck the since-1990 abandoned military hospital.

At about 5 am on Sunday morning, the fire brigade was called to the scene of a fire. In front of the burning building, rescue workers encountered four people, some of whom were seriously injured. Among them was a municipal security employee. It could not be clarified how the fire had started.

Later that night, the fire was brought under control, with post-extinguishing work still ongoing. Around 40 firefighters were deployed. Investigations into the cause of the fire continue; arson is suspected. Councilman Alfredo Cushman, whose constituency includes the building, spoke of decades of investment neglect and deliberate decay. This, he said, posed a safety risk and allowed such devastating fires to occur. Since it was unclear whether there were still people in the building, firefighters began extensive search efforts. In the process, the bodies of five people were found, whose identities could not yet be determined as a result of the fire.

EPILOGUE

A warm summer light shone on the meadow. It smelled like hay. Nettles lined the edge of the spruce forest that surrounded the clearing. Amidst the chirping of birds, scattered cars could be heard from the distant highway.

"Hey, Piper, I think we made it."
"Wow! Take a look at these cars."

Glancing across the meadow, Mia spotted a Camry already overgrown with branches. Further back, a station wagon was rotting away, while a blue Golf in decent condition was parked right at the forest's edge. It even had license plates on it—however, the registration had already expired.

"What incredibly beautiful motifs!" Mia unpacked her camera and roamed around the station wagon, while her friend Piper wandered through the high grass. The place impressed her. Although they were in the middle of nowhere, someone must have parked all these cars here a long time ago.

Who might that have been? When she arrived at the Camry, she took a look inside. Vandals had slashed the upholstery and ransacked the glove box. Walking around the car, Piper noticed that someone had scratched their names into the paintwork. It said, "Ryder + Tami." Rust had stained the spots. Although it seemed rather childish to Piper, she found the carved names romantic in some way. Anyway, no one had ever done that for her so far.

After browsing around for a while, she slowly returned to Mia, who had just photographed the station wagon.

"So, how far is it to these barracks?" she cautiously asked.

"Hmm, that's still quite a bit," Mia replied, "but I don't know if it's too risky?"

"Do you believe the rumors?"

"What kind of rumors? Like the murders?"

"Uh-hu."

"Allegedly, a serial killer has been wreaking havoc there."

"Oh, how exciting!" She giggled. "Like in a horror movie?"

"Worse. They had real blood!"

"We better switch on the cam!"

The two Urbexers strolled across the meadow. Mia held the camera in front of her. This way, she believed, she would not miss a good motif.

"So, have you shot anything good yet?" Piper asked after a while.

"Unfortunately not, although ..." Mia raised her eyes and peered over the camera. "Wait a minute."

"What?"

"I think there's another photographer over there."

In fact, there was a young man walking around a rusted pickup truck. Just like Mia, he had a camera with him and was snapping photos from all different angles.

"Hey, do you think he's all alone?"

"Let's find out!" Excitedly, Piper ran ahead and reached the boy first.

"Hi. Say, can you help us?" it burst out of Mia. "Could you please take pictures of my friend and me on the truck?"

Without turning to them, he replied, "Sure thing, ladies!" A black hood was pulled over his head. Due to the camera in front of him, his face was not visible. "Light, camera and … pose!"

When Mia tried to hand him her camera, he refused. "Later! I'm a pro and constantly looking for new models. So, I'll take a few shots for my portfolio, if that's okay?"

Smiling, Piper gave Mia a nudge. "Well, of course it's okay!"

The girlfriends smiled at the camera, turned, got in the car, and showed their best side. The camera whirred, one image at a time.

"Ain't doing this for the first time, are you?" A sheepish smile came across their faces. "We should do some more of you. I might be able to book you for one of my photo shoots. Would you like that?"

"You bet." — "Sure thing."

"I know another location, a better one. Have you heard about the old barracks?"

Mia and Piper paused.

"Yes, we did. But isn't it dangerous out there?"

"I heard there had been a fire there."

"Not if you're there with me. I also promise it will be quick. Short and sweet, so to speak."

"Hm …" They hesitated. "We barely know you."

"Yeah, what's your name anyway?"

The man put the camera down for them to see his face. They were scared at first. There was a large scar on the right side of his face that looked like a burn. Then, however, he laughed. His bright eyes and beautiful smile made the ugly scar disappear.

"It will be a great adventure, I assure you. An unforgettable experience." He reached out to them. "Pleased to meet you, ladies. I'm Zander Regan from Regan Executives."

Oh my God, these poor girls.

Will they survive? Or will Zander once more prevail? As you've witnessed in 'Urbex Predator,' the darkness can be relentless. While our story here has come to an end, I invite you to stay alert. For lurking in the shadows, a predator awaits, ready to embark on a new nightmare. Our tale may be over, but in the world of horror, the hunt never truly ends.

My next release is scheduled for late 2024. If you would like to be an ARC (Advanced Copy Reader), please email me at jens@jensboele.com.

Thank you for embarking on this chilling journey with me. I hope you've enjoyed every spine-tingling moment in 'Urbex Predator.' Your support means the world to me, and if you've found this tale to your liking, I'd be honored if you could take a moment to leave a review on Amazon. It's a small gesture that makes a world of difference for indie authors like me.

If you'd like to stay in the loop about my upcoming stories, special promotions, and exclusive behind-the-scenes insights, consider joining my email list. I promise not to flood your inbox, only the occasional exciting update.

Chilling regards,
Jens and the 'Urbex Predator' team

Made in United States
North Haven, CT
09 February 2024

48520296R10236